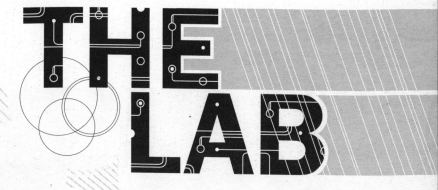

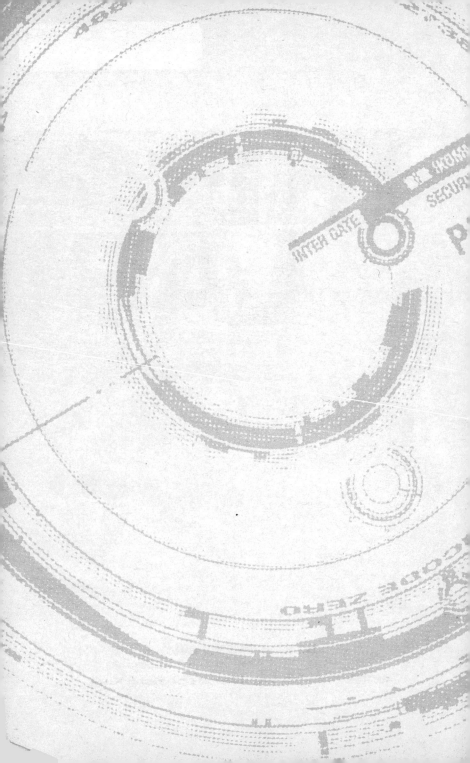

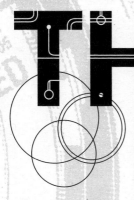
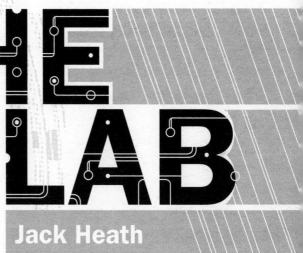

THE LAB

Jack Heath

SCHOLASTIC INC.
New York Toronto London Auckland
Sydney Mexico City New Delhi Hong Kong

For Kate, who always believed in me

First published 2006 in Pan by Pan Macmillan Australia Pty Ltd.
First Scholastic printing by Scholastic Press in 2008.

ISBN: 978-0-545-07595-4

12 11 10 9 8 7 6 5 4 3   9 10 11 12 13 14/0

Printed in the U.S.A.   40
First Scholastic paperback printing, October 2009

The text type was set in Adobe Garamond Pro.
Book design by Christopher Stengel.

ACKNOWLEDGMENTS

Thank you first and foremost to my parents, Ian and Barbara, who always encouraged me to read and supported my dreams of becoming a writer, and to my brother Tom, who was always eager to see my work and has always stuck by me.

I owe a debt of gratitude to Kate Griffiths, who read many different versions of this book with incredible patience and enthusiasm. I must also thank Paul Kopetko, who pointed out many of the inaccuracies and impossibilities in this book — and who, like a true friend, didn't mind when I kept them in anyway.

My sincerest thanks go out to the following people for reading early drafts: Billy and Tom Griffiths, Jonathon Hilhorst, Eugene Lawrenz, Christopher Macphillamy, Brendan Magee, Amanda and Michael Rawstron, Libby Robin, and Sue Willis. I couldn't have done this without your criticism and encouragement. Thank you to everyone else who expressed an interest in my work — I hope it's worth the wait!

Thank you to the hardworking team at Pan, who have been amazing from day one. I am particularly grateful to Claire Craig, who has enhanced and strengthened this book in ways I would never have thought of, as well as representing my interests throughout the process. Special thanks are also due to Cate Paterson, who first read my submission and gave it the thumbs-up.

Family, friends, colleagues, and readers. Thanks are due to all of you — I hope you enjoy this book.

The city is spreading. Soon only numbers will be pure.
—*"High Ground," Tim Freedman, B. Fink (Black Yak)*

Nobody's perfect.
—*Unknown*

PROLOGUE

PROLOGUE

This was not a normal day.

The infant watched from behind the polished glass as the blurred madness continued in the Outside. The Watchers were moving faster than usual, faces shiny, eyes wide. Many of the lights had gone out, but the ones in his glass enclosure were still burning brightly, above and below him.

Shapes flitted around in the Outside. He sucked in another breath of the oxygen-rich water and observed.

Now I am watching them, he thought. *And no one is watching me.* He giggled and clapped his hands together, and for a moment his enclosure glittered with bubbles.

The Outside darkened slowly. The Watchers had all vanished. Grey shadows were creeping over everything. Control panels wavered in the haze. Floor tiles wobbled unsteadily and vanished beneath the inky fog.

Soon the Outside was shrouded in black. The smoke draped itself over the enclosure like a charcoal blanket, and the darkening landscape rippled out of existence.

The water began to get hotter. The infant began to breathe faster.

Anger and fear surged through his veins. He clenched his teeth, narrowed his eyes, and panted roughly, releasing small bubbles of oxygen from his little lungs. He thumped on the glass with his tiny fists and kicked it with his stubby feet. His limbs slammed against the glass with strength that denied his size, making the enclosure rattle in its supports. The baby felt the vibrations and sensed he was close to escape.

He beat on the glass with his palms, harder and faster, desperate now. The water was becoming painfully hot — his skin was stinging and it was getting harder to breathe. The glass shook more and more. The baby gave the glass one mighty kick, and the enclosure broke out of its supports. It slid off the support pillar and fell into the void. Now completely weightless, the baby inside screamed with excitement.

The enclosure slammed down onto the tiles. The baby covered his naked head as glittering slivers of glass mingled in the air with the sparkling water and fell together, splashing and shattering like rain. As the last pieces of the enclosure tinkled to the floor, the baby took his first breath of air.

Smoke filled his lungs. He choked and coughed, mouth open wide, his tongue poking out and his little body shaking. He struggled to stay upright on his hands and knees, and spat some broken glass out of his mouth. Water and blood trickled from his lips as he raised his hands in the air, trying to find a handhold, something to climb up to or lean against. But his hands found nothing, and he fell forward.

One of the panels behind him exploded. Shards of plastic hit the floor around him, and the smoke in the air was lit for a few seconds. The underbelly of the cloud above was pierced by thousands of tiny sparks. He lifted his head off the floor and gazed up in awe.

This was the *real* world.

The baby's prison lay in pieces underneath him, and as the smoke became thicker he began to wish he was back inside. But he couldn't go back — and he couldn't stay here. There was a way to hide from the black cloud above him. There had to be.

He stood up and walked forward clumsily, until the sizzling black mist swallowed him up.

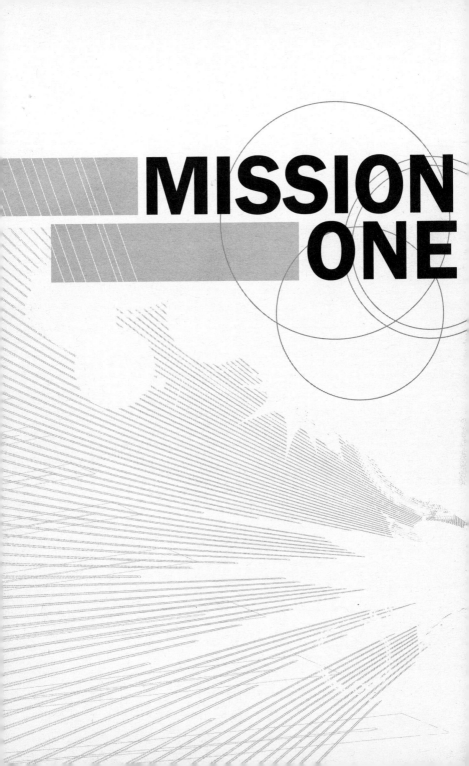

MISSION ONE

SIX OF HEARTS

He was still searching for the USB when the first alarms sounded. The defused lock on the roof must have been found by security. The soldiers would be here any minute now, searching for him.

Fine. The sooner his mission was over, the better. He foraged through the office with renewed urgency.

All the LCD screens in the room began to flicker as they shut themselves down. He could hear steel doors sliding closed, magnetizing, locking. Voices shouting. He blocked out all distractions, as he had trained himself to do, and continued searching through the desks.

They probably don't know where I am yet, he thought. *I've got at least thirty seconds before they figure that out, then another thirty before security gets here.*

Plenty of time.

The fluorescent light above his head flickered and went out, but he could still see. The skylight he had entered through only moments before was open, and cold grey daylight oozed through like a thin and wavering lifeline. Splintered rays slashed out from the broken glass on the floor.

He paused for a split second and then grabbed the USB off the table. *Even if it's the wrong one,* he thought, *there's no time to keep looking.*

He couldn't leave the way he'd come in — the guards would be on the roof waiting for him. Placing the USB in an airtight pocket case, he sprinted towards the door.

If I had been in charge of this facility, he thought, *I would've just contacted security via radio, and not sounded the alarm. Now I know that they know I'm here — whereas they could have caught me by surprise.*

Unless . . . He faltered momentarily as he headed towards the door. Could it be a trap? Had they sounded the alarm just to lure him into the open?

He shook his head. No. If they had already known he was here, he would be dead by now. In any case, he thought, he had no choice but to leave this way.

So do it. Hurry.

He slipped quickly through the door.

The bells and sirens were louder out here: pounding, buzzing hoots that shook the floor.

A long hallway stretched out ahead, leading to a sharp corner at the end. It was lit only by crimson emergency lights glaring down from the ceiling, reflected in the waxed floor tiles.

The instructions from King's mission brief echoed through his mind as he ran.

The central corridor is the only way of getting from the laboratories and offices to the administration and the exits. You will have to use it.

This was the most dangerous part of his route — there was nowhere to hide if they found him in this corridor. However, the security doors at each end were open. This was the only way through without clearance.

Go. Quickly.

He ran along the tiles, sneakers gripping the surface, steadily picking up speed. The corridor must be about two hundred forty meters long, he guessed, but only about six meters wide. That's one thousand four hundred forty square meters of floor space. Given the corridor is about five meters high, that's a volume of seventy-two hundred cubic meters.

Good, he thought. *It matches the blueprints I studied.*

A few seconds later, he only had about sixty meters to go, and he was still picking up speed. He was like a dark shadow, flitting silently through the red glow.

Suddenly a squad of seven guards rounded the corner ahead of him, moving in his direction.

The guards wore fiberglass helmets and Kevlar body

armor. They were all armed with Eagle OI779 automatic rifles and steel truncheons.

They hadn't seen him yet. But soon they would.

Seven people in a corridor six meters wide, he thought. *No way through, and I can't pass them on either side. Can't risk trying to slide between them and knocking them down — they don't look light and their boots are armored. I can't go back — I'd be a sitting duck. All the exits are this way.*

Can I go over *them? It's worth a shot. . . .*

Even as the guards saw him and shouted, he was swerving. He hit the wall with his left foot and pushed up, landing on the ceiling with his right. One of the angry red lights fuzzed out as it crunched beneath his sneaker. Two more steps and he was on the other side of the ceiling; one more and his left foot was on the opposite wall. Then he landed on the floor again, spun around, and kept sprinting with the squad of guards behind him. Flight time: 2.1 seconds.

He could hear the guards turning behind him, shouting in alarm, wondering what the phantom flitting over their heads had been. He'd moved so quickly they hadn't even had time to take their guns out of their holsters. Once again, he blocked out all distractions.

The mission was paramount.

On the north side of the front entrance to the facility is a water processing plant — it provides most of the drinking water for the surrounding seventy square kilometers. The dam and processing plant are legit — they've been on the site longer than the suspects have. As far as we can tell, all the Code violations happen in the main facility — that's where they design the drugs, maybe manufacture them, too. Try not to interfere with the dam or anything in the water processing building — that's none of our business.

Trouble is, the plant isn't far from the building, so it actually makes up part of the fence, and there's plenty of security guarding the perimeter all around the area. The entrance on the north side will be your best bet for escape, particularly since they won't be able to chase you in vehicles if you go via the dam. There are steps on either side of it, so once you reach the bottom, you can follow the Leshuar River out of the enemy territory.

He could see the front entrance up ahead — a squat kiosk surrounded by humming digi-cams. The whole foyer was deserted; the security staff had presumably been called in to look for him. Not wanting to press his luck, he didn't even slow down.

The sun was rising in front of him, a blazing white smear behind the locked glass doors. *It's a strangely clear day,* some corner of his brain thought. *It's weird to see daylight through the fog, let alone the actual sun. I need to get northside, so if the sun is there at this time of day, I'm facing east, and north is on my left. Still matches the blueprints. Excellent.*

He turned left, and felt cool, fresh air on his lips. He was facing another short corridor leading to the exit, but between him and the outside world there was a barbed-wire fence, with two guards behind slightly darkened glass (reinforced and bulletproof, he guessed). Behind the wire was a grassy field, a fresh green relief from all the red darkness. The field sloped down away from him, below a grey sky. He couldn't see what lay beyond.

He sprinted towards the fence and, about six meters from the gate, he jumped.

The guards looked up, alarmed, as he whipped above their heads. Before they could open their mouths to shout, he had slammed into the fence. No sooner had he hit the wire than he was climbing, scrambling up as swiftly and carefully as a spider. He was over the barbed wire before a second had passed, without having touched a single spike. Hitting the ground on the other side, he rolled forward and dived down the slope he found in front of him, out of sight of the guards behind the glass.

He froze for a moment against the cool soil. No sound of gunfire, vehicles, or any kind of pursuit. He was safe — for the moment.

Standing up and dusting himself off, he looked around. The field was flanked by thick forests to the left and right. Farther down the slope in front of him, he could see the dam, a grey slab in all the green.

He knew that all the "nature" around him was an illusion. He was on the edge of a park, designed to make the viewer feel as if he or she lived in the days before ChaoSonic and Takeover, when there had been bubbles of city inside vast horizons of hot desert, grassy fields, and lush forests, instead of one sprawling city with freckles of artificial nature trapped inside it. ChaoSonic felt that nature parks would keep the population docile and compliant. Maybe they were right.

The spires of the facility towered behind him; he could still hear the alarms. By now the owners of this facility had probably realized that he was an agent of the Deck, and that they were facing exposure if he got away with the USB.

Time to leave, he thought.

The dam is a full-scale one, about four hundred meters vertically. It's made of concrete with a steel framework inside; there are service stairs on both sides. There's a spillway at the bottom — a narrow tunnel that goes deep into the riverbed, so excess water can escape into an underground storage tank and the riverbank doesn't flood. There aren't any guards, but there will be some kind of barrier — a way of sealing off the dam in the event of an emergency.

Be careful. The officials in this company are rich, smart, and ruthless — there's no way to guess what they're capable of.

He set off towards the huge grey monolith at a fast jog, considering King's information. It seemed to be accurate; the dam, at least, was about four hundred meters high, one hundred fifty wide, twenty thick. There were rusty chains dangling all over it like thinning bronze hair, which might once have been used to lift things to the upper section of the Leshuar River. Water was cascading from the top of the dam and slamming into the river far below, causing its width to bulge before settling into a cleanly cut flow farther downstream.

He ran towards the stairs.

When he reached them, he looked down. They were as straight as an arrow, made of stainless steel, and they stretched all the way down to the bank of the river below. There was no guardrail on either side. There had to be about two thousand steps, he estimated. Each was about thirty centimeters across, fifty centimeters wide, and twenty centimeters deep. Total distance to the bottom: about six hundred meters horizontally, and four hundred meters vertically. All together, about six hundred thousand cubic meters of steel.

He began to run down the stairs. The metal hummed beneath his sneakers as they slammed down into the frame, making it vibrate.

After only a few seconds, the trees above were out of sight. He paused for a moment, checking his surroundings uneasily. He was about twenty meters below the top of the dam — a hundred steps down. There was still no sign of pursuit.

This is easy, he thought. *Too easy. And that's a very bad sign.*

Why weren't they following him? He had millions of credits' worth of incriminating data on the USB in his jacket — blueprints for deadly weapons, toxic drugs, names of dealers, and locations of manufacturers. Why weren't they trying to stop him?

Maybe the USB was blank. Maybe he'd picked up the wrong one, or they had known he was coming and put a dummy one in the right location.

Maybe the whole thing was a setup.

He looked down. The stairs still seemed to be humming, even though his feet weren't moving. Was there some machinery operating inside the dam, or was the water causing the rumbling beneath his feet? He looked around, then paused.

He was standing still. But the stairs were moving beneath him.

It only took him a moment to work out what was happening: The staircase was retreating back into itself. The steps were sliding backward until they pressed up against the dam, becoming bricks in a flat steel tower. The route he had taken down was steadily vanishing.

There will be some kind of barrier, a way of sealing off the dam in the event of an emergency.

I guess I've found it, he thought grimly.

There was no way back up. And in a matter of seconds, there would be no way down.

He began sprinting down the staircase, even as it continued to slide into itself. His feet pounded the stainless steel beneath him. Moments later he was about sixty meters from the top of the dam. Now ninety — more than four hundred steps gone.

But that wasn't fast enough — the wall behind him was advancing steadily, and there were very few steps left between him and a three-hundred-meter free fall.

The cliff face of stairs was very close on his heels now. He had only seconds to decide what to do. Should he grip the wall behind him and try to hold on? No chance — without hand-holds that was impossible. Should he try to jump back up the dam and grab the top? That was a hundred-meter vertical jump, with no run-up or preparation. He was strong, but not that strong. Could he keep running? The wall would push him off the staircase any moment now.

They do seem keen to kill me, he thought. *At least this means that the USB is probably genuine.*

There was nothing else to do.

He jumped.

ZERO METERS PER SECOND

He could feel the pause, the short moment of hesitation before free fall. Time stood still for a moment as he saw the dark river again, a slippery, writhing snake three hundred meters below.

Then he fell.

The air above his head seemed to push him downward. Because he had jumped sideways, towards the dam, the water around him obscured his vision. Even as gravity scrambled his insides, even as the blood and adrenaline pumped in his veins, even as he calculated that he was falling at about thirty meters per second, he noticed crystal droplets of water floating around him, seemingly still but for small shivers and wobbles.

He had jumped sideways for a reason. Landing in water would not kill him, even from this height. If he had landed on the base of the staircase, he would certainly have died. But falling into the river would not be fatal, not for him. Not even from three hundred meters up.

Still, it was not going to be comfortable. He braced himself in midair, bending his knees and pointing his toes. He squinted into the wind as it rushed past his face.

Then he saw the sign. It was at a bend in the river a bit farther downstream — a white metal board on top of a grey post. CURRENT WATER DEPTH: 0.75 METERS — NO DIVING.

Seventy-five centimeters.

He gritted his teeth. There was no way he could fall this far into water that shallow. Even if the impact didn't kill him, it would break all his bones and he'd drown trying to lift his head above the surface.

Again he blocked out all distractions. He ignored the water. He ignored the dam. He ignored the river below. Instead he reached forward for the rusty chains dangling from the dam.

He grabbed one, and his innards gasped as he suddenly stopped falling. The hanging droplets of water came to life and sped down, out of sight. The rust burned his hands as he slid down for a few meters, but he held on.

With a *crack,* the chain snapped. *Not helpful,* he thought. They were weakened by age and rust — they might even have been forged before Takeover. He let go as he started to fall, and reached for another to slow him down.

He gripped the next chain tightly, and one of the links above broke. Rusty metal splinters darted out, grazing his palms. But he had stopped falling for a moment. *So far, so good,* he thought. Back to zero meters per second.

Then he fell again, grabbing another chain wildly. Every time he grabbed one, he lost some of his falling speed.

He knew that if he grabbed the chains too frequently, he would run out of unbroken ones and be killed when he fell the rest of the distance. But if he waited and fell for too long in between stops, the act of grabbing the next chain could break it right away. Or if it didn't, the jarring halt would snap tendons in his shoulders, leaving him helpless for the rest of the fall.

He compromised by grabbing the chains just before he felt that doing so would risk injury. Beyond that, there was nothing he could do.

The wind whistled through his hair. His wet clothes flapped against his skin as he fell. *If I am going slowly enough when I hit the water,* he thought, *I will live. I've survived worse than this — I was made to.*

The water far below was now crowded with the fallen chains, writhing slowly like drowning worms as they sank into the white froth.

The next time he reached out through the hovering water, he used both hands and grabbed a chain with each.

He came to a very sudden stop, nearly tearing the ligaments in his arms. But it had stopped him for an entire second.

His arms were very strong, but the chains weren't. The one in his right hand split, so he quickly swung his arm around and grabbed the other with both hands. He could feel his weight stretching the metal.

Crack! It snapped. Hovering, he looked down again.

Sixty meters, he thought. Still more than enough to break

his legs, even if it didn't kill him. He needed to lose more speed.

He reached for the next chain, but his hands gripped empty air. He whirled his arms around, but there were no more chains.

The concrete dam was clean shaven. He had used up the last of them.

The dim sun burned down through the smothering fog. The water fell past him. The shallow river far below continued its rippling. Then the pause was over and he plummeted into the void.

He thrashed and flailed around, sending sprays of water in all directions. *I'm going to die,* he thought. Not being shot by ChaoSonic soldiers, not in an explosion while rescuing civilians, not executed by well-meaning fundamentalists nor dissected by Lab scientists. Just by falling a really, *really* long way. Then, if he were lucky, drowning.

His stomach clenched. Blood pumped. Gravity kept pulling at him, and he kept accelerating. The wind tore at his hair and beat at his unprotected face, making him squint. Drops of water crawled upward across his body, as though trying to escape the impact. His heart vibrated crazily, and the adrenaline flowed freely at the thrill of speed. At just a few meters from the water, he calculated that he was falling at more than thirty meters per second — a hundred ten kilometers per hour.

He bent his legs slightly and braced himself for the impact, clenching his teeth.

Then he hit. His feet smashed down into the river, sending up showers of snowy white spray. He shot into the water, expecting the riverbed to break his fall at any moment — but there was nothing below. He was sucked down into a dark tunnel until he could only just see the light of day far above him.

What happened? he wondered. *Why is the water so deep here?*

Then he smiled. He had landed in the spillway. Flight time: 36.3 seconds.

He reacted quickly. He was exhausted, he needed to rest. But if he didn't swim, he'd end up in the water storage tank and drown.

He spread his arms, kicked his aching feet, and stopped sinking. Holding his breath, he started to push upward. The weight of the water thundering down from the dam pressed him back, and he could feel that he was being sucked towards the storage tank, like a scrap of food heading for a kitchen drain.

The light of the sun wafted towards him like a lifeline, and he pressed on.

His head burst through the surface and he took a deep gasping breath. The roar of the water and the white spray deafened and blinded him for a moment. Forcing his eyes open, he scanned the area and spotted the riverbank in the distance.

Moments later he was dragging himself out of the water and clambering on all fours, when he shook his body violently like a dog. He climbed to his feet, checking that he still had the USB and that the water hadn't penetrated the case.

There was no time for rest. Agent Six of Hearts took a deep breath and began running back to base.

THE DECK

The inquisitive digi-cams hummed and buzzed softly — recording what they saw and transmitting millions of digital images to screens inside the building. A thousand pictures of a single face were taken as it slipped swiftly under the ever-watchful digital eyes.

The people in the foyer glanced across as Six stepped through the revolving door. Like the digi-cams, they focused on him, recognized him, and then turned back to their work. He walked silently across the shining floor towards the reception desk, ignoring the dynamic sculptures and colorful paintings, the elaborately carved desks, and the sparkling ceiling high above — a daytime substitute for a clear night sky. The electric stars were mirrored in the trail of small puddles that followed his path across the foyer. His short black hair and dark coat were still dripping.

There was a large bronze plaque shining on the wall behind the reception desk. On it were printed the words SAVE US FROM OURSELVES. Six ignored it, as he always did.

At a hundred seventy-eight centimeters, Six was the shortest agent in the Hearts department — most of them were good at their jobs simply because they were so big, giants of one ninety, one ninety-seven, and even two hundred two in one case. This gave them more power, more physical leverage, and faster running speeds than most.

But underneath the long black coat Agent Six always wore, his body was pure muscle. Everything not covered by his clothes (sharp profile, pale skin, white teeth, thin fingers) looked typical, but Six could lift more, run faster, and jump higher than any other agent at the Deck, no matter how tall. At sixteen years old, he was the youngest agent, too. He had been there since he was only thirteen, when the Deck had been founded. Although ChaoSonic now controlled most of the organizations and facilities in the City, there were still vigilante groups like the Deck that had pledged to uphold the moral and social values of the Code. They were determined to stop any illegal activity that might endanger the people of the City.

Six stopped in front of the large polished desk, and the man behind it looked up. He was in his late twenties, tall and lanky, with cinnamon skin and green-grey eyes — the sort of man who would have looked out of place anywhere. He was dressed in an ash-colored suit that was too short in the arms; he kept tugging absently at the cuffs as if trying to stretch them.

"Hello, Six," he said, ignoring Six's drenched clothes. "How are you?"

Six held up the USB case and slid it across the desk. "Buzz me in," he said.

The receptionist raised his eyebrows, but didn't appear overly surprised. "It's good to see you made it back okay," he persevered, "but you didn't answer my question."

His eyes roamed around the foyer as he spoke, rarely meeting Six's. He seemed to be absorbing every detail of the activities of the people around him, watching them eat and talk and laugh, as if their actions had some special significance that only he could see.

The receptionist was a stickler for politeness and pleasantries. Every time Six checked in at the Deck, his time was wasted by this man. *It's a good thing that I'm the patient type,* Six thought. *A good thing for him, at any rate.*

I could humor him, Six reasoned, *and imitate the way he speaks. It would be easy enough, and I could get back to work more quickly. But then he would be encouraged, and would expect conversation from me the following morning, and the morning after that. I would become trapped in a loop of civility. No, this method is far better — one day he will yield and forget his efforts at politeness. Then I will be free to work in peace.*

"I am well. Thank you. Buzz me in, please," Six said flatly.

The receptionist sighed as he slid the USB case into a slot under his desk. He produced a plastic card, placed it on a metal square on the top of his desk, and pushed a nearby button. Then he held out the card, finally making eye contact with Six. "I have a name, incidentally," he said with a wry smile. "But I've been here as long as you have, so you've probably worked that out."

Six took the card from him and turned away.

"It's Grysat," the receptionist continued. "Feel free to use it in the future."

Six ignored him and stepped into an elevator. Behind him the receptionist shook his head and turned away to greet more visitors.

The elevator was uncharacteristically full. *Just my luck,* Six thought.

He recognized the other occupants instantly as low-rank Deck agents: two from the Diamonds floor, where the reconnaissance, research, and forensic work was done, and one from Hearts — a field operative, like Six. They were all new to the Deck, probably with few skills and a sparse understanding of the Code. The one from Hearts was Agent Two — Six had never learned the names of the Diamonds.

He rarely encountered anyone from Clubs, where agents were trained, or Spades, where internal issues were investigated. Agents from these suits only came to this building under special circumstances.

The other agents smiled at Six as he pressed a button. He greeted their smiles with a blank stare and then turned to face the doors.

"Good morning, Six!" one of the Diamonds said as she slipped her paperwork into her binder, apparently expecting conversation. "How's it going?"

"Well," he replied.

There was a pause.

"Did the op at the water station go okay?" Agent Two asked. He tugged his fingers distractedly through his short, curly hair.

The doors opened and they all stepped out into the basement. Six turned away without replying and walked down the corridor.

"Maybe it went badly," Six heard one of them mutter as he walked away.

Six smiled to himself.

The linoleum clicked a tongue at him in time with his footfalls. He walked purposefully down the corridor until he reached a smooth black door with a silver heart printed on it. The number six was embedded inside the heart.

Agent Six slid his card through the disarm slot, and the door swung open silently. He stepped into the office, carefully shutting and arming the door behind him.

He flicked on his computer and began to type deftly. He made no errors, never hesitated, and didn't change a single sentence. He finished, reread, and saved the document in under a minute.

MISSION REPORT: 8066-7144-2731
AGENT NUMBER: 06–4 (Six of Hearts)
LOCATION: Leshuar Research Complex (LRC)
BRIEF: Retrieve Universal Serial Bus (USB), serial no. 0095-2766-9375 with minimal damage to on-location equipment, terrain, personnel, and within set time limit. Standard Deck

Code applies. (Access code: Delta Nine Four Oscar Seven Seven Kilos)

AGENT IN CHARGE: 13–4 (Agent King of Hearts)

MISSION DESCRIPTION: Entered LRC through skylight in B block (0646 hours), second floor (west building) and removed USB immediately. Exited facility through A block (0654 hours), second administration (north building), second floor, and left Leshuar area via north water processing plant.

GENERAL CASUALTIES/INJURIES: None

DAMAGE TO AREA: Load-bearing implements and equipment on Leshuar Dam damaged. Evidence of presence in building (office reshaped), superficial damage to building interior (broken emergency bulb, one), and exterior (broken skylight lid, one).

ESTIMATED COST: 54,000 standard credits

DAMAGE TO PERSONAL PROPERTY: Water damage to mobile phone (Digi-Call 091), radio (multifrequency transmitter, 2226).

ESTIMATED COST: 5,300 standard credits

NUMBER OF KNOWN SIGHTINGS: None

ESTIMATED POTENTIAL FUNDS INTAKE: 800,000 standard credits

Six printed the document, folded it neatly in half, and slipped it into his pocket. He switched off the computer and printer, then stepped out the office door, locking it securely behind him.

His footfalls echoed through the silent corridor, which smelled of soap and disinfectant.

It wasn't long before he reached the next door. Like his, it was black, but instead of the silver heart, this door had KING inscribed on it in silver lettering. Six touched the door handle lightly with one finger and heard the buzzer whirring inside.

There was a pause. Six knew that he was being examined by hidden cameras, and that if he tried to enter before they had finished, he would be electrocuted automatically by a generator in the door.

The door disarmed and swung open, and the man behind the desk smiled as Six entered.

"Hello, Six," he said cheerfully, winking one of his narrow green eyes. "Please, sit down."

King had his feet on the edge of his desk, and was resting his head on the back of his tall, dark chair. He was forty-one years old, and his face was creased into a hard-edged frown that confused people at first, as he was not suspicious by nature.

Six sat down as King scratched the back of his neatly shaved head — a subconscious gesture of trust and security, Six knew from experience.

Six handed the mission report to King.

"Thank you," King said. "Let me see — what have we here?"

He unfolded the paper, fastened a reading monocle, and scanned the document quickly. He looked up when he had read the whole page.

"Only eight hundred thousand credits in the PFI? You didn't see anything particularly valuable?"

"Just computers, printers, faxes, scanners, photocopiers," Six said. "As you said in your brief, the Code violation was in theft of information and design of weapons."

"So they were working out ways to kill people rather than actually doing it," King commented.

"The locations of factories, storage facilities, and the names of dealers and buyers are on the USB."

"So we've got shutdown with the data you recovered," King conceded. "That's good. But you know as well as I do that by the time we get there, most of those factories will be deserted, and most of the dealers will be in hiding — or dead."

"Hiding isn't as easy now, not with the triple C system."

ChaoSonic had started to enforce a new policy — everyone needed a ChaoSonic Citizen Card, or triple C, to buy anything. ChaoSonic said this was to ensure that all citizens received equal benefits and security from the company. But it also neatly forced people to let themselves be catalogued. If you had a triple C, there was nowhere you could hide from the company. Despite the Deck's best efforts, ChaoSonic's stranglehold on the people of the City had become a little tighter.

"The arms and drug dealers probably work for ChaoSonic, anyway," King said. "And there was nothing of much value to take. Correct?"

"Correct." Six's expression did not change.

King put his feet down on the floor. "We need funds, Six. We need to bust someone doing practical experimentation. Or, better still, proper manufacture. Computers and photocopiers are easy to sell, but too cheap. If we could flog the pieces of a quantum constructor, or a botline — that'd be worth a bundle."

Six was silent. King frequently complained about lack of funds.

"Law enforcement must've been easier when there were governments to pay the enforcers," King grumbled. "And when there were actual laws to enforce, for that matter."

"We uphold the Code," Six said. "It is enough."

"But it's getting harder, Six. I'm old enough to remember what the world was like before, but you're not. These new agents coming in aren't. Who knows what the Code will be in another ten years' time?"

Six said nothing.

"But no, of course," King said with a wry smile, "you'll uphold whatever Code there is, provided there's money in it for you. Isn't that right, Six?"

"Yes." There was no point in denying it.

"The fate of civilization is not your concern?"

Six was silent.

"Well, just remember that in fifty years, I'll be gone. That world is not my problem. But you'll still be here then. You have to live in the City that we're saving. Remember that."

31

Six nodded. It was quicker than arguing about such issues.

King glanced down again at the document Six had given him. "And you'll outlive me by a very long time if you keep getting mission results this good. This is first-class work. No known sightings? No one saw you at all?"

Six shook his head.

"A job well done, as usual," King said with a smile, taking off his monocle. "Excellently done, in fact. The Jokers will be pleased."

Six didn't know who the Jokers were, though he suspected King did. They supplied key intelligence for missions, they made significant contributions to the Deck's funds, and they chose which agents worked for the organization.

"The usual amount will be transferred to your account," King said.

Six nodded again.

"Excellent." King took the sheet of paper and placed it in a tray for filing. Then he opened a desk drawer and produced a large black folder. "And in the meantime, here's a hard copy of your mission details for tomorrow."

Six didn't pick up the folder. "I read the e-brief," he said. "I know them."

"I know you do. Take it anyway."

"It increases the risk for me to have it on paper," Six said. "Why keep it written down when I know it all in my head?"

"Because it increases the risk for *me* to keep it here," King said. "You can memorize all those codes and numbers — the other agents can't. And if I don't print out missions for you and I do for everyone else, that would draw attention to both of us. We don't want that, do we?"

Six shivered. He knew King was right. Too much scrutiny and the Spades might discover who he was or, worse, the Lab might find him — and he didn't want to think about the consequences of that.

King shrugged. "You are much better at defending yourself than I am. The times you needed me to look after you are long gone. You're looking after me now."

Six looked at him in surprise. King rarely mentioned their history. If people knew that King had found Six as a baby and subsequently raised him, there would be many questions asked. King had said it was safer for both of them to appear neutral.

"Destroy it if you have to, but take it," King continued.

Six couldn't argue with that. He took the folder.

"You'll be back for your makeover at 0600 hours tomorrow?"

"Of course," Six said. He slipped back out the door without another word.

CHAOSONIC

An hour later Six was back in the fog. The wind was blowing from the south, where most of the industrial activity and factories were, so the air was thick with pollution. He was completely enveloped in the dark carbon stain.

The fog shortened life expectancy dramatically. While almost all houses had a ChaoSonic air-cleansing apparatus installed in their vents, the average lifespan of a human being had dropped by nearly twenty years since Takeover, when the grey mist had become permanent.

Of course, the rich lived longer. They had implants that oxygenated their blood so they wouldn't strain their lungs trying to drain life out of the rotting air. At the other end of the spectrum, there were billions of homeless people who rarely lived to see their mid-thirties. Then there were the hippies. They lived in the tiny parks dotted throughout the City. The GM trees were efficient at cleansing carbon dioxide out of air, it was true, but the hippies didn't live long, either. Six knew that gradual asphyxiation was just one of the many ways to die in the City.

Six's lungs were more efficient at processing the tainted air than those of probably anyone else in the City. Under his skin there were slender scraps of DNA from those very same GM trees — Six could draw a little life from carbon dioxide as well as oxygen, so he managed to get more from the air than most other people.

Well, he thought, as he looked at the starving man asleep on the concrete and the rich teenager buzzing by on his motorized wheelchair, *everyone gets dealt their hand. Some people have it good; some people, bad. And even if I wished that things were different, they wouldn't be.*

So forget it. This is an unproductive line of thought.

The trouble was, for all his mental, physical, and financial advantages, on a day like today, when the southern wind was blowing, he could hardly see through the fog. His 20/20 vision, however useful most of the time, did not make him an X-ray machine — Six couldn't see more than a few meters ahead through this fog any more than he could see through the brick and mortar wall to the side of him. But he probably had a better chance of not bumping into people than most other pedestrians, because of his quick reflexes.

When he finally saw the ChaoSonic patrol up ahead, he had to make a fast decision.

They were only about five meters away from him.

"Your triple C, please," the patrol leader said to a woman

in front of Six. He looked like a giant, skinny cockroach, with his black breathing apparatus, reflective orange goggles, and clawlike armored gloves.

Six was in trouble. He couldn't use his fake triple C — it was flagged. Yesterday he'd tried it during a random check, and the alarms had gone off. The cockroach-men had immediately drawn their weapons; Six had been lucky to survive the encounter.

Should he try to bluff his way through, make up some excuse for not having his ChaoSonic Citizen Card on him? Should he locate a man with a similar face and body, and steal his?

Could he try to slip through the checkpoint unnoticed? The crowd of people was particularly dense here. But the guards would be expecting that — they'd have a way of dealing with anyone who tried to escape.

Six looked around him. He was very close to the checkpoint. He must have passed some security officers already. It was their job to arrest or kill those who bolted when they saw the checkpoint. He hadn't seen anything — maybe they were plainclothes security, or maybe they were too far away in the fog for him to see. Or there were digi-cams designed to photograph anyone who tried to escape so they could be filed by face-scan and located later.

"Your triple C, please," the cockroach said again, this time to a homeless man. The man pulled a grimy card out from one of his tattered socks, and handed it over. The guard scanned it and handed it back, with a grating "Thank you."

Six knew he had few options. He couldn't bluff his way through; at the very least they'd photograph him, and he was too close to the Deck to allow that to happen. If ChaoSonic found the Deck headquarters, none of the agents would last very long.

He could take them by surprise and fight his way through, or he could turn back and face whatever resistance lay that way.

Better the devil you know than the devil you don't. Six knew that this proverb made more sense than most. He had no idea what was behind him, yet he could see the four soldier-cockroaches in front of him. It would seem that logic was on the proverb's side — except that whatever hostile forces waited behind him, there would be at least as many in front.

And there was another problem. Although ChaoSonic insisted that random triple C tests were just to make sure that everyone had a card and was therefore receiving equal benefits from the company, Six suspected that they had a secret agenda. It wasn't just to ensure that everyone was catalogued; it was also to weed out Deck agents. And Six could feel the rising panic in the pit of his stomach when he thought about his own secret suspicion: They might be looking specifically for *him*.

The Lab was a division of ChaoSonic. If they had somehow worked out who he was, they would be scouring the City for him.

And if that were the case, he wouldn't be able to fight his way past them. Against these soldiers he would not have the element of surprise. They would have been well briefed about his capabilities; even if they didn't know specifics, just a quick study of his history would be enough to warn them to be heavily armed if they expected to encounter him.

"Your triple C, please," the guard asked Six coldly.

"Sure," Six said smoothly, his heart pounding like a drum. "I know I have it here somewhere. . . ."

Six reached a hand into his pocket, shuffled it around, and pulled it out again, reaching towards the soldier. Before the soldier had time to realize that Six wasn't holding anything at all, Six had snatched the guard's gun from its holster and was firing it into the air.

People screamed and started to run away from the checkpoint. Suddenly Six was at the back of a mass of people — running, they thought, for their lives.

The guard lunged forward to grab Six, but his hands gripped empty air. Six had vanished.

Suddenly the airwaves were thick with transmissions, and guards' radios crackled all around.

"Suspect sighted."

"Where?"

"I lost him in the crowd."

"Don't let anybody leave! Establish a perimeter!"

But it was too late for that. There were only ten guards, and more than three hundred people. The guards were well equipped to handle one or two people trying to escape, but not a whole herd of civilians running for their lives.

"Open fire! Kill them all!"

"No!" a voice crackled. *"He'll be gone by now."*

From his vantage point around the corner, Six breathed a sigh of relief. But he wasn't altogether satisfied — they were still much too close to the Deck.

One way or another, this wasn't a safe place to be. Six slipped into the fog, and escaped deeper into the City.

THE WATCHER

The house sat among its neighbors, as inconspicuous and ignored as an ant in its nest. It was small, functional, and had an armored appearance to it; there were dark metal sheets on the roof, and the windows were opaque. There was a security floodlight trained on the front yard, glaring suspiciously at the cars that droned past, waiting for trespassers on the lawn so it could blind them. There were alarms behind the door, adorned with numbered buttons, which sternly awaited the arrival of an intruder so they could swiftly electrocute him or her with small, sharp wires, stopping the heart instantly. A satellite dish on the roof moved in a slow circle, maintaining constant reception from all the mechanical creatures that drifted around Earth, invisible to the naked eye.

A window near the front door suddenly became clear. Agent Six peered in through it, carefully scanning the room for anomalies. Satisfied that everything was how he'd left it, he clicked his remote control and placed it back in his pocket. The window became opaque again.

Moments later, the front door rattled. One at a time, four different keys disarmed four locks. The door swung open, and Six typed in the nine-digit combination to turn off the alarm. The electric wires slid back patiently into their slots.

Six walked methodically through the house, checking each room. Everything was as still as death. A vague, uncertain humming emanated from the refrigerator. Its LCD was blank. The television's sole light, a tiny red dot, flicked on and off twice per second. There was one bed in the house — a firm, narrow bunk with a gun under the pillow.

He found nothing out of the ordinary, so he went to the bookcase, where hundreds of dusty books squatted on shelves. *The Politics of Modern Society* — *A Study of Anarchy*; *Warfare: Tools and Strategies*; *Whitman's Encyclopedia of Physics and Chemistry*; *The World Since 2000*. On a separate shelf rested titles of a different nature: *The Human Genome Project*; *DNA and Genes*; *Splicing Genes to Affect Growth*; *Beyond IVF*.

He removed a copy of *Philosophy and Its Application in Today's Society* from his pocket and placed it on the shelf. He had bought it before returning home. *If philosophy is the wisdom of the world's greatest thinkers,* he had thought, *then I should at least develop an understanding of it.*

Some of the books on the shelves were biographies, and some were biographies of people Six was sure could never have existed. Since Takeover, the line between fact and fiction had become so blurry that no one was sure who had actually existed and who had been made up for entertainment. Harry Houdini, Long John Silver, Julius Caesar, Jesus Christ, Hamlet, Bruce

Wayne, Socrates, Sherlock Holmes, John McClane, Ludwig van Beethoven, James Bond, Eliot Ness, Adolf Hitler, Ned Kelly . . . who was real?

Who knew what life had been like all those years ago? Who could be sure, when no one who had seen those times was now left alive to say?

The computer perched on the edge of a black fiberglass desk, lights blinking as Six approached. Under the desk was a crisp, clean strip of carpet. Under the carpet was a steel trapdoor. Under the trapdoor was a shallow concrete pit, empty except for cockroach carcasses in the corners.

Six pulled on a pair of latex gloves as he sat. A few clicks of the mouse, taps on the keys, and he was satisfied that he had been paid for today's mission. He switched off the computer, peeled off his gloves, and tossed them into the steel garbage bin. The bin hummed unobtrusively as it heated the gloves, melting off Six's fingerprints. No prints were left behind on the keyboard, either.

Six walked down the hall to his training room. As he moved, narrow beams of light and shadows danced around his feet. They ducked and waved, weaving and playing in rings and loops around his legs.

The light came from the mirrors that were placed in every room. Laser torches had been placed at the front and back doors, and their beams hummed right through the house, guided by the mirrors. If anything moved in any room, the beams would move or break, changing the lighting conditions throughout the house. If anyone was in the house, Six would know about it as soon as he or she moved.

Six walked into his training room. It was cube shaped — about five meters on each side. Its walls were painted pristine white. The room contained a flat screen built into the wall, a digi-cam on a tripod, a black rubber mannequin bolted into an aluminum track that ran across the floor, and a black nylon jumpsuit with a stopwatch sewn into the wrist.

Six slipped into the jumpsuit and flicked a switch on the watch. Circular patches on his wrists, elbows, hips, knees, and ankles began to glow. There were also glowing spots on his chest and his back, right in front of and behind his heart. Reaching into a breast pocket, Six removed a luminous adhesive disc and attached it to the side of his head.

Crossing the room, he switched on the digi-cam. The flat screen on the wall flared into life, and immediately rendered an artificial image of Six. The copy mimicked his movements as he examined it. Its body was largely the same as his, but it had no face, fingers, or hair.

The computer wasn't really displaying him, Six knew. It was hypothesizing his movement and posture, based on the digi-cam's readings of the signals from the glowing discs on the jumpsuit. If the camera were switched on while the jumpsuit was folded neatly on the floor, the screen would display Six as a tangled mess of broken bones.

Six touched the screen, and a menu appeared. He selected UNARMED COMBAT DRILLS, STRIKING DRILLS, then

COMBINATIONS. A list of strike types appeared, and Six chose AERIAL STRIKES, HOLDS, KICKS, and PUNCHES. He hit NEXT.

A list of thousands of files appeared in alphabetical order. Six selected QUADRUPLE STRIKE BACK FLIP v2.5.

LOADING appeared on the screen. Six approached the mannequin as its silvery eyes began to glow.

This mannequin was Six's training dummy. He had purchased it from a mercenary who specialized in torture, and he had made some special modifications himself. Inside were many broken circuits that would sound an alarm if they were connected. Six had wired the dummy up to function like a human body. Any strike to it that would cause pain to a human being triggered a distorted buzzer; any strike that would cause a human being to lose consciousness made a clear *ping* sound. Anything that would kill a human being caused the mannequin to power down, as a short hum, falling rapidly in pitch, was emitted.

Six tested the dummy, putting his hands around its neck and squeezing. First came the buzzer (pain), then the *ping* (unconsciousness), then the dummy powered down (death). Everything seemed satisfactory.

The screen on the wall beeped. An image of Six appeared, crouching in front of a generic enemy soldier. When a *blip* was heard, the image sprang up into the air, slightly towards the soldier, and did a backflip in slow motion. On the way up, it punched the soldier in the abdomen with its left fist, and then used its right foot to push off his chest and fly higher. When it was on its back at the highest point, it put its left foot on the soldier's face and pushed off again to finish the flip. When it was almost right-side up with its feet nearing the ground, it executed an uppercut to the soldier's jaw, using the last moments of momentum from the spin to add power to the blow.

Six's image hit the ground in a crouch as the digital soldier staggered backward. Without pause, the image stood up, stepped forward, and neatly caught the soldier before he hit the ground. It held its opponent for a moment in a bear hug, with the soldier's arms pinned against his sides and its right foot ready to trip him if he should struggle. Apparently satisfied that its opponent was unconscious, digital Six lowered him to the ground.

The real Six nodded to himself. *Excellent,* he thought. *I can have this sequence perfected before dinner.*

The dummy powered up and raised its rubber arms into a fighting stance. It slid along the aluminum track with a hydraulic hissing until it was in the center of the room.

Six crouched, and waited for the computer's signal.

Blip.

Six jumped forward. Only moments after his feet had left the ground, he had already punched the dummy in its synthetic midriff with his left fist. The rubber sank in slightly, the grating pain buzzer sounded, and the mannequin rolled backward along its track as it doubled over a little. Now hovering right above the dummy, Six slammed out his right foot and pushed off the mannequin's torso. The pain buzzer sounded again, and Six lifted a little higher. Now he was facing the ceiling, and beginning to fall — the light fixtures were barely a meter above his face. He kicked the dummy in the head with his left heel and heard the rubber skull snap backward. The buzzer crackled again as he spun in the air, now upside down. The floor came into view from the top of his field of vision. Then the dummy's feet dropped into his line of sight. Then waist. Then torso.

Now!

Six swung his right arm up and cracked his fist into the mannequin's jaw.

The dummy's rubber head popped off and bounced along the floor.

The power-down death hum sound was played, and Six landed nimbly on the floor. Flight time: 1.7 seconds.

The headless dummy slumped backward, and Six didn't bother catching it. It clattered to the ground.

The move was supposed to knock an attacker unconscious, not decapitate him. Six sighed. This was going to require more training than anticipated.

Six touched a few buttons on his ancient microwave and watched his homegrown GM vegetable soup circling inside. The microwave was long since obsolete — food was now manufactured to react with oxygen, creating its own heat. It came, in specially sealed electronic packages that required a triple C to be opened (this served to starve those without a government file). But Six had no card and no file. He didn't really trust anything manufactured after ChaoSonic took over supply of the City's electronic needs — anything you bought could have bugs in it. Tracking devices, microcameras, digi-monitors. Any electrical object could have another electrical object inside it. And whenever you used a triple C, whether it be for a scan, a purchase, or just opening a meal, a signal was sent to the ChaoSonic mainframe, acknowledging your location.

Six couldn't let them find out where he was. If the Lab ever caught him . . .

He glanced nervously over his shoulder and checked that the light beams were still steady. He zipped up his jacket to stop the shivering.

The microwave pinged.

He flicked on the television as he sipped his soup. It was smooth and chalky in his mouth. He checked the news on each channel for mention of himself, the Deck, the Lab, or anything to do with phase two of the Human Genome Project — Project Falcon. There was nothing.

After dinner, he read *Philosophy and Its Application in Today's Society*. He studied Descartes, Socrates, Aristotle, Plato, Hume, and many others who were less well known. He sat motionless for half an hour, his long fingers rapidly turning the pages.

Once he had read the entire book, he wiped it clean of his fingerprints with a white cloth, and then put the cloth in the incinerator.

Six climbed the glass stairs to the attic and crouched in front of a tiny window, ignoring the milling cockroaches. The

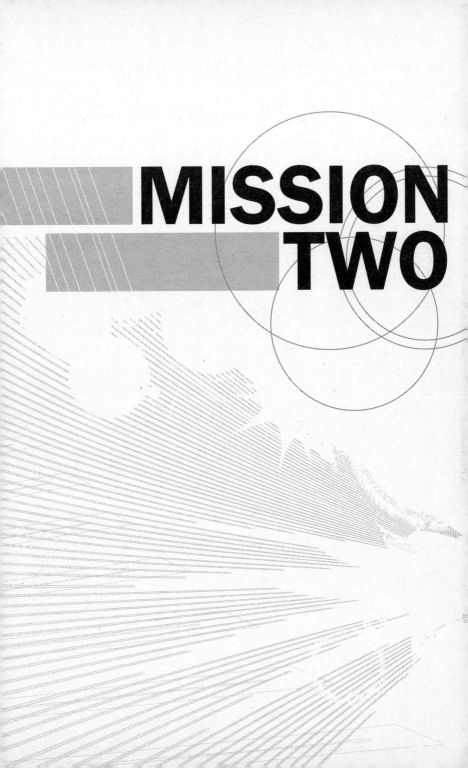

MISSION TWO

CHANGING FACE

"Hi, Six!" Jack said. "Ready for your next mission?"

Six sat down and leaned his head back against the headrest.

"I'll take that as a yes," Jack said, undaunted. "I've heard lots of exciting things about these undercover missions! I heard from Five that —"

"Please get to work," Six said.

"Just being friendly, Six. It wouldn't kill you to try it, you know."

Six grunted. Like Six, Jack had worked at the Deck since its formation, and for those three long years Six had never enjoyed his company. Jack's enthusiasm for his work and the agents he served hadn't dimmed at all, much to Six's displeasure. Although he was twenty, Jack had the bright, curious demeanor of a child, and an endless supply of boyish excitement. His long, strawberry blond hair was always knotted and tangled, and his reddish-brown eyes were always wide with delight. He was always smiling and laughing and talking. *And talking and talking and talking,* Six thought, gritting his teeth. So damn chirpy — completely unaware of the grim reality of the City around him. They say that ignorance is bliss, but Six didn't understand why bliss had to be so loud.

Jack was rummaging through his equipment. "Today I think I'll tan your skin slightly," he was saying, "give you brown eyes, a mole or two, and make your hair sort of mahogany-colored, okay? Then . . . maybe I'll lengthen your eyes a bit. Sound good?"

"Please hurry up," Six said. He wanted to be on his way as quickly as possible.

"Okay. You're not in a cheery mood today, I see. No worse than any other day, of course. Off we go!"

Six stared at Jack coldly as he removed two contact lenses from a grey case on his desk.

"Open wide," Jack said. He held Six's eyelids apart and dropped in the lenses. Six felt them attach themselves to his eyeballs.

"Good. I'll do the hair next. Actually, it's not mahogany after all. 'Chestnut rust,' it says on the packet. Incidentally, ChaoRinse shampoo will have no effect on the dye, so when you want to go back to normal, just come to me. Or you could just leave it as is —"

"Don't you have other work to do?" Six asked.

Jack sighed. "Just making conversation," he said to himself.

Dodging a glare from Six, Jack stepped around behind

him and used a soft brush to paint the dye onto Six's hair. Six could feel it seeping right down to his scalp.

Jack continued to talk as he painted. "Because of the nature of this mission, your equipment is rather limited. They'll almost certainly scan you on your way in, so guns, bombs, and knives are out as far as combat equipment goes. Not that you often use those things. You will, on the other hand, be able to have a plastic microphone in your collar, a button-cam in your breast pocket, and a Deck-issue, four-prong electrical discharge generator."

Six snorted. "You mean a taser."

"Basically. But a rather powerful one. Anyway, provided that none of these things are switched on when they do the scan, you'll be ushered through before you can say, 'None of my equipment was on during the scan.' Okay?"

Jack picked up a hair dryer and started drying Six's hair. "You'll be wearing all designer clothing," he continued. "It's probably the most expensive outfit I've ever seen. So do me a favor and try to bring it back in one piece."

"So you can keep it when I'm finished?"

"Yeah, right," said Jack. "There'll be other missions where agents need to look classy, so we'll be keeping the suit in storage. Although I wouldn't mind a suit like this. I'm —"

"Are you talking," Six asked, "for your benefit, or mine?"

Jack had finished drying Six's hair. "Mine, I guess." He sighed. "Gee, I barely recognize you already," he said happily. "And we've still got lots more work to do!"

"Who's going to be online?"

"I was just getting to that," Jack said. He put down the gel container, washed his hands, and produced some tan cream. He began to rub it into Six's face. "Agent Two will be at an on-site location, and the radio is preprogrammed to a frequency you can reach him on. Although if you need to, you can change the frequencies on the radio. Just push the up button to switch it up, or the down button to switch it down. You'll have to take it out of your ear to do it, though."

"Mmm." Six couldn't open his mouth; Jack was still rubbing in the tan cream. A few seconds later he had finished, and the floury smell of the cream filled Six's nostrils.

"Only two more things to do!" Jack fished around inside his case and pulled out two flaps of artificial skin, one with freckles on it and the other with a scar. "Hold still, please."

He touched the flesh between Six's right eye and his ear and pulled it backward slightly. Then he stuck on the scar to hold it in place. Six could feel that his eye had changed shape; it had become longer and narrower.

"I wish I could be a field agent," Jack said dreamily. "Go to interesting places, meet new people, get paid to run around and stuff. A car chase would be good, or one of those jump-out-of-a-plane infiltration jobs!" He repeated the shaping action on the other side of Six's head.

Six had never understood how Jack could work at the Deck for three years and still be so blind to the horrors they fought every day. "Meet new people, and kill them," he said. "It's the good life all right."

"But you don't," Jack said. "I've seen your mission results. We all have. You never kill on missions; you avoid it at all costs."

"Other people try to kill *me* on a regular basis. It's not like your 'Secret Agent: Interesting Places, New People, Car Chases' brochure."

Jack smiled. "I'm just going to smooth the transition between face tone and chest tone," he said, ignoring Six's comment.

He unzipped Six's shirt and pushed aside the fabric.

Six's torso should have been covered with surgical scars, marks from deep cuts and heavy bruises, and even a bullet wound in his right shoulder. But thanks to Six's doctored metabolism, supercharged heart, and incredible immune system, his chest looked muscular and healthy but for a few patches where the fine hairs had not regrown.

Jack suddenly paused in his work. "I didn't know you had dog tags!" he said.

Six grimaced. Before reporting to Jack he always turned the chain around so the dog tags were behind him where Jack wouldn't see them. They must have slid around to the front again.

"'Sender J. Lawson,'" Jack read, "'Infantry.' Who's he? Some kind of relative?"

Six snatched the tags out of Jack's hand and slipped them back behind his neck.

Jack scooped some tanning cream out of a silver container. "I used to wear my father's ring. . . ."

Please, no more, Six thought.

"The tags are none of your business," he said. "Are you nearly finished?"

Jack zipped up Six's shirt. "There. Your own mother wouldn't recognize you now!" he said. "But one last thing . . ."

If I had a mother, you'd probably be right, Six thought. *But you could never guess what my childhood was like.*

His face remained blank, and Jack didn't notice anything wrong when he began to paint Six's face again. "A mole here, some more freckles there, a scar under the neck, and a touch of sunburn under the eyes. Perfect! All done!"

Six looked in the mirror that Jack was holding up, and as usual after Jack had done his work, he saw a complete stranger glaring back. The man he saw had a darker face than Six did, his hair was reddish-brown, his narrow, dark eyes were black and mysterious, and his face was riddled with tiny, natural-looking marks.

"What do you think?" Jack asked hopefully. But he didn't seem surprised when Six got out of the chair, grabbed the taser and the outfit from Jack's desk, and left the room without answering.

Six walked down the stairwell to get to his car. His almost silent footsteps were amplified by the thin metal and cold brick walls. Six didn't like elevators — the speed at which they moved was outside your control, they could be shut down by external forces, there was no easy way to escape them if you were trapped, and you never really knew what was waiting on each floor. In a stairwell, if you opened the door and didn't like what was on the other side, you could just slam it shut and run for your life.

Six opened the exit door and left the stairwell, entering the underground parking lot. He headed towards his car.

A sudden noise made him pause. What was that? Just the scuff of a shoe on the concrete — tiny, almost inaudible, but he had heard it. He glanced around uneasily. It didn't look as though anyone was there. . . .

A door slammed somewhere behind him. Six whirled around immediately, but no one was there. Rows and rows of parked cars were illuminated in the blue-white glow of halogen lights. The whole parking lot was empty.

No one was here now, but someone had been.

Six crouched down and looked under his car. No evidence of tampering, no bombs apparent. He looked at the locks on the sides, the trunk, and the hood. No sign of anything amiss.

He stood well back and hit the remote control on his keys.

The car disarmed itself. Six waited for twenty seconds, about the time it would take for an assassin to make certain he would be in the car.

Still nothing happened.

Satisfied that no traps were set for him, but still uneasy, Six climbed into the car and closed the door. He started the engine and drove towards the exit.

There! A flicker. One moment a man had been leaning against the wall — and the next he was gone.

Six floored the accelerator and zoomed up the ramp, out into daylight.

Looking around, he saw that no one was following him, no one was looking at him, there were no helicopters or planes overhead.

But Six knew for certain — he was being watched.

UNDERCOVER

"Mr. Macintyre," the woman in the Wanderer said. "I'm Earle Shuji. At last we meet in person!"

"The pleasure is entirely mine," Six said, with what he judged to be a disarming smile. He reached down to shake the hand of the woman in the wheelchair.

"I felt that given your patience online, I should give you the tour in person. I'm very flattered that you've taken such an interest in our work here, Mr. Macintyre."

"Again, the pleasure has been mine," Six replied. "I very much look forward to doing business with you. And please, call me Scott."

Six appraised Shuji. She was classy looking — her gold-tinted brown hair was tied back in a fashionable rather than practical way, and when her lips parted, dark with understated but expensive lipstick, they revealed a polished white smile. Her face suggested arrogance, but if this was indicative of character, Six thought as she looked him up and down with her chocolate-brown eyes, she was hiding it well in front of her prospective business associate. It was hard to judge her height. Almost certainly she was not disabled — Wanderers were currently fashionable with the rich, so most people on the street in wheelchairs were likely to be perfectly healthy.

The rich of the City are so greedy, Six thought. *That greed is how they became so rich. However, the same people would gladly buy things they didn't need, like a wheelchair, making their own legs redundant. What a stupid, stupid world.*

Six slowly scanned the room he was in.

It was a foyer, tiled in a pristine white. None of the edges were sharp or square; the furniture was rounded and smooth. Besides the entrance, there was only one door, which blended almost seamlessly into the polished white wall.

A receptionist in a dark suit sat behind a silver counter with headphones in her ears. Six could hear the music playing, although he suspected that most humans would be deaf to it. He turned his shoulders as he looked around, so the button-hole camera in his vest could take in the whole room.

"That's good, Six," Agent Two said, his voice buzzing through Six's earpiece. *"Keep it up."*

"Now, if you'll indulge me for a moment," Shuji was saying, "I'm going to have to ask you to hold still while you are scanned." She clicked her fingers, and a guard in full battle gear emerged from behind the door.

"Of course." Six stood with his legs slightly apart and his arms spread wide, inviting the guard to search him. The guard approached.

"Check out the gear on that guy," Six's radio observed. *"Full Kevlar body armor, anti-flash goggles with night-vision attachment, gas mask with biochemical filtering, ChaoSonic digital scrambler radio, Falcon 17 automatic rifle (probably an upgrade of the M41-A 10 millimeter), retractable titanium combat knife, and ChaoSilent fittings on his boots. This guy must have gone into the ChaoSonic defense site and just clicked 'Add all to cart'!"*

Indeed, Six thought. This was no security guard — this was a commando. Someone who was probably not just prepared, but *expected*, to kill during his shift. Still, Six thought, there would be weaknesses. The digital scrambler radio, for example, had a computer chip in it. An electromagnetic pulse or a strong magnet could corrupt it, and the soldier wouldn't be able to receive messages from his comrades.

Six smiled to himself. No one ever expected the magnet.

"Hold still," the soldier growled as he set up the scanning apparatus. His voice was deepened and distorted by the gas mask.

"Six, we're going to cut radio contact for a moment," the earpiece said. *"Sit tight."* There was a click as the transmitter was switched off.

The guard held up the scanner and turned it on. It looked a little like a black horseshoe with a power cord snaking out from the back and two short prongs emerging from the top on either side of the guard's gloved hand. When the power was switched on, the batteries sparked to life and a line of crackling energy joined the two ends of the horseshoe.

The soldier pointed the scanner at Six's torso, then at each of his limbs, then at his head. Apparently satisfied, he switched the device off.

"Remote support is back online, Six. We're getting audio and visuals, loud and clear."

"Thank you again for your patience, Mr. Macintyre," Earle Shuji said. "This is Mr. Neeq. He will be your bodyguard for the duration of your brief stay."

Six nodded politely to the guard. Neeq didn't respond; he just stared with his reflective goggled eyes.

"Please, follow me." Shuji revved the Wanderer and drove it over to the door, which slid open. They all went through it.

The receptionist in the headphones didn't look up.

This mission was a straightforward rescue. Shuji had captured different experts to work for her, and was planning to execute them once their tasks were complete. Six was to get a layout of the building and transmit it to the Deck. He was then to meet up with one of the hostages in the bathroom and be taken back to the holding area where the rest of the hostages were. He would barricade them in while Deck agents stormed the facility.

"You'll appreciate, of course, the need for security in a place like this," Shuji was saying as they walked down the flawless white hall. "Not only do we have to deal with the usual vandals, saboteurs, terrorists, and spies from other companies but, between you and me, we also have to avoid the local vigilante groups, particularly an organization called the Deck. Sometimes those kinds of people take an unwelcome interest in our activities."

Six raised an eyebrow. *So,* he thought, *she knows about the Deck.* "They have a moral opposition to your work?" he asked.

"Apparently so. They seem to believe that bots are dangerous, because they will replace human beings in the workforce."

"Will they?"

"Eventually, yes." Shuji shrugged. "If we're going to get right down to the speculative side of things, I foresee two possible outcomes for the reasonably distant future. One is that bots will do all the jobs requiring any manual labor at all, and humans will only be necessary for thinking tasks. This sounds unpleasant until you give it due consideration. Yes, it means that humans will be effectively removed from the workplace. However, the only reason humans need to be in the workplace is to earn money for themselves. If everything is done by bots, all goods and services will be free, because bots have no need of money, and therefore won't be paid. Soon, money will stop changing hands completely. Not long after that it will be only a vestigial concept and, not too much later, it will be gone completely. The human race will finally be at rest, and everyone will just do as they please at their leisure for their entire lives, while the bots do all of the work."

"Forgive my cynicism," Six said, "but that doesn't sound like the most likely outcome of bots replacing humans in all jobs."

Shuji chuckled. "Your cynicism is forgiven, Mr. Macintyre, because you are right, of course. Far more likely is that unemployment and poverty will suddenly sweep the City, the already fragile economy will collapse, millions will starve to death, the rest will die of disease or old age, and the bots will keep doing things alone until their batteries run out many centuries from now. But these problems will not be in our lifetime, I suspect."

"Incredible," Two said. *"What a shameless, evil witch. Try not to lose your cool, Six."*

It hadn't occurred to Six to lose his cool. He was admiring the ChaoSilent fittings on the guard's boots — a mechanism that would silence a soldier's every footfall by simultaneously emitting a phase opposite to the sound.

Rumor had it that ChaoSonic was working on an upgrade to their technology that could cancel out any noise at all triggered by the activities of soldiers — even vehicle movement and gunfire. Ironic, Six thought, given that ChaoSonic owned most of the organizations in the City anyway, and there was no reason for them to even have a defense force, let alone make the one they had more powerful.

The boots didn't matter as far as he was concerned, anyway. When Six of Hearts didn't want to be heard, he wasn't.

"It is no concern of mine," Shuji was saying. "If the end of the world was going to be prevented, something should have been done long before either of us were born. You and I are witnessing the final death throes of the human race, Mr. Macintyre. It can't be long now before cultural habit and routine break down completely throughout the populace, and complete amorality follows the lawlessness in which we have lived our lives."

She's smarter than most, Six thought, as they approached the titanium roller-door at the end of the corridor. But what was a woman with such clear insight doing in a Wanderer?

"Bots will neither cause the end of the world, nor prevent it. They may indirectly throw a few more scraps of garbage onto the heap under which we are already buried, and perhaps accelerate the process of our downfall. But I need to eat. And, particularly if there is no future, I feel obliged to enjoy the present."

She slipped her finger into the gel in the scanning terminal next to the roller-door. The terminal pinged.

"Access granted," it announced. *"Welcome, Dr. Shuji."*

Doctor, Six thought. As if there were such a thing as a university anymore to give qualifications like that. She really did think highly of herself.

The door rumbled aside, and Six's eyes widened at the sight before them.

THE PERFECT KILLING MACHINE

"What the . . ." the earpiece stammered. *"They've already gone into production.* Serious *production."*

Six agreed. He had seen botlines before, but nothing of this magnitude.

Steam thundered up from hundreds of engines and furnaces. A massive conveyor belt chugged its sluggish way around the cavern. Electricity crackled constantly between the enormous pockmarked, wirelike roof and the chrome spires attached to every station. The air was filled with the clanking of gears and the hiss of hydraulics from thousands of mechanical limbs doing their various tasks of welding, soldering, assembling, and molding.

And at the end of the conveyor belt, bots were being put into cases. Their polished, symmetrical bodies and expressionless plastic faces glinted in the light of the furnace fires and the electrical storm above.

Six was completely shocked. He had never expected the bots to be in construction already. Their contact among the hostages had told the Deck that as far as he knew, no manual laborers had been recruited to begin production, so apart from a few prototype bots, the entire project was in the theoretical phase. In fact, when Six had been briefed, he'd been informed that no botlines were currently at a stage where they could begin mass construction, except for one in a different branch of ChaoSonic called Gear.

And these are combat bots, Six thought. *These are armored and aerodynamic — and armed,* he added mentally, when he saw the Swan KM909 rifles molded into the bots' wrists. *Gear doesn't make soldier bots, he thought. They make androids for manual labor tasks, like heavy lifting and routine assembly —*

Then it hit him. He scanned the floor of the cavern quickly, searching for a worker who was facing him. He saw one, and the bald eyeless head confirmed his suspicions. "Bots building bots," he whispered.

Shuji grinned. "That's right. We bought a few hundred from Gear, assigned them their tasks, and soon the pace of production was triple what Gear themselves can do. It surprised me that they didn't think of it first, actually. Perhaps they got sentimental and refused to dump their employees." She chuckled. "Or, more likely, they're up to something we don't know about. Of course, the beauty of this system is that it's totally leakproof. Bots don't sell secrets to competing branches; nor do they feel a moral obligation to tip off the vigilantes about our activities."

She was right, Six knew. Usually the Jokers, the two mysterious spies who ran the Deck, could tap into at least one source from any company and learn incriminating secrets, but no one knew that there were operational soldier droids in this facility already. Shuji could have bought the droids herself, had them shipped over to her facility by any of a thousand courier organizations, and given the bots their duty instructions with no one having any idea what she was up to.

"Keep stalling her, Six," Two said. *"The source isn't ready to roll just yet."*

"So, the soldier bots," Six said to Shuji. "Do they function as well as in the promo designs you gave me?"

The woman in the Wanderer grinned wickedly. "I thought you'd never ask," she said.

Shuji led Six into a testing lab, while Neeq watched impassively. The laboratory was superbly clean and tidy. There was a chrome table in one corner with nothing on it, and a tinted-glass window high on one wall. All the staff and testing apparatus were, Six suspected, behind that glass, watching from above. The light in the room was provided by fat neon tubes built into the walls and similar ones hanging from the ceiling, which were so bright that Six had to squint against them until his sensitive eyes adjusted.

"A demonstration bot will be here in just a few moments," Shuji said. "In the meantime, let me explain how the testing process works."

Six guessed that she was probably wearing a wire, and that their conversations were being monitored. This way, she could appear perfectly prepared for everything, because her staff knew exactly what Mr. Macintyre was being told. When she had informed Six that a demonstration bot was on its way, a company operative had probably hastened to arrange one.

"In the early stages, of course," Shuji said, "all testing and training were theoretical. My technicians simply programmed the Central Processing Units with some basic vocabulary, strategy, knowledge of physics, weapons information, and priority code. The real fun started when we brought in some trained soldiers to fight the prototype bots with a variety of weapons. Then we analyzed the results and reprogrammed the bots accordingly."

"How did you stop the soldiers from leaking details of your activities to the general public?" Six asked, already knowing the answer.

"They believed that we were testing body armor, not droids," Shuji said smoothly. "We told them that the bot used was a Gear product, reprogrammed and dressed like a soldier, because we couldn't risk harming human beings in our tests. Trust me, Mr. Macintyre, no one but you, me, and my staff knows the truth about what we do here."

The data the Jokers had obtained said that all the soldiers had been kidnapped from security organizations and vigilante groups like Six's own. They had been imprisoned and forced into a fight to the death with prototype bots. Those who had refused had been starved and tortured. After days in excruciating pain, without food or hope of rescue, most soldiers had chosen to fight the bots. Those who didn't had been executed by Neeq and the rest of his team. But even those who had fought and won had not been freed; instead, they had been forced to compete against more and more advanced models until the soldier bots had reached perfection and the last soldier had been killed.

The technicians and engineers had been kidnapped as well. The Deck suspected that as Shuji's theoretical development of the project was nearly complete, all the programmers were scheduled for execution. She was not a woman to leave witnesses.

But Shuji has already begun production of the soldier bots, Six thought. *Perhaps we are already too late.*

His thoughts were interrupted as the titanium laboratory door rumbled open. Another commando dressed like Neeq stepped into the room, carrying a steel coffinlike case.

The soldier placed the case on its end in the center of the floor. He nodded to Earle Shuji.

"The demonstration droid, Dr. Shuji," he said, his voice crackly and gravelly through his gas mask.

"Thank you, Mr. Crenshaw," Shuji replied. "You may return to your duties."

The soldier turned and nodded to Neeq, who was standing by the door. Neeq nodded back, and Crenshaw left, rolling the door closed behind him. Six heard an ominous clank as the soldier locked and bolted the door from outside — presumably out of habit. This was probably the very room that all those men and women had died in.

Shuji rolled over to the case and unlocked it.

"Scott Macintyre," she said, "it is my pleasure to present to you . . ."

She opened the lid.

". . . the perfect killing machine."

Inside the case was a soldier bot.

Six looked it up and down. It was more or less humanoid in shape, but with some bulges in the wrong places — for example, the bulge on its right wrist from the built-in Swan, and the bulge on its left wrist where a flashlight was attached. The hands were narrow, with long, thin fingers. The head was featureless except for two silvery eyes. Instead of a mouth, the bot had an amplifier on the front of its left shoulder, with a directional microphone next to it for receiving audio.

"Runs off a plutonium battery with a half-life of a hundred seventy years — the bot is operational for all that time," explained Shuji. "It can lift weights of up to nearly one ton, run at speeds exceeding sixty kilometers an hour, and hit a one-centimeter bull's-eye from a range of nearly one hundred thirty meters, provided that its Swan is well maintained — which it always will be, because the bot does all the maintenance itself. As for vision, hearing, reflexes . . . don't even ask. The thing literally has eyes in the back of its head — and the top, for that matter. Its senses are more effective than those of any man alive."

Six raised an eyebrow.

"While it obviously isn't suitable for a traditional IQ test," Shuji continued, "let me tell you that this baby is *smart*. All that genuine AI requires is the ability to learn, so it can change its own programming within certain parameters."

"Asimov's Three Laws of Robotics?" Six ventured.

She grinned. "What good is a soldier bot if it can't kill people? Its advanced CPU will detect, analyze, and plan the eradication of any threat in a matter of moments. It has been programmed with all the latest in combat strategy. It can do anything from directing a battalion of soldiers to victory to winning a game of chess. And all its systems are completely impervious to EMP."

"How did you manage that?" Six asked.

Shuji winked at him. "Trade secret," she said. "Incidentally, the bot is not as fragile as it looks, either — that plastic coating you see is only a few millimeters deep. Underneath it there's a steel exoskeleton that is much tougher than Kevlar. You could park a three-ton truck with its front wheels on the torso and you'd barely leave a dent — so it's bulletproof, just for starters. It has an internal-temperature conditioning system inside that automatically adjusts the heat of all systems to match the air — thermal vision won't pick up the bot at all. Also, this means it's nearly indestructible as far as heat and flame go. A direct and sustained blast from a Phoenix flamethrower would wipe off the plastic skin, but leave the exoskeleton and all systems intact. Also, when you combine temperature efficiency like that with this kind of pressure resistance, you've pretty much got a machine that can't be destroyed in an explosion. It wouldn't survive a nuclear blast, but grenades, rockets, and even plastic explosives will still generally leave it standing."

Six was beginning to get worried. If everything Shuji said was true, then these bots probably weren't just a step towards the end of humanity — they may well be the end itself.

The Deck agents were clearly thinking along the same lines.

"Are we hearing all this correctly?" Two said in his ear. *"This is much worse than we expected."*

"Allow me to demonstrate some of its combat skills," Shuji said, smiling. "Mr. Neeq, if you please."

"Agent Six of Hearts," the earpiece crackled, *"your mission priorities have now changed. A layout of the building is no longer required as there will be no time to formulate a strategy before we move in. Understood, Six? Just get the hostages and get out of the crossfire."*

This is getting extreme, Six thought. There were probably Deck teams moving in to cover every entrance right now.

"The source will be ready soon, Six. We'll keep you posted. As for now, keep stalling her. Buy us some time."

"Because this is only a demonstration bot," Shuji was saying, "its Swan is not loaded with bullets. Instead, it will fire semi-solid capsules of UV-receptive paint. This is one of my favorite demonstrations — the hostage demo. Just watch."

Neeq grabbed Shuji roughly with his left forearm around her neck and crouched behind her, his right hand pointing his Falcon at her head. Immediately the bot opened fire, and capsules smacked against Neeq's armor.

"Stop!" Shuji called.

The bot stopped firing. Neeq stood up. Six couldn't see any evidence that the fight had taken place.

"Mr. Neeq," Shuji ordered, "turn on the black light."

Neeq crossed the room to a switch beside the door and pulled the lever down. All the lights went out.

Six's eyes adjusted quickly. The room was bathed in a dim glow of royal blue, emitting from the black light overhead. He was in darkness, as were Shuji and the bot. But Neeq was glowing. He had splatters of luminous paint on his helmet, goggles, and boots. The paint covered much of his body armor as well.

The bot had shot him dozens of times, without hitting Shuji at all.

"Mr. Neeq," Shuji commanded, "resume your previous stance."

Neeq crouched down with his left forearm forward and his gun arm up, exactly as he had been when he was hiding behind Shuji. Six squinted, not quite sure what he was looking at. Then he saw it and his eyes widened.

The fluorescent paint on the soldier's armor was an exact silhouette of Shuji!

"You'll notice that not a single drop landed on me," the woman in the wheelchair said out of the darkness. "Nor did any hit the wall behind me. As I said before, the bots are deadly accurate with their weapons. This one left a two-centimeter safety margin around me in case I moved, and another margin of the same width around Mr. Neeq, to avoid hitting anything behind him. According to its programming, it would have kept firing until it could no longer detect Mr. Neeq's heartbeat if I hadn't told it to stop. Mr. Neeq, the lights, please."

Neeq pushed the lever back up, and the neon bulbs exploded back into life. Six squinted against the glare. "It follows your orders?" he asked.

"Yes. Yours, too, if I tell it to." She grinned. "Bot, you now have shared ownership. This is your new owner. Follow his orders." She smiled at Six. "Happy birthday."

Six waited, but the bot didn't respond.

"It doesn't really respond unless it considers it a necessity," Shuji said. "Try an order."

"Bot, stand on one foot," Six said.

The bot lifted one leg into the air and stood stock-still.

"There you go," Shuji said, beaming. "Bot, resume previous stance."

The bot put its foot back on the ground.

"It still follows my orders, too, because I said shared ownership. But once you buy them, they will be entirely yours."

A puddle of fluorescent paint had formed around Neeq's boots. "It's not terribly, er . . . *subtle* in its approach, is it?" Six commented.

"It can be," Shuji said. "This is another of the bot's little tricks — an old one, but a good one. Bot," she said, "camouflage."

The bot vanished.

Six tensed. He had seen a quick flicker of movement before the bot had disappeared in front of his eyes.

"Projection," he guessed. "The bot puts a thin covering on its front, receives a DV feed from behind, and projects the footage onto the inside for invisibility." He had seen the bot swiftly don a cape of some kind.

Shuji laughed. "Well done, Mr. Macintyre. That is indeed the essential core of the camouflage technology. However, it's even more sophisticated than you've guessed. Please, look at it yourself."

Six walked uneasily around the invisible bot. He could see a flickering around the edges, and sometimes the things he saw through it were blurred or distorted, but somehow it was hidden from *all angles*.

"The plastic covering doesn't just hide the front; it covers the whole bot, like a poncho or a cloak. Once we finished that function, we decided to name the bot Harry."

Six didn't understand the reference.

"After Harry Potter, Six," Agent Two said hurriedly. *"Children's book character of pre-Takeover times. He had a cloak that made him invisible."*

"After Potter, I presume," Six said smoothly. "How quaint." He chuckled appropriately.

Two snorted. *"Nice save, muggle. I thought you read books!"*

Shut up, Six thought.

Shuji continued. "The digi-cams that receive the feed are at its feet, so they film from underneath the cloak. And there are three of them, so it can project from all sides. Also, the digi-cams are mobile, so when there's only one threat — in this case, you, Mr. Macintyre — the digi-cams rotate according to your movements and always project the relevant image." She shrugged. "There are drawbacks, obviously. The bot can't actually *move* in camouflage mode, nor can it attack. And it has to rely on the digi-cam feeds to see, which are less sophisticated than its eyes. Still, I have no doubt that this technology will be useful in the field, and the bot can switch back very quickly."

She demonstrated. "Bot, standard!"

With a faint swoosh, the bot reappeared. Its expressionless face gazed at Six.

"I talk to it in simple terms only out of habit. The early models couldn't understand anything more complicated than noun-verb-noun sentences. But we've come a long way since then; Harry has probably understood our entire conversation. How are you today, Harry?"

"I am functioning satisfactorily, Dr. Shuji," the bot replied.

"As you can see, the conversation won't be scintillating," Shuji said. "By the way, the bot can swim, too. Harry, show Mr. Macintyre your webs, please."

The bot held out its hands and extended its fingers. With a *ching* sound, the fingers became connected by silver plates.

"There is also a propeller in each of the feet. On that note, while it is not technically capable of actual flight . . ."

The bot jumped into the air, and a blast of flame appeared behind it. It hovered menacingly just below the ceiling of the testing lab.

". . . it *does* have a built-in HR905 jet pack, with which it can jump up to fifty meters vertically, and levitate at any height it jumps to."

The bot shut off the jet pack and landed on its feet with a resounding *clang*.

"Scott," Shuji said, "I think you'll have to agree that this machine is the biggest advance in weaponry in centuries."

"She's working towards the sale, Six," Agent Two said. *"We still need a few more minutes on the source, or we won't be able to save those hostages. Stall her."*

"The air tank that Force is working on has got nothing on this," Shuji was saying. "The new laser rifle from Gear is showy, to be sure, but it's a commercial gimmick, not a serious weapon. It's not in the same league as my soldier bots. The targeted DNA virus that the Lab is designing . . ."

Six's head snapped up.

". . . will be nowhere near as effective or as immediate as this, just as Project Falcon, their superhuman assassin project from twenty years ago, wouldn't have been this good, even if it had worked."

She knows about Project Falcon, too, Six thought. *She's obviously had dealings with the Lab before. And if I didn't know better, I'd say that was a challenge.* "How is Harry on hand-to-hand combat?" he interrupted.

"Superb. Its reflexes are the best you'll ever see, as is its strength, speed, and coordination. In short, it's nothing less than perfect, as with all its systems. Why do you ask?"

Six looked at her evenly.

"I want to fight it," he said.

"What?" Six's earpiece crackled.

"What?" Shuji demanded.

"I want to fight it," Six repeated.

"Mr. Macintyre," Shuji said, suddenly nervous, "I really don't think that's a good idea."

"*Six, no offense,*" Two said, "*but that thing could kick the stuffing out of you. Bad idea, man.*"

"If it's as good as you say it is," Six said to Shuji, "then it should have no trouble beating me, and it won't be damaged."

"Damaged?" Shuji said incredulously. "It's *immune* to damage! It's the safety of my number-one business associate that I'm worried about!"

Six raised an eyebrow. "I've won the North Tarriga Bay Tung Wu Do championship three times in a row," he lied. "I'm the best kickboxer you'll find this side of the Tower, and I was middleweight champion of the City for two years." He adjusted his collar modestly. "When I was younger, of course."

There was a pause.

"Is this a joke?" Shuji asked finally.

"I'm perfectly serious," Six said. "I assume the bot has a non-lethal mode?"

"Well, yes —"

"Then switch it on. I can handle myself, believe me." He walked to the center of the room and stood still.

"Mr. Macintyre —"

"*Mr. Macintyre will be safe, Dr. Shuji,*" the bot interrupted.

Six and Shuji stared at it.

"Preliminary medical scans indicate that this is the fittest, healthiest human being I have come into contact with," the robot continued. *"He has no diseases, heart conditions, or any other factors to consider that are beyond my control. While I am in non-lethal mode, he will not come to harm."*

"That thing is creepy," Six's earpiece said. *"I hope you know what you're doing, Six."*

"Well, you have been warned," Shuji said finally. "Non-lethal mode notwithstanding, this won't be pleasant. Are you sure you want to go through with it?"

Six nodded firmly.

"Very well. Mr. Neeq, take Mr. Macintyre's coat."

"No thank you," said Six, shrugging off the big soldier's hands. "I'm fine."

When he looked back towards the bot, it had vanished.

Invisibility cloak? Six wondered. No, the machine definitely wasn't there.

Six dived to one side as the droid plummeted out of the air and splintered one of the floor tiles with its fist.

"In a real combat situation," the bot rasped, crouched on the floor, *"the first strike will always take the opponent by surprise."*

"Mr. Macintyre," Shuji said, after a pause, "I think this is a bad idea."

"Why?" Six asked. He pointed to the bot. "It's quite correct." Then he leaped into the air with his arms stretched wide and his fists clenched, spinning like the blades of a helicopter, before sending a fist crashing down towards the bot's steel skull . . . only to have his blow halted millimeters above the droid's head as it grabbed him by the throat and held him in the air. Its synthetic eyes scanned him again.

"You are not like the others, Mr. Macintyre," it said.

"No," Six agreed. *You killed the others,* he thought. *But you won't kill me.*

Six grabbed the steel wrist of the hand that was choking him. Then he forced his chin down into the fingers. The robot let go as its synthetic knuckles bent under the pressure.

Six fell to the floor, landing hands first. Springing back like a cat, he swiftly twisted his torso and kicked the bot's legs out from under it. As the bot fell, Six flipped back up onto his feet and darted backward so it couldn't do the same to him.

The bot hit the ground with a *clang*. In the blink of an eye it was on its feet again.

"No," it said. *"Not like the others at all."*

There was no change to the tone of its voice, but Six assumed that behind that dark masklike face, a very advanced CPU was working hard to assess the situation and figure out what it was dealing with. *I must not win,* he reminded himself, *or my secret will be out.* Shuji knows about the Lab and she knows about Project Falcon. If I win, she might put two and two together. He ducked as the bot flew overhead, steel boot first.

Not that winning would be easy, he thought.

He grabbed one of the bot's arms as it flew overhead, and then threw the machine to the ground. It landed on one hand, wrapped its ankles around Six's neck, and tossed him away.

Six hit the wall with a thump. He thought he heard a tile crack behind him, but all of his bones were intact. The robot was clambering to its feet very quickly, but to Six's eyes it was all happening in slow motion. Six jumped straight up and twisted his body sideways in midair so both his feet were pressed against the wall. Then he pushed off and rocketed horizontally towards the robot's head, fist first.

This time, his fist connected.

The bot shuddered as Six knocked it over. He was on top of it before it had time to get up again. Pushing against the ground with one steel foot, the bot threw off Six's weight and pounced upon him. But by the time it hit the ground, Six was no longer under it.

Six jumped high into the air behind the bot. *The strike from above,* he thought as he rose. *That's the bot's weakness.*

The bot switched on its jet pack and followed him up.

Fine, Six thought. *I can trick it.*

In midair, he threw a punch at the bot's chest. The bot blocked it easily, but as it did, Six grabbed the outstretched mechanical arm with his other hand, pivoted off it, flipped upward, and let go.

Suddenly the bot was blinded. All of its eyes had ceased receiving. It flailed its arms around, trying to strike its opponent. It switched the feed from its eyes to the digi-cams in its shoes. They were functioning, but they couldn't locate Six, either.

Six was doing a handstand on the robot's head, with his coat covering all of its eyes. He wobbled precariously as the bot flew around the room with its jet pack, searching for him with the digi-cams in its feet.

The bot paused.

Six could picture the circuits buzzing in its synthetic brain.

Only the crackling of the jet pack marred the silence.

"Six, are you receiving? The source is en route, I repeat, the source is en route. He'll be at the bathroom in seven minutes — so if you're still alive in three, get going."

Silence again.

Then the bot flipped upside down, with Six still holding on to its head, and cranked the jet pack up to full.

It's insane! Six thought wildly. *It's doing a kamikaze dive for the floor!*

He let go of the head and pushed off with his feet, throwing himself clear.

He landed on all fours. As soon as his limbs touched the ground, it shuddered with an ear-piercing *clang* as the robot slammed into it headfirst.

Six collapsed on the floor in a crumpled heap, briefly disoriented by its shaking and the noise in his ears. The sound rang out like a bell, reverberating around the room and against the walls and floor.

Flight time: 9.9 seconds.

Six stood up and dusted himself off. *This,* he thought, *has been an interesting —*

Bang! Six was knocked over as a robotic fist hit him in the solar plexus.

Even as he fought to stay conscious after the force of the blow, Six flipped over backward and landed on his feet. For a moment he struggled to breathe.

Bang! He was hit again in the same place. This time when it knocked him down, he stayed down.

The thing sure packs a punch, he thought, wheezing. *But now that I'm on the ground, I bet it follows standard ground-fighting techniques — which means that its movements can be predicted. This fight isn't over yet.*

As he had expected, the next steel limb to fly at him was a foot. He wrapped his right arm around the ankle, and before the machine had time to react, he reached with his left and grabbed the bot's other leg. Then he lifted it into the air and slammed it against the tiles like a giant hammer on a strength tester at a carnival.

Six pounced on the bot, crouching with one foot on its throat. Immediately its arms whipped up and its hands wrapped themselves around his neck. Six quickly put his hands over the top of the bot's and slid his fingers underneath to stop the bot from choking him.

There they paused, in a temporary truce.

"You fight well..." the bot said softly. *"Agent Six of Hearts."*

Six gasped. How did . . . and then he realized something. The bot's voice had not come from the amp; it was coming from *his own earpiece!*

The bot could receive radio waves. It had heard his radio transmissions.

"Your genuine title explains some, but not all, of your abilities," the bot continued. *"You are still hiding many things."*

Six squeezed the synthetic hands tighter. There was a long silence.

"All right," he said finally. "Enough." He lifted his foot off the robot's neck, and the robot immediately dropped its hands from his. Six dusted himself down as the bot clambered to its feet.

"Well," he said, turning to Shuji, "I'm satisfied. The machine can fight after all, and what's more, it can fight well. Our business deal will proceed as planned, if you are agreeable."

Shuji looked at him for a long time, tapping one of her fingers against a tire on her wheelchair. Then she said, "Where did you learn to fight like that?"

"Stay in character, Six," the earpiece hissed.

"I've seen some very old movies," he said with a smile. "Now if you don't mind, I require the use of your bathroom facilities before we conclude our business here."

Shuji nodded. "Of course. Mr. Neeq, show Mr. Macintyre to the bathroom."

"Thank you," Six said. "A pleasure to meet you, Harry," he said to the bot. "Farewell, until next time."

The bot nodded slowly.

Six and Neeq walked out the door, and it rumbled shut behind them.

"Bot," Shuji said, "back in your case." The bot complied, shutting the door behind it.

ONLY HUMAN

"Well, that robot certainly can fight," Six said.

Neeq said nothing.

"And that was in non-lethal mode, of course," Six added. "I wouldn't have stood a chance if it had been in standard mode."

Neeq said nothing.

They were walking down the same corridor as before. With its limited human staff, the facility only required one bathroom — and it was close to the entrance, so visitors had no excuse to go deep into the building. This was a design flaw that the Deck was about to exploit — the hostages had to use the same bathroom as the visitors.

The conversation wasn't going well — it was more of a monologue, really. Six needed to put the soldier at ease so he didn't see Six as a threat, which was going to require significantly more effort now that Neeq had seen Six fight the bot.

Slight tactical error there, he thought. *I got carried away.*

"So," Six said now, "how long have you been working here?"

"Twenty months," Neeq growled.

"I suppose you've seen the work being done, then, right from design to testing."

"Yes."

"Listen, between you and me," Six said, turning to face the guard as he walked, "how efficient are the work processes? Are they . . . *streamlined*? I mean, in your opinion, do Dr. Shuji's strategies make full use of her resources?" His smile vanished. "Everything I've seen today is satisfactory, but I'm no fool — I know that this is merely the tip of the iceberg."

Neeq hesitated.

"It will be, of course," Six said, "in your best interests to help me. I need security staff of my own, obviously. Although no one has ever attempted to infiltrate any of my various offices and facilities, a man with as much money as me still requires . . . insurance."

Neeq made up his mind.

"I can appreciate your concern, Mr. Macintyre," he said, "but it is misplaced. Dr. Shuji's sense of business is as faultless as it appears."

Smart man, Six thought, *and tactful. But it would appear that I've won him over as I intended.*

Moments later they turned the corner and the bathroom door came into view. Neeq slowed as he saw there was already a guard waiting by the door.

"You have guards for your bathrooms, too!" Six said approvingly. "Security certainly is tight here."

"Why are you here?" Neeq said to the other guard.

"Dr. Shuji's orders," came the reply.

"Which orders?"

"I'm protecting . . . an employee."

Neeq tapped the side of his head — a signal, Six suspected, to go to closed-circuit communications. The rest of the conversation would be done over the radio waves, in private.

"Hang on, Six," his earpiece said. *"Just patching you through to their frequency now."*

". . . we both wait out here, he will try something," the other soldier was saying. *"He knows that the project is nearing completion, and that his time is nearly up. If Macintyre goes in alone, he will see his chance."*

"Agreed," said Neeq. *"I will go in with Macintyre. You wait here."*

So far, so good, Six thought.

"This way," Neeq grunted, talking through the mask again.

Six followed him through the door into the anteroom.

The bathroom was one of the cleanest Six had ever seen. The mirrors glittered like gems, and the polished marble walls and floor shone in the light from the softly glowing light notches.

The guard stood motionless by the door. Six wandered over to the end cubicle and stepped inside.

Even as he was closing and locking the door, he was weighing his options. Neeq wasn't close enough to the cubicle door for Six's ideal attack strategy — he could have just kicked the door out and knocked Neeq down with it. He had to think of something else.

He was fortunate at least that the anteroom between the bathroom and the hall outside was a long one, with granite walls. The guard outside was unlikely to hear any noise softer than gunfire. This still left the radio as a problem, but the soundproofing was better than nothing, and it gave Six a few options.

One: He could slide under the door or cubicle wall and kick Neeq's legs out from under him. But this soldier was well trained, and Six bet on a thirty or forty percent chance he'd be shot before he reached striking distance. Not good odds.

Two: He could jump over the toilet wall and land on Neeq — the gap between the wall and ceiling was about eighty centimeters, so he could do it. But without a run-up and with the forced angle of an ascent that vertical, the strength of the blow would come entirely from gravity. There was no way Six could put any of his muscle power into the attack, and Neeq was a big man. There was every chance that Neeq would just throw Six to the ground and shoot him. Likelihood of survival with this strategy hovered at only around fifty or sixty percent.

Three: Six could keep up the pretense of cooperation until he'd already come out of the cubicle, and then improvise an attack while he was washing his hands or exiting. But Six knew that as soon as he left the cubicle, Neeq would be on the alert again — not because he suspected that Six was up to something, but because he knew that there was a hostage in the next cubicle, and this was his best chance to escape.

Chances of survival: around eighty, perhaps ninety percent.

That seemed to be his best option right now — or was it?

Six smiled to himself as he began unfastening the bolts that connected the cubicle wall to the frame that was fixed into the tiles at the back of the cubicle.

Fortunately, these weren't standard bolts. Each one was a powerful iron magnet that connected the cubicle wall to the metal rods stuck into the main wall of the bathroom. If the bolts had been screws, then Six would probably have needed a screwdriver to get them out. But with the magnets, he could pull them right off with a bit of effort.

"Dr. Shuji must have her own private bathroom," Six said aloud, as he worked. "The toilet paper in here is only two-ply!"

"She's probably got some bot specially designed for the job," came a shaky voice from the next cubicle. "Already poised to hit the market, the ultimate bathroom accessory — a robot that dispenses five-ply toilet paper."

Theoretically, the code words were supposed to be so innocuous that Neeq wouldn't become suspicious. *But,* Six thought, *if I were him, I'd be on my guard as soon as either of us said anything at all. At least now I know I'm saving the right person.*

With a silent pull, the last bolt in the wall came loose. Six slipped it into his pocket and braced himself.

Now!

Six slammed one foot against the wall that the cubicle shared with the next one, and shoved his hands against the wall he had disconnected from its frame.

The wall exploded outward, skittering across the floor tiles and striking Neeq's wrists. Neeq cried out and dropped his Falcon. Six scrambled off the floor and quickly rechecked his surroundings. Neeq must have moved — but at least he was unarmed now.

Neeq reached for his earpiece.

Six lashed out with one foot, slapping Neeq's head. Neeq still tried to touch the button on his earpiece, but Six had it covered with his foot. Neeq angrily swung a fist at Six's skull, but Six twisted to one side, neatly dodging the blow, and then retaliated with a strike of his own: an uppercut to Neeq's jaw.

Neeq's gas mask popped off, and he grunted in pain. Giving him no time to recover, Six ducked around behind him, grabbed his hands, and then held his elbows together with one arm. Neeq grunted again as his arms were forced behind his back. Six slid a hand up to Neeq's neck and pressed his fingers in behind a gland.

Neeq immediately slumped into Six's arms, out cold.

Six lowered him gently to the ground, and listened carefully. Nothing. There was no sign that the guard outside had overheard the brief scuffle. "Mr. Hoz!" he whispered. "You can come out now."

A man came out of the cubicle next to Six's. He had black hair and pale, greenish eyes. He had probably been quite a handsome man before Shuji's goons had captured him. Now he walked with a slight limp, his clothes were ragged and torn, and his face had several disfiguring purple welts.

"Thank God you're here," he said, his eyes beginning to fill with tears. "Thank you so much for coming. I never thought I'd make it. . . ."

To Six's surprise, Hoz stepped forward and tried to embrace him. With more instinct than thought, Six parried Hoz's arms away, spinning him around, and grabbed him by the shoulders.

"We're not out of trouble yet," Six said. "Put these on." He began stripping Neeq's unconscious body.

Hoz shakily put the uniform on. The fit wasn't perfect, Six thought, but close enough.

Six dragged Neeq into a cubicle and sat him down on the toilet. He closed the door, locked it, and climbed over the wall.

Hoz was waiting for him by the door, wearing Neeq's uniform.

"You know what to do?" Six asked.

"Yes." Hoz's voice was garbled slightly by the gas mask.

"Then let's go. We have to hurry things along — the situation is worse than we thought. As soon as the guard outside is out of sight, take that uniform off or you risk being shot by Deck agents. Clear?"

"Yes," Hoz said. "Crystal."

"And try to hide the limp," Six said. "Got it?"

"Got it."

"Follow me."

Six pushed open the bathroom door, and they stepped outside.

The remaining guard froze when Six exited. He turned to Hoz.

"Mr. Darris," Hoz said. "Your man is still in there." He hesitated. "If he's still there in another ten minutes, perhaps you should . . . check on him."

The guard nodded slowly. He understood the implied message — the prisoner was procrastinating. Put a stop to it. He opened the bathroom door and stepped inside.

"Go," Six hissed. "Go!"

He and Hoz sprinted up the corridor — or rather, Hoz sprinted, while Six jogged.

This man has been imprisoned for at least eighteen months, Six thought, *working on the AI programming for the bots. He hasn't seen daylight in all that time.* He would have been on a minimum food ration, with little sleep, no exercise, frequent beatings, and the threat of death constantly looming over him.

And to top it off, he's only human.

All that considered, he was running pretty fast. He was probably very fit once.

Either that, or he was pushing himself to his absolute

limits. He knew what he had to do to survive, so somehow he was finding the strength to do it.

Six admired that. It showed logic and determination. He picked Hoz up with one arm and slung him over his shoulder.

Immediately Hoz sagged, his completely drained muscles all relaxing at once.

"I can make it," he said.

"You can't."

"If the guard sees us —"

"He won't." Six put on an immediate burst of speed.

Within moments they were around the corner. Six lowered Hoz to the floor.

"Mr. Hoz," Six said. "Can you still hear me?"

"Yes."

He's still conscious, Six thought. *A good sign.*

"You . . . run fast."

"Save your energy. Speak only when spoken to," Six said. "I need you to show me where the hostages are being kept."

"It's in the west corner."

"I know. But I don't know how to get there. We couldn't get blueprints for this building."

"This corridor will lead you to the northwest side. Turn left, go to the end, and down two flights of stairs." He coughed. "It's not far. They had to put —"

"They had to put you near the bathroom, I know." The Deck had guessed rightly that Shuji would want the hostages to leave their holding area as little as possible, and so she had made the bathroom close by. They had used the bathroom as the meeting place with Hoz so he could lead Six quickly to the others.

Six helped Hoz remove Neeq's uniform and put it on himself.

"Mr. Hoz, try to stay conscious," he said. "You can rest when we get you to safety. It is imperative that we get to the other hostages immediately. If we don't, then Darris will radio security before the Deck agents storm the building, and they'll be prepared for the attack. If he radios them before we even arrive at the hostage room, then they'll kill both of us on the spot. Understood?"

Hoz nodded wearily.

Timing was crucial to this mission. Everything so far had been a ruse to ensure that when the Deck agents reached the guards posted outside the hostage room, one of those guards would be Agent Six. The taser in Six's pocket was strong enough to knock down a big man. It couldn't kill anyone, but a shock to the head or neck would result in an immediate temporary blackout. Six was to subdue any of the sentries who attempted to harm the hostages when the Deck agents appeared. That way, none of the enemy soldiers would escape (the agents were moving in from every entrance) and the number of casualties among the prisoners would be zero.

Six was wearing Neeq's uniform now, complete with the

IF YOU WANT TO LIVE

Okay, Six thought. *Here goes nothing.*

There were two sentries posted outside the door. One was standing at ease, cradling his Falcon; the other was sitting in a chair. They both nodded to Six as he approached the door. Six nodded back and shoved Hoz forward roughly. He didn't like doing it, but he didn't want the guards to smell a rat. Hoz whimpered convincingly — genuinely terrified of them, Six guessed.

One of the sentries pressed a button.

The door slid open.

Six grabbed Hoz by the shoulder.

They were both walking towards the opening . . .

. . . when the radio in Six's stolen helmet exploded into life:

"Attention, all personnel! Emergency! Emergency! We have an escaped prisoner, working in conjunction with an intruder!"

It was Darris.

Shuji's voice came through the headset, icily calm.

"The intruder and escaped prisoner are to be terminated on sight. Consider them dangerous. Prison guard team, kill the hostages and protect the western entrance. I repeat: Kill the hostages and protect the western entrance."

"Did you hear something?" the guard who'd been standing at ease asked Six.

"Only a burst of static," Six replied. "Probably interference from another facility, or a solar flare. I'll check with the radio crew once he's taken care of." He pointed a thumb at Hoz. "I'll get approval from Shuji to contact the radio crew from the landline inside."

The guard sitting in the chair said nothing. This was because as soon as he had heard the word "attention" in his helmet, Six had swiftly blasted his neck with the taser, knocking him unconscious. He wouldn't have heard any of the message before he blacked out, still propped up in his chair.

The other guard hadn't heard anything either — he had a magnetic bolt from the toilet wall stuck to the side of his helmet. It had demagnetized all the data in the descrambler chip in his helmet, making his digital radio completely useless. Six had put the bolt there so fast the guard hadn't even seen him move.

"Yeah, make sure you do that," the still-conscious guard was saying. "Something weird's going on today; I can feel it. Get him inside."

Relieved, Six pushed Hoz through the doorway.

Some of the prisoners glanced up as Six and Hoz stepped inside.

"I'm in the holding area," he whispered.

"Copy that, Six," his earpiece crackled. *"The strike teams are being given the green light. Expect us to reach the holding area in seven minutes maximum. Good luck."*

The ceiling was painfully low. Six almost had to stoop to fit in the room. Unlike the rest of the facility, the holding room was not styled with polished chrome and rounded edges — this was a filthy concrete basement.

Rickety steel tables sat on the gritty floor. The lights were cheap, bright neon globes. There was a stain on the wall in the corner. Six thought it looked like blood.

There were about thirty people in the room.

A woman forced a smile for Hoz as he collapsed onto the floor. She didn't look at Six.

A man in his thirties was sobbing in the corner. He ignored them both. A girl in her early teens cradled her head in her hands.

How ironic, Six thought. *She must be incredibly gifted with computers for Shuji's henchmen to kidnap her.* Some people are just unlucky.

An older woman sat on a table, staring into space, probably thinking of better days. Was she old enough to remember pre-Takeover times? Six wondered. That'd give her something better than this to think about.

The door rumbled shut behind them. Six took off his mask.

"Your attention, please," he said loudly. "My name is Agent Six of Hearts, and I am employed by the Deck. Deck agents are currently on their way into the facility. In approximately six minutes" — he set his stopwatch as he said this — "your captors will be arrested and you will be rescued."

No one spoke.

"You need to calmly but quickly set up a barricade with these tables," Six continued, "staying low at all times. Lay them on their sides, with the tops facing the door, and stay behind them. I want you to remain there until I say it's safe to move. Do I make myself clear?"

More silence.

"Excellent. Move!"

No one budged.

"This is essential to your survival," Six shouted. "Your best chance is to do exactly what I tell you, when I tell you. Build a barricade out of these tables *right now!*"

A handful of people stood up. Some looked down at their filthy bare feet. Some went to the tables, but there were still people sitting on them. A few sat back down on the concrete.

"I'll get them to do it," Hoz mumbled. "You do your job — guard the door." He dragged himself to his feet and shuffled as quickly as he could over to a bare table. Then, straining with all his strength, he lifted it onto its end.

The woman who had tried to smile joined him. The teenage girl stood up, too. A young man started work on another table, and the man who'd been crying joined him.

Soon the room was in motion.

Six went to watch the door. He crouched just to one side of it, prepared to spring as soon as a guard entered. He gripped the taser firmly in one hand.

And now, he thought, *we wait.*

"Attention, prison sentries," Shuji's voice said in Six's helmet. *"Have you reached the west entrance yet?"*

Uh-oh, Six thought.

"Prison sentries," Shuji said again, *"have you reached the west entrance? Have the hostages been executed?"*

There was no reply, of course. Neither guard could hear her; one was unconscious and the other had a jammed radio.

"Attention, all units," Shuji said. *"Those who are currently defending the entrances stay there. All those who have not yet reached the entrances, head to the hostage holding area immediately. Kill the hostages and await my instructions."*

Oh no, Six thought. "How many soldiers am I looking at?" he asked.

"There have been surprisingly few soldiers attacking our entry team," Two said, *"so I'd guess they're all at your end. I'd say that you're looking at at least two hundred troops."*

Six groaned. Two hundred soldiers! He'd never be able to fight them all off.

"What's their ETA?"

"The nearest groups will reach you in about two minutes."

Okay, Six thought. *Time for a change of plan.*

"Can you get me a helicopter?" he asked.

"Sure. How many civilians have you got in there?"

Six did a quick head count. "Thirty-two," he said.

"We have a Mother here — it holds about thirty. More than that, I can't promise."

All right, Six thought. *Time to get out of here.* He turned to face the hostages working on the barricade.

"In approximately ninety seconds," Six said loudly, "this room will be stormed by more soldiers than we can fight, and the Deck agents are not going to reach us in time."

The hostages looked at him.

"You need to do exactly what I say if any of us are ever going to leave this building. Understood?"

Nobody moved.

Six sighed. "Come with me if you want to live," he said.

BREAKOUT

Thirty-two escapees and one Deck agent sprinted through the gleaming chrome corridor.

Come on, move faster, Six thought, turning his head to watch the stragglers. *The farther we are from the hostage holding area, and the quicker we reach the edge, the less chance we have of running into enemy commandos.*

Too late.

Four soldiers appeared at the end of the corridor. The goggles of their black masks reflected the ragged, terrified hostages as they skittered to a halt and tried to run in the other direction.

The escapees at the front saw the soldiers first, and they were the first to turn and flee. The prisoners behind crashed into them, and the whole crowd wobbled with confusion and panic.

"No!" Six roared. "Stand your ground!" With a tensing of calf muscles, a push of hamstrings, and a flick of his ankles, he was in the air, hurtling towards the soldiers headfirst.

He barreled into the air, arms outstretched and fists clenched, looking like a black broadsword thrown hilt first.

Six didn't quite make it as far as the soldiers. About a meter away he opened one fist and put his hand on the ground, then used the momentum of the leap to swing his legs around, spinning horizontally, and kick the legs of the first two guards out from under them.

An instant later Agent Six was on his feet, and the two guards hit the ground like bowling pins. Six stepped immediately to one side as Falcon bullets riddled the ceiling.

He ducked out of the way as a combat knife whistled overhead, held by the third commando.

Six spun around and punched the guard's abdomen, using all the strength of his turn to add force to the blow. He heard a *crack* as the guard's Kevlar vest bent and snapped, leaving the soldier wheezing.

Six swung his gloved hand down and jammed the taser against the back of the soldier's neck. The man thrashed around for a moment and then slumped to the floor.

Six looked around. There were four. He'd only knocked out three. Where was the fourth soldier?

He heard the click of a safety catch being adjusted.

The fourth soldier had been smarter. When Six had begun his attack, this guard had run back out of the fray, giving him plenty of time to take the safety catch off and level his Falcon at the hostages from a distance.

He was now pointing the gun at the head of the teenage girl.

She saw him and tried to move. But she was sandwiched between other panicking hostages and couldn't force them aside.

In the split second that Six realized she'd never make it out of the way in time, he made eye contact with her. Six could almost feel her raw terror.

The guard's finger reached for the trigger.

Six scooped up a Falcon from one of the unconscious guards and dived forward.

Hoz grabbed the girl by the shoulder and shoved her aside, leaving himself in the line of fire.

The guard pulled the trigger and the Falcon shuddered. Hoz opened his eyes. He hadn't been hit!

Six lay facedown on the floor of the corridor — he had taken the bullet.

The guard paused for a moment, confused. His finger was still depressing the trigger of his Falcon, but the gun wasn't firing.

Ah. He flicked the safety dial from semiautomatic to automatic, and reached for the trigger again.

Six fired two shots.

One bullet hit the soldier in the kneecap. The man yelped as his leg broke.

The other hit his hand, and he dropped the gun.

The soldier stumbled, staggered, and fell.

Six switched his safety dial back to the off position and clambered to his feet, unclipping Neeq's broken Kevlar vest as he did so.

That *hurt,* he thought, prodding his bruised ribs with one finger. Those Falcons packed a punch.

The soldier was writhing around on the ground as Six approached. Six pulled off the soldier's helmet, and jabbed a pressure point near the soldier's ear. Immediately the man was still.

"There'll be more coming," Six said as he turned around to face the hostages. "We're nearly at the elevator, but we'll have to hurry."

This time, the prisoners didn't need to be told twice. They moved.

When they arrived at the elevator, it was sealed shut, as Six had anticipated.

"Emergency override and identification codes required," the terminal intoned.

Six slipped in his skeleton card and switched on the transmitter. The transmitter began trying all of the thirteen billion possible combinations at a speed of a hundred million per microsecond.

"Agent Two," Six said as the transmitter did its work, "I need to know all the frequencies being used in this mission."

"We're on 140.85," Two said. *"Shuji and the guards are on 141.80; 141.12 and 140.96 are civilian frequencies with people listening in. Gear is using 141.52, and 140.15 could be picked up by another vigilante base."*

"And that's everyone?" Six said.

"That's right."

Six pulled out his earpiece and scanned the frequency up to 140.48 — a channel no one had any reason to be listening to. He would only be heard by devices that listened to *all* channels, and he knew of only one.

"Hello, Harry," he said. "This is your owner speaking."

"Access granted," intoned the terminal. The elevator doors hissed open.

The hostages started to move in.

"This is what I need you to do . . ." Six began.

Less than a minute later, the last of the hostages was inside the lift. Six pushed the button for the roof impatiently.

There was a long pause. Six hoped Shuji hadn't disabled the elevators. These people were in no condition to climb stairs.

There was a window in the corridor. Six leaned to look outside. No sign of the helicopter yet.

He looked the other way down the corridor . . . and saw a platoon of soldiers appear at the end.

Six pulled his head back inside the elevator. He pressed the button for the roof again. Nothing happened. He jammed his finger down on the CLOSE DOOR button, but there was no response.

He leaned around the elevator door again and saw that the soldiers in the corridor were coming closer.

"Hoz," he whispered, "the helicopter will be on the roof. Follow the pilot's instructions, get everyone on board as quickly as you can, and get out of here."

"Where are you going?" Hoz asked, alarmed.

"There are soldiers coming down this corridor," Six said, keeping his voice low so he wouldn't panic the other hostages. "They'll be at the door in seconds. I'm going to distract them."

He took a few deep breaths. Then he crouched low and pulled the pin from a PGC387 stun grenade on his belt.

He could hear the soldiers coming closer.

Six jumped into the corridor and threw the grenade towards the approaching commandos. They halted, startled. Six covered his eyes as he landed, shielding his retinas from the light.

Crack. The grenade exploded and the whole corridor flashed a dazzling white. The soldiers staggered back, disoriented. Six ducked around the corner as a hail of bullets sparked across the floor. They chipped the walls and cracked the window.

The elevator dinged, and the doors slid shut. The hostages were now on their way to the roof.

But Six was stuck here with a platoon of soldiers.

He didn't have many options. There was no way to get to the elevator without putting himself in the line of fire. And the soldiers were blocking the only route to the stairs.

He considered going the other way down the corridor and looking for an alternative exit. Then a group of soldiers rounded the corner in the distance, blocking off that route.

He hit his earpiece. "Harry," he said, "I'm going to need your help. I'm on the thirteenth floor. Are you still outside?"

"Yes."

"Get ready — I'm coming down." Six could hear the soldiers coming closer to the corner he was hidden around, staggering their fire to make a continuous barrage of bullets.

He climbed to his feet. He crouched.

Then he raced forward, dived, and smashed headfirst through the window.

Don't panic, he thought. *You might make it through this yet. . . .*

And then he was sucked down into the void.

The fog surrounding the building was almost impenetrable. The sun was a pale stain on the grim dome of the sky, and no other buildings were visible. Most of the light came from floodlights around the perimeter.

The side of the building had vanished from view, but the ground wasn't in sight yet. Six estimated that he had fallen about forty meters and was going at a speed of more than three hundred meters per second.

The ground was visible now, just a hundred meters away. That meant about one-third of a second until impact.

Six bent his legs at the knees out of habit, though he was going much too fast for bracing himself to be anything but ceremonial. In a fraction of a second he'd be dead meat —

BANG!

The shock of the impact reverberated right through Six's body. He cried out reflexively.

Hang on, he thought. *I shouldn't have felt that. I should have died instantly, without feeling a thing.*

"*We meet again, Agent Six,*" the bot said. "*Is this satisfactory?*"

Six looked down and saw the ground about four meters below them. Flight time: 8.0 seconds.

"Yes," he said, looking up at the machine that had so neatly caught him. "This is exactly what I wanted."

NO ONE EXPECTS THE MAGNET

By the time Six arrived in the foyer, the conflict was over. Shuji's security force had mostly surrendered and been arrested, and the remainder had fled the building.

"Did the hostages make it out?" Six asked Agent Four.

"Yeah, they're all safe. Great work, Six!"

"*Freeze,*" hissed a voice from behind Six.

Six didn't move. Shuji!

The other agents reached for their weapons.

"Don't even think about it," Shuji said. "If anyone draws their gun, your best agent dies. Or else he does one of his miracle tricks and gets out of the way, but then one of you will take the bullet. Understand?"

"What do you want?" Six asked coldly. He'd get her talking. Relax her for a split second.

"I want you all to get out of here and never come back. However, I'm willing to negotiate. I'd settle for safe passage away from here, and one hostage as insurance."

Six thought quickly. What could he use? He had his gun, but she'd shoot him if he turned. "You think you can hide from us?" He had his taser, Neeq's armor, two iron bolts from the bathroom . . .

Iron. Yes . . . that could work.

"I can," Shuji was saying. "I have more money than God; I could hide from anyone. Anyone will turn a blind eye if they think it's in their interest to do so — it's just a question of finding the right price . . . or threat."

"I'll be your hostage," Six said.

"Nice try, *Scott*. Don't come any closer to me than you are now. In fact, take three paces forward. Away from me."

Six complied. As he moved, he slipped one of the remaining magnetic bolts from the bathroom wall out of his thigh pocket and held it against the front of his taser. Then he bent the four wire prongs, wrapping them around the iron bolt in a coil formation. He made eye contact with the Deck agents.

They all got ready. None of them knew what to expect, but they all knew Six's reputation. When he was nearby, you braced yourself.

"You," Shuji said, pointing to one of the agents. "Take that armor off, strip down, and come with me. And don't even think about touching your weapon."

Six hefted the taser and the iron bolt. Now combined, with the taser prongs coiled and the bolt attached, this was no longer just a taser.

Six switched it on and whirled around. It was now an electromagnet.

Shuji's gun was ripped from her hands. She yelped with shock. The Deck agents held their rifles in place and tried to keep back as the metal in their outfits dragged them towards Six. Shuji's Wanderer started rolling towards the humming taser.

Six turned it off, caught Shuji's gun, and tossed it away.

"Game over, Dr. Shuji," he said.

The Deck agents handcuffed Shuji and lifted her out of her wheelchair.

"How much?" Shuji yelled. "You're not fools! *How much to buy my freedom?*"

"I think you'll find that our agents are emptying your account as we speak," Six said, without looking back.

"People like you pay our salary!" Agent Four said, chuckling.

Shuji hung her head, apparently giving up. Then, as the agents carried her past Six, she lashed out with one foot.

Six shifted his head slightly without looking up, and the strike swished harmlessly past him. Then he reached back and pinched a nerve in her calf, causing her leg to cramp and making her cry out with pain.

"Who *are* you?" she screamed. "How can you do that?"

"I have no name," Six said softly, without turning to face her. "I can do it because I have to."

"Don't you *dare* get cryptic with me," she hissed as the agents hauled her away. "We will meet again."

Six watched her go.

The bot entered the foyer. *"It appears,"* it said, *"that events here have been satisfactory to you."*

Six nodded. "Largely thanks to you. I'd like you to find my car outside." He handed the bot his keys. "Conceal yourself in it." He smiled. "I will definitely be able to find uses for you," he added.

The bot nodded and left the building.

That, thought Six, *is how conversation should be.*

DEBRIEFING

Six reread his mission report as he walked towards Queen's office. *Not bad,* he thought. *What's that quote about six impossible things before breakfast?*

He touched her door handle and heard the buzzer.

"Come in," she called, and Six entered.

Though Queen was in charge of just as many missions as King, and was his equal in rank, her office was smaller and seemed more lived-in. The walls were covered in photographs and news clippings, with a painting on the wall adjacent to the window.

Queen was thirty, and just over one hundred seventy centimeters tall. Her shoulder-length brown hair was not tied back, and hung over her left eye. She slowly rotated a glass paperweight in her left hand, keeping her head tilted towards it, looking at Six sideways as he approached. As usual, this made Six uneasy. When Queen spoke, he could see that her thoughts were moving in a different direction from her words. She had the habit of leading her conversations towards one conclusion and then catching Six by surprise with another.

Six handed her the mission report. She placed it on her desk without reading it — Six guessed that she already knew the facts.

"Six," Queen said, "this is the best bust we've had in many years."

Six nodded.

"This is going to solve all our financial difficulties for months," Queen continued. Her pale blue eyes met Six's. "Thanks to you. As always, your work is completely beyond reproach."

Six met her gaze, but said nothing.

"These mission stats are impressive, Six. Other agents would die happy having done just one mission even half as well." She put the paperweight carefully on her desk. "And for a sixteen-year-old, what you've done is just incredible."

Six frowned. He didn't think his age was relevant to the work he did, and he didn't want to be treated like a child. "Where are you going with this?" he asked.

Queen shrugged, then rested her chin in her hand. Her hair cascaded over her fingers. "I just wondered how you felt about that."

I have no feelings about it, he thought. *I'm satisfied, that's all.* "What's my next mission?" he asked.

"King said he wanted to talk to you about that," Queen said. "Whatever it is, good luck."

As Six left the office, Queen watched him thoughtfully.

"Congratulations!" King said. "Another amazing result — but this time with heaps and heaps of cash as an added bonus! I knew we'd wind up nailing a rich one sooner or later. Now look at us! We're rolling in it! The agents can all get pay raises, Jack can get the new equipment he's been begging for, and it's a big step towards getting our own satellite instead of always trying to piggyback onto ChaoSonic ones. Brilliant! Sixty-two million, nine hundred and forty thousand credits!" He paused. "Is that including the cash from Shuji's account?"

Six shook his head.

"Yesssss!" King pumped his fists in the air. "Have you told Queen?"

117

"Yes."

"What did she say?"

Six frowned. "Nothing relevant. She's a bit weird and creepy."

King rolled his eyes. "People say that about you, too, sometimes. Remember that not everyone knows you like I do. And there is more to pleasant chitchat than just killing time, Six. It strengthens trust, friendships, and bonds between people. You know that other people aren't like you. I'm not denying that. But they need their rituals to function smoothly with one another. The Deck will reach its fullest potential most quickly if you don't disrupt the harmony of our working environment. Just pretend you like the people you work with, okay?"

"Okay."

"Good. One more thing — you took a lot of risks this last mission."

There was a pause.

"We both know that," King continued. "And I've seen all your mission stats in the records. You *always* take a lot of risks."

Six said nothing. Where was King going with this? Did he want Six to draw less attention to himself?

"Six, the best agents have three things going for them. Brains, ability, and *luck*." He sighed. "You've unquestionably got all three. But as a result, you take many more risks."

"What do you mean?"

"The other agents admire you, Six," King said, "because you never kill. You are so smart and so skilled that you manage to incapacitate your enemies without killing them, and still complete the mission. However," King leaned forward across his desk, "this is one of the hardest things I've ever had to tell you, and it'll be even harder for you to come to terms with it. But listen to me — it's not just a possibility, it's a *certainty* that one day your luck is going to run out. When it does, you might have to choose between killing or being killed."

Six closed his eyes as he listened to King's words. The image of Sender J. Lawson invaded his head.

King leaned back in his chair. "You've saved a lot of lives. You will save many more. And I know, even if you don't, that you are a good person, and better liked than you think. So when you make the choice between sparing the life of a man who would kill you or saving your own, I hope you will bear that in mind."

King pinched the bridge of his nose with his fingers, squeezing his eyes shut. Six knew that he was feeling weary.

Six got up. "Is that all?" he asked flatly.

King scoffed. "Of course not. Sit back down — but before you do, close the door."

Six did. King examined the papers in front of him.

Six raised an eyebrow. "What is this all about?" he asked.

King looked up from the folder. "I've found them, Six. They're still being led by Methryn Crexe."

Six's jaw dropped. His arms erupted into goose bumps and his stomach squeezed painfully.

No, he thought. *Please, no.* His heart thudded against his ribs so loudly that he almost couldn't hear King's next words.

"I'm sorry, Six, but I'm almost certain that I've finally found the Lab. And with it, most of the people who spawned *you.* It seems that Project Falcon is still in operation."

MISSION THREE

NO CHOICE

King's eyes narrowed, searching for a reaction. Six hoped he wasn't shaking visibly.

"I don't think the Lab gave up after the fire that destroyed their facility," King continued. "There were rumors about them, of course, but I think they went into hiding until the time was right. Now that ChaoSonic owns just about every-thing — everything except us — the Lab is back, and stronger than before. The Diamonds tell us that they've made several advances in therapeutic and medicinal treatment, and they've even made some changes to the original genome used in Project Falcon.

"If they've still got a fully mapped genome to work with, then the chances are that they've still got data from their first experiments. They'll probably still have your DNA on file."

Six fought his rising panic. It was getting hard to breathe. "What does this mean?"

"It means a number of things," King said. "One: They plan on continuing, and they'll be looking for funds. So they'll be dealing with some very rich, and therefore very dangerous, people.

"Two: They'll be beefing up their security. They'll have learned from the arson attack sixteen years ago. They're going to be hard to penetrate, and they'll deal ruthlessly with anyone who tries. The closer they get to the crucial stage in their plan — presumably, actual gestation — the more alert they'll be. So we'll have to move quickly and *carefully*.

"Three: They'll be trying to find and eliminate anyone who has the power, the motive, or the evidence to stop them. And you have all three. *And* they probably have your DNA."

Six's palms were slippery with sweat. He still couldn't believe it. *The Lab,* he thought. *They're coming for me. It's my worst nightmare come true.*

"So all this adds up to one thing. . . ."

Six braced himself. *I'm going to get thrown out of the Deck,* he thought. *King can't risk me staying, so I'm out on my own again, with a ruthless corporation after me.*

"You're on your own," King said grimly. "Your next mission is going to be a one-man act."

Six's eyes widened. He hadn't expected *that*.

"I need you to take on the whole Lab investigation yourself, firstly because I trust you more than anyone else in this building; secondly because physically and mentally you are better equipped than any other agent here; and thirdly because if any other agents took the job, they might end up discovering your origins, and the Spades could find out. That would be very nasty for both of us. We'd both end up in the Visitors Center."

The "Visitors Center" was the Deck's cell block. The punishment for being a genetically engineered ChaoSonic assassin would be life imprisonment. And the punishment for King, for concealing one within the Deck, would be nearly as bad.

"I know the risk," Six said, cool on the exterior but terrified inside. "What's involved in the mission?"

King put on his monocle and spread an array of photographs on the desk. He pointed to the first one. "This is Methryn Crexe. Forty-one years old, probably has a vague recollection of the days before Takeover. Senior official within ChaoSonic, pretty influential. He hasn't got a file here, but that doesn't indicate good character — the most dangerous kind of code-breakers are the ones smart enough to evade capture. Shady background, inherited a lot of money at a young age when his parents died. They were the founders and owners of a very successful pharmaceuticals company. They died in suspicious circumstances and Crexe inherited the company. He helps to fund the Lab with money out of his own pocket, but he earns it all back when the profits come in. He handles the deals with the other branches of ChaoSonic, so he's the lead PR man as well. When he's not running the actual experiments himself, he's running rings around the spies from other sections of the company, and around us. Got it?"

Six looked at the photograph. The man within it glared slyly back at him with large, dark eyes.

"Yes."

"Good. Next, there's Kligos Stadil. Age unknown, but I'd guess thirties. Started out as a bodyguard for a ChaoSonic official, then accepted a contract to kill him and found the life of a hit man to be to his liking. He was recruited by the Lab about five years back; Crexe probably pays him enough money to make it safe to trust him. He now controls security for the Lab, which means he's in charge of sheltering them from all outside parties, including us. Try to avoid his attention — he'll go down for his crimes later."

The picture showed a tall man with a thin, bony face and scarred, scabbed hands. His eyes were covered by greasy strands of a low-hanging fringe. He didn't look particularly dangerous, but Six never assumed anything.

"Go ahead," Six said.

"This one is Retuni Lerke. He worked for the original Crexe pharmaceuticals company, and may have had a hand in the deaths of the owners. He associates with Crexe in many other ways, but there's one that concerns us in particular. This man was in charge of Project Falcon — and he's still working for the Lab, though I'm not sure in what capacity. He's an expert with most biological sciences. But then, you know that."

This photograph showed the first face Six had ever seen. He was older. Thinner. Balder. But he had the same eyes, the same pale, curious stare. This man had designed and created him.

"Lerke is extraordinarily dangerous. He's rich, respected, ruthless, and very, very clever. Stay out of his way. Destroy his company, erase his project, steal his data, and smash his job to pieces, but avoid a face-to-face confrontation at all costs. Understood?"

Six looked at Lerke. From the day he had first awakened, he had seen that face on the other side of the glass, looking at him with pride, awe, smugness, concern, and, sometimes, chilling glee. Six had no intention of going anywhere near Lerke — if anyone was going to try to dissect Six, it would be this man.

"Those are all the names I can give you for now," King said. "I'm hoping you'll bring me back some more after your first assignment."

"Which is?"

"To get all the information you can about what they're doing at the Lab, ideally with photographic evidence. Once you have the information, we can analyze it and work out the best way of short-circuiting what they're doing."

"And just how am I supposed to get this information?" Six asked.

"Simple," said King. "By breaking in to the Lab's head-quarters. We need to find the Project Falcon lab."

Six controlled his shock. "Are you serious?" he asked.

"Deadly," King said. "There's no one else who can take them down. And if we don't, clones of you will be sold to the highest bidder and used as bodyguards and assassins.

Then the City will be far beyond anarchy. It'll be totalitarian fascism, because the rich will decide who lives and who dies."

He locked eyes with Six. "This isn't easy. I know this mission sounds insane on the surface, and I know neither of us wants you to die. But I also know that we have no choice."

Six glared across the table. King was right, of course. Just like Hoz, when he had kept running alongside Six even though every muscle had screamed at him to collapse.

Recognizing a lack of options was often a matter of life and death.

Six was still edgy in the shower at home. The news about the Lab had rattled him badly. Even as he scrubbed the grime and dried sweat from the day's mission off his skin, he kept pausing, thinking he could hear faint noises in his house.

It's just nerves, Six told himself. *My ears are playing tricks on me; there's no one in my house.* Just the same, he got out of the shower and toweled himself off quickly. He didn't let the towel cover his eyes at any time, for fear that if he closed them, when he opened them again he would be looking into the reflective goggles of a Lab security agent. Or a grinning scientist with a needle.

Or a clone of himself, one who was trained to kill rather than protect . . .

Six knew he should rest, so he would be best prepared for the mission tomorrow. But he wasn't tired. He knew that if he went to bed now, he'd simply lie awake all night, afraid to close his eyes for fear that his past would sneak up on him with a bloody scalpel.

He wandered down to the training room, where he had replaced his homemade training droid with Earle Shuji's demonstration bot.

"Can't sleep," he explained unnecessarily to it. "Is it all right with you if we do some combat drills tonight?"

"Yes," the bot said. *"That is all right with me."* It gestured at the flat screen on Six's wall. *"I have been studying your practice routines. Most of them are excellent."*

Six wasn't comfortable with the level of intelligence the bot displayed. Although it had saved his life earlier that day, it was still just an electronic appliance.

Six slipped into a fighting stance. "Let's go, Harry," he said.

THE SEAWALL

"The next flight over the Seawall is at 12:20 PM." The squinty-eyed woman behind the counter pointed at a metal chair. "Take a seat."

Six remained standing. Looking out the window of the charter office to his left, he could see the Seawall — a huge, intimidating monolith that blocked the horizon for as far as he could see.

ChaoSonic had put the wall there. From their point of view, too many of their consumers had escaped the continent via the sea, never to return. They had usually left by ship or submarine, so they could escape the notice of ChaoSonic.

The big corporation had put a stop to it — a rather unsubtle one, Six thought. They had built an enormous wall, a hundred sixty meters high, all the way around the City. Then they had drained out all the seawater trapped inside. What had once been a beach was now a grimy but profitable parking lot, and what had once been the only escape route for refugees from the ruthless company was now just another dead end.

Now ChaoSonic truly had a captive market.

Six had been seven when the Seawall was built. For those first seven years he had almost been able to see the horizon through the fog, and then suddenly, over mere weeks, the sea was gone, replaced by the giant concrete structure.

Soon, you could hardly even see that, unless you were close. The fog got worse, and had pretty much obscured everything.

Now the only way you could leave the City was by plane or helicopter, and they were all tagged. ChaoSonic knew exactly where you were going the moment you checked in. If you ventured too far out, they shot down your plane. They insisted that it was entirely possible to leave, of course, and that the planes were actually being shot down by terrorists on the other side of the Seawall. But the chartering companies got the message when they started to lose aircraft in vast quantities: Don't leave the City. Everybody stays here.

So they changed their flight plans to go only from one side of the City to the other, except for a few designated trips to artificial offshore islands, from which ChaoSonic made all of the profits from sales and accommodation. And airlines continued their rigorous checks to make sure you were who you said you were, and that you didn't intend to go too far out.

Except here, Six thought. This station only took you to one place — a small mining rig just outside the Seawall, one of many such offshore facilities and miniature towns. Hundreds of oil miners checked through this station every day to get to work. The terminal Six was using didn't bother checking for ID, firstly because they would do it at the other end, and secondly because there was no plausible reason to go there unless you worked there. ChaoSonic didn't care about people going to this rig — there was no way you could possibly leave the continent, given that the chopper only had enough fuel to get out to the rig and back. Once you were there, the only other way of leaving was via speedboat. This could get you to some of the other offshore facilities, but a single tank of fuel wouldn't get you anywhere near any of the other continents.

Six didn't mind. One of those other facilities was the Lab headquarters, and that's where he was headed.

"Your chopper's here," the squinty-eyed woman said. "That'll be eight credits."

Six had wondered about visiting the other continents. There was little reliable information about what lay out beyond the offshore facilities, and even less about how to get there, but Six was sure it could be done somehow. Now, as he looked out of the helicopter window at the ocean below, ignoring the miners and drillers and oil-refining workers, he pictured himself in a speedboat with plenty of spare fuel tanks, drinking water, and freeze-dried food. He was gunning the motor and watching the spray at the back of his boat kick up into the air. He didn't know where he was going — he was holding a map that was blank except for the City and millions of kilometers of empti-ness. But he knew that somewhere in that emptiness there were other landmasses, and with enough fuel, he was bound to find them sooner or later.

He came back to reality when the helicopter touched down on the concrete at the oil rig. As the blades wound down, slowing to a halt, the miners all clambered off.

Six waited until the last man was on the ground before climbing out himself.

He took a deep breath, ran over to the edge of the landing pad, and jumped.

As he plummeted through the air, towards the big blue sea, he suddenly felt like a child again. There was no Seawall between him and the ocean. Once again, he could almost see the horizon.

When he hit the water sixty meters below, his feet pierced the surface like a knife and he slipped right in. He plunged to a depth of nearly eleven meters before the traction of the water and his own buoyancy slowed him to a halt.

The sea was very dark at this depth — like an oil painting of shadows and silhouettes, drenched in murky navy blue.

Something bumped his leg. He looked down and his eyes widened.

Immediately he started swimming upward, and a few seconds later he had breached the surface. A shortfin mako shark was not something he wanted to interfere with.

Sharks were some of the oldest creatures in the world, Six knew. They'd had more than four hundred fifty million years of evolution to perfect their physical design, but had remained largely unchanged for at least seventy million years. There was plenty of evidence to suggest that sharks similar to the ones of today had preyed on oceanic dinosaurs.

Six himself had some shark DNA — his strong skin and regenerative cartilage were thanks to this. Sharks had outlived the dinosaurs sixty-five million years ago, and now that the Seawall had gone up and people in the City had given up fishing, it looked as though they were going to outlive humans, too. Six couldn't stand up to that kind of grim, tenacious perfection. The sharks had his respect — he would gladly step aside for them.

The shortfin mako was an average-sized shark, but very aggressive and predatory, and not averse to the taste of human flesh. Six swam in breaststroke to avoid splashing too much, towards the speedboat he knew would be tethered to a support strut of the rig. The bulletproof bodysuit that Jack had given him was surprisingly lightweight, and he found he could move easily across the water.

Once he'd hot-wired the speedboat and set out for the Lab, it was almost like his fantasy. There was food, fuel, a map, drinking water, and a fin of spray behind the boat.

I could live out my dream right now, he thought. *I could forget the Lab and go looking for the new world in a way that no one has really done for hundreds of years — with a blank map, an empty horizon, and no concept of what I'll find.*

But then his thoughts closed in on themselves. It was possible that there was a world out there untouched by the violence and greedy corruption that plagued the City — but on the other hand, maybe there would be another Seawall waiting for him. Maybe every continent of the world was the same: an urban industrial purgatory run by corporations and populated by captive markets.

This is why Six never went out to sea. As long as he never looked for it, there was a chance that paradise was just over the horizon.

Looming out of the fog, standing on a red steel spider-like structure, was an enormous slab of cement with grimy windows and rusty fire escapes clinging to it on all sides. There was a construction site attached, containing a few cement mixers and a crane. Rising up, impaling the concrete chunk of the building, was a glittering glass tower with smooth rounded sides and a flat top. The building resembled a dirty concrete monster that had been speared with a polished glass sword.

The Lab's headquarters.

An office building on a rig. A huge rig, big enough to have streets and shops on it. Six could see pedestrians walking along the edges, cars driving past behind them. Though these things were common now on offshore facilities, Six still found the appearance strange.

He examined the structure of the building carefully. No apparent security. Concrete at the base, glass at the top — not unusual, as far as modern architecture went. It fit in well with the other buildings on the rig; grey and green seemed to be the dominating colors. The building was too short to be a tourist attraction, but too tall to be a hotel. It had no sign or label anywhere on it.

Perfect for illicit purposes, Six thought. The structure had nothing at all to draw attention to it. In fact, for a moment Six wondered if he had been given the wrong coordinates and address. But the building fit the blueprints he had seen. This had to be it.

I'm going into the lion's den, he thought. *If they catch me, and figure out who I am . . .*

He started thinking about the needles. The surgery. The knives and drugs and the ever-watchful machines that would hold him in place with clamps and chains. He breathed deeply for a moment, fighting the rising panic. He had to do this; there was no other way.

He tethered the boat to one of the support struts underneath the center of the structure. Using magnetic hand clamps, he climbed up the strut about thirty meters to the metal ceiling. The water lapped gently below him; besides that, he could hear nothing.

There was a grill in the metal wall above, leading to the drainage tunnels of the rig. Six deftly produced a fifty-centimeter crowbar and prized the cover off the grill. He swung up into the tunnel, and had vanished into the darkness before the cover hit the water below.

He landed on the floor of the drain with a splash, but the water didn't penetrate his airtight sneakers. He replaced the crowbar in his suit and zipped it back up, shivering slightly against the damp. He began to creep through the dank, gloomy drain.

It was a very long, dark, rusty metal tunnel, with tiny pinpricks of light piercing the drainage holes and filtering up into it. The place smelled of salt and grease. Six was ankle-deep in murky black water, which flowed towards the opening he had made.

Wasting no time, and carefully scanning his gloomy surroundings, he broke into a light jog, the water gurgling around his feet. There was no sign of any security yet, but there would be guards down here somewhere. He felt suspicious rather than relieved — they must be farther up the tunnel, he thought.

As the water flowed underneath his feet and the walls flew by, he saw a light in the distance. It was a flashlight, but the bearer was invisible in the darkness.

There was a manhole in the ceiling of the tunnel up ahead; Six could see slivers of light and a ladder on the wall — but he would have to sneak past the person with the flashlight first. He advanced slowly.

A few meters from the guard, Six's foot slipped on something beneath the inky water. He stumbled slightly, but regained his balance before falling. Water splashed around his legs as he righted himself.

Suddenly the flashlight was pointing at him. The bearer of the flashlight had heard the splash, and had now seen Six.

Before Six could move, eight shots were fired. And he was hit by three bullets.

Six reeled backward with the force of the impact. Thanks to the bulletproof suit, he was only bruised by the shots, but he knew that wouldn't last. And if the guard sounded the alarm, the four hundred soldiers who worked for the Lab would soon be hunting him — with twelve hundred reinforcements on the way. This wasn't good.

Six dropped to the floor and rolled into the darkness to his right. Icy water trickled down his collar as he left the beam of the flashlight.

The guard whirled around, searching for Six, the light scanning the rust-covered walls. Six waited until it was on the other side of the tunnel, then jumped up into the air.

The guard heard the splash and turned. But Six was already gone, clinging to the manhole in the ceiling. He flattened his body against it like a lizard on a stone.

The guard walked beneath him, moving farther away into the tunnel; Six was closer to the ladder now. He realized that his best chance to get away was to climb up through the manhole. Quickly he pushed open the cover.

By the time the guard had seen all the light pouring into the drain, Six was climbing up. But the guard was quick — he looked up and shot Six twice more.

Six felt the bullets slam into his back. He fell back down into the drain, but as he did, he pulled the manhole lid back on. The soldier was enveloped in blackness, and as he raised the flashlight, it was kicked out of his hand.

Six could still see. The darkness wasn't absolute, and his eyes were almost as strong as those of an owl. He slammed his foot up into the guard's chest. The guard flew up into the air and hit the roof, his back taking most of the impact. Then he fell and landed facedown on the floor with a thud, just as Six moved the manhole cover again and a flood of light poured briefly into the tunnel.

Darkness and silence fell.

The guard recovered quickly and picked up the flashlight. There was no point trying to hit an enemy he couldn't see. He raised the flashlight and aimed his Hawk, but he still couldn't see his assailant. He swung the light around all over the tunnel, but saw nothing. Six had gone.

Up in the Lab's basement parking lot, Six was sprinting away from the manhole, dodging pillars and parked cars. He needed to get out of this facility, *now.*

It would seem that King had misjudged the situation. The Lab's security was already too tight to infiltrate. They were shooting to kill. The Deck needed a full-on strike team in here, not one pathetically outnumbered agent.

Six hoped that the bullet holes in the fabric of his suit were enough evidence of Code-breaking activities, because he was getting out of here and he wasn't coming back.

An alarm sounded, and he ducked behind a pillar in the parking lot. This was bad — *really* bad.

All the guards in the building had been alerted now. Exits were being locked, digi-cams and guards were searching for him, and there was nothing he could do.

He gritted his teeth. Should he go back the way he came? Look for another way out?

Even as a bullet slammed into the wall beside his head, releasing a cloud of dust and grit, he was scrambling to his feet. He sprinted away from the sound of gunfire, but he knew he couldn't outrun bullets from Eagle OI779 automatic rifles.

Six crouched behind a parked car. He could hear the soldiers coming closer. *I need to get out of here,* he thought desperately. *But I'm surrounded, I'm trapped.*

There! Just a few cars away, he saw a door marked FIRE EXIT. The guards hadn't reached it yet.

A chattering Eagle tore his cover to bits. He dived to one side, rolled, and was on his feet running.

The narrow windows near the ceiling were shattering above his head. He hunched his shoulders to protect his neck and kept running as broken glass rained down. Bullets thudded into the walls around him.

The car riddled with bullets exploded. Six felt the heat sweep across his back — he hoped it had been caused by a spark and not by a grenade. The gunfire stopped momentarily, the shooters presumably ducking for cover in the explosion.

Six kept running. He ripped the pocket off his bodysuit and caught his radio as it fell. "This is Agent Six of Hearts," he yelled, "requesting immediate assistance, over."

Looking up, he saw the fire door right ahead of him. It might be locked, but it didn't look too solid. Six sprinted straight at the door. Just before he reached it, he turned sideways and jumped, shoulder first.

The door snapped completely off its hinges and shattered into large splinters as it slammed into the wall behind. Six skidded through the doorway.

"Deck HQ, do you copy? This is Agent Six of —"

Something hit him in the face, and he was suddenly blind.

"Got him," he heard a voice say before he slipped into unconsciousness.

PRISONER OF THE LAB

Where am I? Agent Six asked himself.

Captured, of course, he answered. *I'm a prisoner of the Lab.*

He could feel a prickling sensation under his left eyelid, and he realized that one of his colored contact lenses must have broken when he'd been knocked out. He reached up with one hand, opened the eye, and started picking out splinters of plastic.

When he opened his good eye, he found himself staring at a gritty, greyish-green ceiling, about five meters up. He looked to the left and saw a wall of the same color. He looked to the right and saw a guard, munching on half a sandwich.

"Hi!" the guard said through a mouthful. "Did you sleep well?" He was smiling, and he sounded genuinely concerned. His features looked strangely familiar — he had piercing blue eyes, a hard-edged profile, and scruffy bleached-blond hair. His lightly tanned chin was coated in light stubble. He looked about eighteen.

His expression had a mischievous quality — he kept looking knowingly at Six, then glancing away. He was slouching on a wooden chair, with both hands on the sandwich. Six saw he was armed with a Raptor semiautomatic, but he'd made no move to point it at Six, or even to take it out of its holster.

"You've been out for, well, a while, I guess," the guard continued. "I don't know who hit you, but it must've been pretty hard."

Six touched a hand to his forehead. *If I were human, I'd be dead,* he thought.

He looked around. The room was very bare: blank walls, no furniture except for the bed he lay on and the guard's chair, and the floor was only about three by two meters.

The door was slightly ajar, and Six could see that the padlock on the other side was broken. *What kind of prison is this?* he thought.

He sat up on the bed, looking around suspiciously. "I'm not buying this," he said.

"You're not buying what?" the guard asked.

Six snorted. "There's no security camera, no alarm switch, only one guard, and the door isn't even locked! Should I feel insulted?" His eyes narrowed. "Or is there something I can't see?"

The guard smiled back at him and swallowed another mouthful. "It does seem a bit undercautious at first glance, doesn't it?"

"No kidding." Six examined the guard's face. *I know him,* he thought. *I've seen him before somewhere.* "You really expect me to take this at face value?"

"Not really, no. I expect you to be suspicious . . . but for what it's worth, I say that what you see is genuinely what you get."

"No infrared cams behind the walls? No fiber optics? No collar mikes?"

The guard shrugged. "Nope. None that I know of, at any rate." He frowned. "I hope not."

Hmm, Six thought. *Time to change tack.*

"I've been in some extremely casual prisons before," Six said, gazing around as though in wonder, "but this!" He was lying — he had never been caught before today, so this was his first experience of captivity since his synthetic womb sixteen years before.

"Well, it's not actually designed to be a cell," the guard said. "I'm not exactly sure what it's for."

Six seemed to have subdued the soldier into a relaxed state of mind. Although he had seemed ridiculously calm to start with. Conversation, he reflected, does have a few good uses.

He reached over swiftly and snatched the Raptor out of the guard's holster. "Tell me how to get out of the building," he demanded, aiming the barrel at the guard's face.

The guard continued eating. "Want the other half?" he asked, waving the sandwich. "Sorry, I didn't mean to be rude."

Six stared at him. "Are you listening to me?"

"Yeah, but the directions are a little complicated," the guard said. "And there aren't any bullets in that gun, anyway. So, are you hungry? I'm on my lunch break, so you may as well join me."

Six had known that there were no bullets in the chamber. He had felt how light it was the instant he had picked it up. But he had hoped that the guard didn't know. A foolish presumption, clearly.

Six dropped the gun onto the floor. "Fine," he said. "How long am I going to be stuck in here with you?"

"Hey, don't be like that." The guard sounded offended. "There's no need to —"

Six's arm shot out towards the guard's chest. His fist raced through the air, a blur to human eyes. But the guard deflected the blow easily, and it hit the wall behind him. The plaster cracked, spilling dust into the room.

The soldier pushed Six back by the shoulder with one hand, and as Six spun around with the force of the blow, the guard's feet lifted up off the ground. He held himself up on the chair with his other arm, and kicked Six's legs out from underneath him. Six tumbled through the air and hit the wall with a force that knocked all the breath out of him — and then the guard's feet slammed into his back. Before he knew it, he was upside down and pinned to the greyish-green wall.

The guard's body was propped up between the two walls of the cell — he had a hand on one wall and his feet pushed Six against the other. With his other hand, he caught the sandwich, which had been flying through the air the whole time.

The fight had taken place in under a second.

"— sound so negative," the guard finished. He took another bite out of the sandwich. "It's nice to meet you, Agent Six. I've been waiting for a long time."

Six had been trying to move, but now he froze, horrified. This man had beaten him in the fight, outsmarted him with the gun, and *knew who he was.*

"Hey, relax," the guard laughed. "It's okay, the Lab doesn't know, just me. . . ."

Six didn't relax. *He's only about eighteen,* he thought. Not old enough to remember the attacks on the Lab. How could he know? Unless . . .

"Okay, I can guess what you're thinking, and I doubt I'm going to do well out of it. So stop thinking for a second. I can probably let you down now; I think I've got your attention."

He removed his feet from Six's back, and Six landed on the bed, arms first. The guard landed back on his chair.

"Sorry about that," he said, scratching his stubbly chin. "I hope I didn't hurt you. I just didn't want you to escape before you heard what I had to say. You're listening now, aren't you?"

Six nodded dumbly.

"You're not hurt?"

He shook his head. As a matter of fact, the guard hadn't caused him any physical pain at all. The whole movement had been very carefully executed, Six thought. Not a good sign —

he was dealing with a pro here. A pro who still looked oddly familiar.

"That's good." The guard grinned. "Introductions first? Of course, I know your name already, but I'm Kyntak. It's a pleasure to meet you."

He extended his hand. Six ignored it as he always did when people tried to shake his hand.

Kyntak shrugged and withdrew it. "All right. I'll tell you how I got here, how I know who you are, and how I can help."

"Why should you help me? And what makes you think I need any help?"

The guard laughed. "I've helped you a fair bit already. Do you actually believe that Stadil would leave you in here with only one guard, with no bullets in his gun, no video or audio monitoring, no physical restraints, and no lock on the door?"

Kligos Stadil — in charge of security for the Lab. King was right.

"He was going to torture you for information right away," Kyntak said. "But I sabotaged his equipment, so it won't be working until they get some replacement parts. They stuck you in here, and I arranged to be in the right place at the right time so I was told to guard you. The video camera that used to be on the wall is under your bed, along with the microphone. I took the bullets out of the gun in case you tried to shoot me. I broke the lock off the door. You were tightly restrained when

I got here — you were tied to the bed, but the ropes are now under your bed, too. You probably could have broken them, anyway. There's a hidden alarm in here, too, but, believe me, I have no intention of using it."

He leaned forward. "After all, I wouldn't want to be caught, either."

Six looked under his bed and saw five lengths of rope, a security camera, a small black square (presumably the microphone), and a large padlock. There was also a Hawk 9 millimeter and a box of ammunition. It was all true.

"I'm not exactly what you'd call a loyal soldier," Kyntak said. "I'm only here because I've been following the Lab since I was a small child. Unlike you, I wasn't able to just let go of my origins. I traced them all the way back to my creation, and then went to seek out the creators."

It all clicked into place.

Six's eyes were wide. He should have guessed. The man sitting in front of him had beaten him in a fight. No one had done that before. Ever. And this was why.

Kyntak had the same genetic structure as Six. He, too, was more animal than man. A product of Project Falcon.

That was why he looked familiar. When Six mentally lightened Kyntak's skin, unbleached his hair, and removed the stubble, his face was almost identical to his own.

It made perfect sense. If one embryo had been obtained for illicit purposes, hundreds or even thousands more could have been cloned from it easily. They would have just needed to take a single cell from the original, separate it, grow and culture it, and then they'd have a carbon copy of it. The Lab wouldn't have wanted to put all their eggs in one basket — several experimental fetuses would have had a better chance of success than just a single one.

This creature, the smiling, scruffy kid in front of him, was the same as Six underneath. A flesh-and-blood robot. A monster. A piece of biological weaponry.

"You weren't the only one born in that experiment," Kyntak was saying, even as Six was working it out. "We two are the same model, Six. Grown from the same genetic plan." Kyntak smiled sadly. "Feels good, doesn't it? To find someone else who can understand?"

"Stay away from me," Six said. "I don't need your understanding."

"So far today you've been shot, knocked unconscious, tied up, and if it wasn't for me, you'd probably be dead." Kyntak sighed. "Believe me, you need all the help you can get — and that's what I'm offering. So be nice."

Six boggled at him. Be *nice*?

"You know who I am, that's a start," Kyntak continued. "Now for what I'm doing here. A courier picked me up after the fire, when I first escaped from the Lab sixteen years ago — his transport had lost power on the speedway and he saw me on the ground near the road. When he fixed the transport, he took me to the first stop in the City and dumped me in an orphanage. It was one of the last to close before Takeover was complete. I stayed there for almost four years. But someone must have noticed how different I was from the other kids, and pretty soon the Lab was after me again in my part of the City. Luckily for me, there were a lot of dirty homeless kids around, and I managed to hide pretty well. And when I realized it was me they were after, I decided to follow them. I wanted to find out what the hell was going on."

He grinned. "Typical childhood, I suppose.

"Anyway, after spying on this company and its members up until I was about ten, I started military training in the City. There was no army to join, of course, but there was a kind of boot camp for ChaoSonic security applicants. Target shooting, athletics, martial arts, kickboxing, endurance races, the works. I studied combat of all kinds.

"When I was fifteen I applied to join the security for the Lab. The physical tests were pretty rigorous, but they never tested my DNA. I figured that the last place they'd look for me would be within their own organization. So they took me in, of course, and I've been watching them ever since.

"I figured that when I had enough evidence to know exactly what they were doing, I'd bring them down, but after a while I stumbled across the Deck. I'd thought that the City was completely lawless, you see — I'd heard the old stories about police and governments and so on, but I never really believed that they'd ever existed. The City had become so big by then that no one could possibly have been looking after it. It was already like one colossal machine that ran itself. But then I found this small, secretive, almost invisible organization trying to uphold the values that safeguard humanity's survival, and I realized that there was someone in charge after all."

We're not in charge, Six thought. *ChaoSonic will never let us control the City.*

"So then I did some research, and dug up you. A boy with a hundred percent mission success rate, so whenever he's around, everyone makes it through. A boy who does the impossible with ease, who works in silence, and has riches beyond the wildest dreams of any orphan like me. Once I discovered that you were the same age as me, it was obvious who you really were."

Not a boy at all, Six thought.

"I decided the Lab might be too big for me to take on my own," Kyntak continued. "I figured that the Deck would send a field agent, a Heart, to stop the Lab before the situation got out of hand again. And you, of course, would be the one. The Lab has a file on you, and you wouldn't want the Deck to find it because the Spades would investigate. The City's big, but you can't hide from anyone forever — friend or foe."

Six felt a chill run down his spine. His glands pushed a little more adrenaline into his system, sensing his fear and preparing for danger. *I'm inside the Lab,* he thought. *Why are we just sitting here?*

Kyntak sighed again. "If the Deck doesn't get us, the Lab will. Lucky us, yeah? Oh well. Anyway, we'll have a better chance if we stick together. I'm glad you're finally here."

The story checked out with all the facts Six knew. *If I hadn't stumbled into King's life,* he thought as he watched Kyntak swallow the last of his sandwich, *I might have ended up like him.* Laughing and joking, like a parody of a human being. A wolf in sheep's clothing — with the wool over his eyes.

I'll have to get rid of him soon, or he could get us caught. But he's as strong, fast, and well trained as I am, so I can't outfight him. I can't try to ditch him immediately. Six gritted his teeth. *He's got me cornered — but with any luck, he doesn't know it. I'll cooperate — for the moment.*

"What happens now?" he asked.

"Now?" Kyntak laughed mischievously. His piercing eyes twinkled. "I've been looking forward to this. I have a disk with all the information and photographs you need for your mission, about what the Lab is up to. Your work here is done. Good to have the pressure off, isn't it? So now, we escape!"

"Just don't get in my way," Six growled.

Kyntak handed him a gun. "Ready?" he asked.

"Yes. Count."

"Okay. Three . . ."

Six crouched.

"Two . . ."

Kyntak copied Six's stance. Six gripped his gun tightly.

"One," Kyntak said.

"Go!"

They burst out of the cell door together. Six slid out into the corridor firing, back-to-back with Kyntak. Almost simultaneously, seven video cameras on opposite sides of the hallway shattered as bullets tore through them. Not a single shot had missed its mark.

Kyntak hefted his gun. "Not too shabby," he said, spinning it on his finger.

"With any luck they'll think it was a power failure in this room," Six said. "But they'll figure it out soon."

Kyntak nodded. "Let's get out of here. This way."

They started to run down the hallway. Like most of the hallways in the building, it was well lit but sparse and narrow. A murky-green tiled floor lay between wooden walls, below a cream ceiling. The corridor stretched endlessly into the distance, the four corners meeting at a point on the horizon.

Six was very uncomfortable. This was an odd sensation for him. He had never seen someone match his running speed before. But there was Kyntak, flying alongside him without breaking a sweat. Six gritted his teeth and increased his pace.

"You want to race, huh?" Kyntak laughed. "Let's go!"

Six glared as Kyntak reappeared beside him and then pulled ahead. Pumping his legs harder, Six caught up.

He was channeling all his physical and mental strength into this. Glancing down, he saw that his legs were a grey blur. Right left right left right-left-right-left right*leftrightleftright* . . .

"Six!"

He looked up again and saw the corner just in time — a very sharp, very sudden left turn in the corridor. Gripping the edge of the left wall with his hand, he swung around it, feet sliding across the tiles. With his heart thudding like a drum, he crouched midstride and slid for several meters before stopping.

Wow, he thought, panting. *I've never run that fast in all my life. Not like me to miss the corner, though . . .*

He looked around for Kyntak, but couldn't see him. *Maybe he slipped and broke his neck,* Six thought, quite pleased at the prospect. He was about to go back to look for him when he heard the alarms and saw the wall near the corner torn up by gunfire. He jumped back as though stung, and slammed himself against the wood.

There were guards in the corridor they had just run through — he could hear footsteps coming closer. Sounded like eight, maybe ten people (which still left three hundred ninety hanging around somewhere else, he reminded himself). Judging by the damage to the wall, these soldiers were armed with shotguns of some type. Probably pump-action Vulture GI446s.

"Hey! Six!"

Six looked around for the source of the voice. Then he saw it — directly above the corner was a metal trapdoor embedded in the cream ceiling. It had been opened just a crack, and he could see Kyntak's eyes.

The footsteps were getting nearer. The boom of the guns was deafening. Six steeled himself and sprinted towards the corner. Sneakers squeaking, legs flying, heart pumping, he headed straight for the wall. "Get out of the way!" he hissed at Kyntak.

Six took a running jump and landed in a crouch on the wall. Then he pushed off again, jumping up through the trapdoor in the ceiling. Inside was an air vent, and he banged into the steel ceiling before clattering to the floor, landing on his back. A moment later, after figuring out which way was up, he rolled over onto his hands and knees.

A hail of pellets crashed into the wall where he had been a split second before.

"Hi, Six!" Kyntak grinned at him. "Who won the race?"

"Shhh!"

Kyntak raised his eyebrows. "Must've been me."

Six glared venomously at him. "Which way to the exit?"

"Southeast. Follow me." Kyntak scrambled off into the darkness, with Six right behind him.

The air vent was slick, smooth, and dark, only about a meter square. Six hated vents with a logical kind of claustrophobia — there weren't enough ways to escape them.

"Here." Kyntak had stopped. "There's a way down onto a fire escape. We'll climb down the side of the building, then we're home free."

Before Six could answer, Kyntak had vanished. Six followed his lead.

FLYING HIGH

Six was on the fire escape. He could see the ocean in the distance. *There's much less fog when you're out at sea,* he thought.

The air tasted of grease, ore, and salt. Kyntak was already climbing down the stairs, the rusted steps clanging under his boots. Six followed him reluctantly.

Looking around, he could see that they were on the southern wall of the building. Six could hear a distant rumbling, but there didn't seem to be anyone around. Despite all the cars parked around it, the construction site was deserted. Evacuated when the Lab went to full alert, he guessed. Looking up, Six saw that they were near the top of the building, still beside the glass part of the tower. The bejeweled sword rising from the grey monster.

The distant rumbling had suddenly become not so distant. Six glanced up. "Yes," he muttered grimly. "I thought so."

A Twin-600 helicopter was descending from the sky, like a giant black insect blocking out the sun. Unlike their almost silent cousin, the Twin-900, Twin-600s emitted a booming, thumping rattle as their blades swirled. It must have taken off from the roof, Six thought, or he would've heard it approaching sooner. They'd never get away in time.

He felt the chopped air press down against his skull. The pounding and whining of the turbines seemed to echo through his brain. The helicopter was huge, a massive mechanical beast with whirling flat blades. Standing in the open hatchway was a soldier wearing Kevlar armor and hefting a Condor 616 chain gun.

"Jump!" Kyntak yelled.

"What?" Six shouted incredulously. It was hundreds of meters to the concrete below.

"Just jump!" Kyntak howled, and he leaped off the fire escape.

With only a split second of hesitation, Six followed him. *If all else fails,* he thought, *I can land on Kyntak to break my fall.*

The moment he looked down, the instant he faced the sickening drop to the construction site far below, the gunman in the chopper opened fire.

As he plummeted through the air, Six saw the glass encasing the tower shatter. Thick lead bullets tore the smooth windows to brittle shreds. He looked up and saw the Condor pumping rapid rounds towards them. Six continued to fall.

This was a familiar sensation — the wind tugging at his body, his guts squirming, throat dry, air slamming upward into his face. But though the feelings were familiar, he knew that he had never jumped this far before onto concrete. And there seemed to be no way of avoiding the ground this time.

I'm going to die, Six thought. *I'm falling hundreds of meters onto solid concrete. And a helicopter is shooting at me.*

Six's heart rate increased. He was whipping downward at an incredible speed. Far below him, the concrete did not seem any closer yet. On his right, out of the corner of his eye, he could see the whirling blades of the Twin. On his left, there was a constant glittering storm of exploding glass. His ears ached from the chattering of gunfire, the acid splintering of glass, the pounding of the helicopter blades, and the wind screaming at him. It all mixed together to become white noise.

Six could see Kyntak below him, falling at the same speed. Kyntak was squirming and flapping through the air, against a distant backdrop of steel, cars, and concrete. He was waving his arms around, and Six realized that he was probably doing the same. But Kyntak was looking up, not down. Now that he had Six's attention, he smashed the window he was falling past with his fist, and grabbed the frame. He stopped falling and held on tight. Suddenly he was rushing up towards Six as Six shot straight down.

Six felt himself yanked out of the air. He gasped as he stopped falling. Kyntak had grabbed his hand, and now they were both dangling from the window frame. Flight time: 3.1 seconds.

"Gotcha!" Kyntak grunted, hauling them both up into the window. Quickly they ducked into the room as another burst of gunfire shattered the air around them. Six's legs wobbled slightly, but he steeled himself and turned to Kyntak.

"Where to now, genius?" he asked.

Kyntak stared at him. "You know," he said, wiping his bloody hand, "you sounded almost sarcastic just then. Didn't that drop give you a rush?"

Six wanted to strangle him. But he maintained an even tone. "What now?" he repeated.

Kyntak crept over to the empty window frame, hiding near the wall. He pointed outside. "Do you see that crane?" he asked.

Six edged over to the window and glanced out, then stepped back. One glance had been enough. There was a large grey crane in the construction site below. It looked pretty strong — reinforced steel, made of wide beams for heavy loads. The top of it was perhaps fifty meters below, the ground about a hundred fifty meters. Six nodded. "I see it."

The droning of the chopper grew nearer.

"Well, if we jump down from here, shoot the gunman and the pilot on the way down, and grab the hook of the crane, then we should be able to make our way across to the control cabin and down the ladder. Then we steal a car and run off."

Six opened his mouth.

"I know what you're going to ask." Kyntak smiled. "And, no, we can't just go through the building to the ground floor. Security will be everywhere. I know these things. I'm supposed to work for them, remember?"

"I'm going first," Six said, and he dived out the window. *Anything to get away from that lunatic,* he told himself, as he plunged headfirst into the void.

As soon as Six was out in the open, he began firing. The Hawk in his hands shuddered, but even while he was falling upside down, his accuracy was flawless. The gunman's feet were knocked out from under him, and he fell silently from the helicopter. Six aimed at the cockpit. The pilot ducked behind his seat for cover.

Six was dropping towards the crane. He could see the tip of the horizontal beam below him, so the hook was below that. He would have only a nanosecond after seeing the hook to grab it.

Idly he noticed that below him a parachute had opened up, like a rippling white flower blossoming. *Hopefully the soldier will be too shaken to join the ranks again,* he thought.

The tip of the crane had just swept past his face, and he lashed out with one arm. The hook was there, and he grabbed it. The sudden stop swung the hook crazily, and Six gripped the underside of the crane on the first swing. Flight time: 5.2 seconds. He climbed up.

Once he reached the top of the structure, he looked up. Kyntak had leaped out of the window, arms spread like a bird, and had just begun to fall. Six stood back, making room on the loading beam for Kyntak.

A straining whine alerted him. The helicopter was slowly tipping over in midair.

He stared intensely, and as he tried to figure out what was happening, he saw the pilot jump out. Another parachute fanned out below him.

Now the Twin was half upside down, and suddenly it was moving. Fast. The whirling of the blades added to gravity to push it down as well as forward, sending it into a tailspin. The motor screamed and then stalled as the helicopter spun out of the sky.

It was heading for the base of the crane.

Six looked up to see Kyntak's falling silhouette. It would be seconds before Kyntak reached him. He wasn't going to make it.

The helicopter hit.

The whole crane shuddered underneath Six's feet. He wobbled at first, but then he ducked down and grabbed hold of the sides of the beam with his hands. The crane was tilting forward, and was slipping farther over every second.

Kyntak's going to miss, Six thought. *I have a second to do something, or it'll be too late.*

Six reached down and grabbed the chains attached to the tip. He pulled up the hook and gripped it tightly. Then he dived forward off the beam, clutching his lifeline with one hand and reaching out with the other. Just as Kyntak flew past, falling like a brick, Six grabbed his hand, and they both swung up onto the beam.

"Thanks, Six!" Kyntak gasped, sprawled across the greasy steel. "I owe you one!"

"Get up," Six said. The crane was still tilting, and it felt as though it could fall any second. He looked down to where the chopper had crashed . . .

. . . and recoiled as it exploded. The base of the crane was enveloped in a ball of roaring flames. It wasn't the heat that Six felt first, it was the energy of the blast as it slammed into him. He was knocked down, and slid off the top of the beam.

Six grabbed the edge as he went over, then dragged himself back up. He started to clamber onto his feet, the heat cooking his face.

The explosion had wiped out any strength left in the crane's vertical support beams, and then had given it a push towards the building. The base creaked and strained. Six could feel the metal moving under his feet; the rumbling spread through his whole body.

The crane began to fall. The world suddenly loomed towards Six, and he leaned back to remain vertical. The metal support struts moaned. Six could see that the crane was going to hit the building very soon.

Simultaneously, he and Kyntak began running along the beam of the crane. Even as the slope became steeper they were sprinting up it — desperation hurling them along at breakneck speed.

They had almost reached the top when the tip of the beam struck the building. The metal bent and the concrete crumbled. A grinding, squealing roar filled the air as the beam started to crumple. The crane was quaking and rumbling below them as it was scrunched against the concrete like a tin can.

Six and Kyntak jumped up to the end of the beam.

For a short second they were in the air, separated from all the movement and noise. And then they grabbed hold of the crane's giant hinge, which had been hanging just above their heads a second before. Part of the building's concrete wall crumbled, and the crane shuddered as it fell inward. They were dangling vertically along the beam as the building came closer and closer.

The crane leaned crazily and began to collapse sideways. Most of the horizontal load-bearing beam had smashed into the building, pushing its way inside the tearing concrete. The main structure of the building had been crushed, and as the crane collapsed over to one side, it was tearing out more of its supports.

Six and Kyntak were riding a huge grey monster as it tore a bigger one to pieces. It was still about fifty meters to the ground from where they hung.

They clambered up until they were standing on the main support beam. It was horizontal, at least. But not for long. This beam was swinging down towards the ground, which was rising up to greet them.

"Jump!" Kyntak screamed.

They both leaped off the beam sideways as it fell out from underneath them. They fell down, past the flames, past the twisting metal, past the falling, crumbling concrete. They fell faster and faster, until they slammed into the dirt in the construction site.

A concrete wall punched Six in the guts, then a dust cloud blanketed him.

TOTAL DESTRUCTION

Six lay back, sucking in a deep lungful of the gritty air. He didn't feel seriously hurt, or even tired — his heart rate was still up from the fall. But the impact had shocked his whole body. Even as the dust cleared he was flexing his joints to see that none had been broken or dislocated.

Up above, he saw the crane disappear to one side. He could still hear the crashing and booming as it attacked the building from below. Soon a screeching sound reached him, followed by a huge thumping clatter that shook the ground beneath him.

Then there was silence.

Six savored the peace for a moment while he tested all his muscles for damage. The dust had cleared slightly above his head now, revealing a painfully white sky. He heard Kyntak coughing and spluttering beside him.

"Are you all right?" Six asked.

Kyntak sat up. His grimy face parted to show perfect white

teeth as he grinned. "Never been better!" he declared. "That was fun!"

"I meant, are you injured."

"Heck no! I feel great!"

Six was almost disappointed. Perhaps he had been hoping that the shock would quiet Kyntak down. *Oh well,* he thought. *I'll ditch him pretty soon.* He stared numbly up into the sky, letting his heartbeat slow.

He could see the building on the horizon behind him, and rubbed his eyes with a dusty hand. *Maybe my vision was affected by the impact,* he thought. The building looked almost . . . curved.

"Six?" Kyntak said. "Can you see that?"

"What?" Six asked, still looking at the building. It seemed to be getting larger.

"The building."

"Yes, does it look, er . . . misshapen to you?" The building was looming over his head now, blocking out the sun.

"Maybe the crane damaged it."

They glanced at each other.

They looked up again.

And then they scrambled to their feet and ran, as the building began to collapse.

They both knew that on foot they'd never get clear of the impact in time.

"There's got to be a car around here somewhere," Kyntak panted.

"There!" Six pointed to a green ChaoSonic Earthride. "Go!"

The building was tearing out of its supports. The hole caused by the crane was making it collapse into itself, like a dead man falling to his knees.

And we are going to be under him when he slumps, Six thought.

All around them there were chunks of concrete falling out of the sky. A huge slab of brick slammed into the dirt in front of Six, sending up a cloud of dust. He jumped over it and kept sprinting as the ground around him became steadily darker.

They had reached the car, and it wasn't locked.

It was an old model, with a key ignition, but Six knew he'd never have time to hot-wire it. As he jumped into the driver's seat, Kyntak threw him a multikey.

He jammed it into the ignition. The plastic expanded to fill the slot, and he twisted.

The car's engine roared to life. Six smoothly clicked it into gear and slammed his foot down on the accelerator. He glanced out the window as the car blasted forward. The wall of the building was nearly horizontal now, just meters above the car roof and falling fast. Concrete and mortar rained down all around them like stones and ash from a volcano.

Six turned back to the wheel. He could see the shadow of the falling monolith in front of the car, creating an artificial night around them. He had to reach daylight in — he looked out the window again — about four seconds.

The car rocketed forward, wheels sliding in the dirt.

Three.

The monstrous grey slab was looming larger, eclipsing the light and bearing down on the car.

Two.

Six clenched the steering wheel, his knuckles white. The ground was zooming by below them.

One.

They were almost out of the shadow. Daylight was visible. The building was almost upon them.

Zero.

The building thundered down onto the ground. The construction site, the crane, the wreckage of the helicopter — everything vanished, crushed under the weight of the concrete. The ground shuddered and cracked. Dust flew everywhere and chunks of cement exploded outward.

The edge of the building's wall slammed down onto the rear fender of the Earthride. The front of the vehicle flipped upward, and Six found himself staring at the sun as the car shot into the air.

The momentum slackened. The car stopped moving. The air carried it, letting it drift for a moment. Six and Kyntak braced themselves.

Then the car smashed into the asphalt, back wheels first. The front followed soon after, hitting the pavement roughly. And suddenly they were back on the road, driving in front of the massive dust cloud, tearing along the street.

The remainder of the glass tower splintered into tiny shards and tinkled musically to the ground all around the car.

Six put his foot back on the accelerator.

"Strong car," Kyntak observed. "Pity about the rear fender."

"Shut up!" Six said angrily. "Did you even see what you did back there?"

"Me?" Kyntak said incredulously.

The huge grey wall of smoke and dirt was gaining on them. It was impossible to see for more than a meter behind the car, and the dust stretched into the sky as far as the eye could see. The rain of broken glass intensified. It looked as if Judgment Day had come and civilization had been reduced to ash.

"Yes, you!" Six turned to glare at Kyntak. "You're the one who said we should escape. You led me down the fire escape. You said we had to jump onto the crane."

"Hey, we're alive, aren't we?" Kyntak frowned. "If —"

"We nearly *died*! Look behind you. Take a long look. What do you see?"

Kyntak looked, and shrugged.

"Nothing!" Six roared. "That's what! Nothing! We destroyed the whole building, not to mention the entire construction site next to it! Now the Lab is gone, and the information you have means nothing! Everyone involved will go underground; we'll never find any of them ever again. And the Lab will know where to look for us now, assuming that not *everyone* was killed in that catastrophe. Dozens of witnesses saw us do things that human beings can't do, and someone's bound to put two and two together. If the Lab doesn't get us, the Deck will! We'll be put down like rabid dogs! You honestly have no idea what you've —"

The door on the driver's side was hit by a hail of bullets. Six ducked down into his seat. Looking in the rearview mirror, he saw that there were jeeps following the car, with guards standing up in the back. All were armed with Hawks or Vultures. More military vehicles were appearing from side streets.

"Oh, yeah, I was going to mention that when you'd stopped yelling," Kyntak said. "They evacuated the building before they sent the helicopter. So no one was hurt when the building collapsed. Thought you'd be relieved."

"How do you know that?"

Kyntak held up a cell phone. "They sent me an SMS, like all the other guards."

"And the Project Falcon lab?" asked Six.

"Not here," said Kyntak. "I was getting closer to discovering its location when you dropped in."

"You shoot," Six said flatly. "I'll drive."

Kyntak grinned and drew his Raptor. Leaning out the window, he fired eighteen shots, emptying the whole clip. As he sat back, five jeeps skidded to a halt, their tires burst. The smell of burning rubber filled the air as Kyntak reloaded.

Six swerved and went into a side street. The car slid around the corner, tires screeching. Six gripped the wheel tightly.

Two more jeeps rounded the corner.

Six and Kyntak were about ninety meters from the edge of the rig. The road curved and bent to go alongside the rim, but Six wasn't planning to follow the road. He floored the accelerator, and the car roared. The wheels spun, and the ground flew past. Within a second or two, they were at the edge. The tin safety barrier crumpled under the wheels as the car sped into the open air.

The deep-blue sea lay far below, sparkling and calm. Behind them, the orange-brown cliff of painted metal rose up into the sky as they flew into the void. Before the car began to fall, they could see the smooth blue sky blend into the grey, foggy horizon and the indigo sea. The air was touched only by the sun and a single puffy white cloud.

This far away from the City, the fog was gone completely.

They both stared in silence for a moment.

The car began its sickening drop. The front nosed forward, and Six and Kyntak found themselves staring at the sea. The wind roared past the open windows as Six pushed the window button furiously to close it. The water approached quickly as the car rocketed straight down.

"Undo your seat belt!" Six yelled to Kyntak.

The car was almost vertical now and falling like a brick. The air rumbled in Six's ears as the car pierced the wind.

"This is awesome!" Kyntak crowed when the sea surface was only meters away. Six braced himself, slamming his hands on the back windshield and his feet on the dashboard.

The car hit. The front crumpled against the surface of the water.

Kyntak and Six were jolted as the car slammed into the ocean. For a short moment the Earthride floated vertically, bobbing and dipping like a cork, then it tipped over, landing upside down.

Crouching on the inside of the roof, Six watched the water flowing in around the door seals. "Kyntak, on the count of three, open the windows so it fills up with water. Then the pressure will be equalized and we can open the doors and swim to the surface. Got it?"

"Ready when you are."

"One."

Six watched the water, almost up to his knees now.

"Two."

All daylight had disappeared — the windows were underwater.

"Three!"

Six pushed the button to wind down his window, and felt the car lurch as Kyntak did the same. He was hit in the face by a blast of freezing water, but he held his breath and kept pushing the button.

His electric window shorted out halfway down, so he leaned back and kicked it, snapping off the remaining square of shatterproof glass.

The car was full of water now. He pushed the door open and swam out into the ocean.

Darkness surrounded him as he felt the bubbles from his mouth wriggle past his cheek. The car sank down into the blackness. Within moments he was blinded by the seawater in which he was submerged. He forced his eyes open against the salt, and saw light coming from his left. Kicking his feet, he swam to the surface.

Fresh air touched his face. He spat out the seawater and pushed soggy hair out of his eyes. "Kyntak?" he called, as he rose and fell on the ripples from the car. He glanced around. "Kyntak?"

He felt something bump against his legs. A shark! He curled into a ball and floated with his head and knees above the water. Sharks were least likely to attack you when you were positioned that way.

"Kyntak," he called. *"Kyntak!"* Then he saw Kyntak standing in the speedboat, peering down at all the equipment in it.

"Gee, anyone would think that you were worried about me," Kyntak said. "Check out this cool speedboat!"

"Bring it over here," Six called to Kyntak.

"I found it tethered to this strut," Kyntak said. "If I had a great speedboat like this, I wouldn't just leave it lying around like that."

"It's mine," Six said. "Now bring it here."

Something bumped his legs again, harder this time.

Kyntak peered down into the water. "Is that what I think it is?"

"Yes, it's a shark," Six howled. "Bring the boat over here *right now*!"

Kyntak grinned. He turned back to Six. "Not until you apologize."

Six's eyes bulged. "For what?"

"For being so mean to me in the car," he replied. "It really wasn't my fault, you know."

"It was entirely your fault, and should the rest of this rig collapse around us, I will blame you for that, too. Bring the boat *over here*!"

"Think before you talk, Six." Kyntak glanced meaningfully down into the water.

Six looked down and gasped. It wasn't a breed he recognized — but it was a lot bigger than a mako shark.

He uncurled from his ball and freestyled furiously through the water. He thought he could sense movement below him, but he wasn't sure. He looked down between strokes.

The shark was huge. It had to be at least seven meters long!

Six reached out and touched the side of the speedboat's hull.

He scrabbled furiously at the side.

There was nothing to hang on to.

The shark bumped his kicking legs again. Hard.

"God, you look so pathetic." Kyntak laughed, throwing down a rope ladder. "I hope none of my buddies from Lab security see me with you."

Six scrambled up the ladder so fast that he was in the boat before the drips from his outfit had rejoined the sea.

"That was childish and dangerous," he hissed, turning back to Kyntak. Then he froze. Kyntak was still laughing.

"That wasn't funny," Six said icily.

"Yes it was," Kyntak gasped. He broke out into fresh bouts of laughter. "You got out of that water so fast!"

"My life was in danger!" Six roared.

"No it wasn't!" Kyntak howled. He slapped his knee. "That was a basking shark! They're huge, but they only eat plankton!"

"You're lying!"

"No!" Kyntak struggled for breath through his hiccups of laughter. "It bumped you to scare you out of its territory, not to eat you!"

Six hesitated. Now that he thought about it, he couldn't think of any sharks bigger than white pointers that had been known to eat people. Kyntak was probably telling the truth.

"We have to get out of here," he said, annoyed. "More soldiers will be coming after us any second."

Kyntak was still laughing.

"Your razor-sharp wit caught me unguarded with its tact and subtlety," Six said sarcastically.

Kyntak's grin became even wider. "Hey . . . that was almost a joke!" He clapped Six on the back, and Six resisted the urge to hit him. "Congratulations!"

"Sit down, strap yourself in, and shut up," Six growled. He stepped up to the prow of the boat and, without checking to see if Kyntak had heeded his advice, gunned the engine and drove the boat into the waves.

DOUBLE DEALING

"Is this line secure?"

"This is Crexe's private terminal. This room, all the adjacent ones, and the terminal itself have been swept for transmitters. The line travels the whole way to your station at a minimum depth of two hundred meters of solid concrete, and I have a satellite searching the base for transmissions and receiving none. Unless you are being monitored at your station?"

"Unlikely."

"Then this line is clean. But we will be brief, just the same."

"Very well. Name your price."

"Sixty million for a scrape of the subject's cells, complete with a blood sample. Another seventy million on top of that will get you a sample of the fresh stem cells, and another ninety million will get you a digital copy of the subject's DNA. The complete package comes to a total price of two hundred twenty million standard credits."

"When were the scraping and blood sample taken from the subject?"

"Today. He had been knocked out and captured. As expected, his stay was brief, but he was out long enough for me to collect some physical evidence and plenty of data about his condition. I highly recommend buying the complete package — that way you can check that the blood sample taken from the subject matches the original genome, and that both of these correspond to the final product when Crexe delivers it to you. My price is insignificant compared to your losses should he try to cheat you when you have no quality control method."

"Indeed. Why did you use the rogue one for the samples? Why not the subject who works for the Lab?"

"Ah, the one who works in security. Have you ever met him?"

"Never. Why?"

"I'm rather proud of him — but this same pride inspires in me a terror of his abilities. That creature is violent, clever, unpredictable, and, ultimately, more dangerous than I think either of us could imagine."

"Your paternal feelings for him are touching."

"Very droll. One way or another, I couldn't think of a way to get samples from him without putting myself at risk — and the agent practically fell into my lap."

"I see. It makes no difference, anyway. The DNA should be the same from the two subjects, correct?"

"Correct."

"Then I agree to your terms. As you know, I am meeting Crexe tomorrow. I will speak to you after this. But one more thing."

"Yes?"

"How do I avoid the agent? The rogue subject? I would not, I think, enjoy a confrontation."

"Do not trouble yourself with that, my friend. The one who works for us is watching him, and awaiting orders. I have Methryn Crexe's word that Agent Six will not be a problem for much longer."

Grysat was sitting at his desk. "Hi, Six," he said cheerfully. "Mission go well, did it?"

"A message for King," Six said, ignoring the question. Dried mud crunched on his clothes. "There's someone I want him to meet."

"Who's that?" Grysat glanced at Kyntak.

"Just buzz King," Six said. "And send him this disk." He put Kyntak's disk on the desk.

Grysat sighed. "Come on, Six. You know the rules. I have no idea who this guy is, so for all I know, you could be under duress. I can't make exceptions for you just because —"

"Look! The mission didn't go well!" Six exploded. "I was shot, beaten up, knocked unconscious, and left to rot in a cell with a chatty guard." He glared at Kyntak before continuing. "Then I helped destroy the building I'd been working in, along with a nearby construction site and a perfectly good car.

Countless jeeps and a Twin helicopter were smashed to pieces, and everything I own suffered water damage. Do you want my repair budget estimate, or will you buzz me in now?"

There was a pause.

"Feel better?" Grysat asked finally.

Six did, strangely enough. But he didn't reply.

"Okay, I'll buzz you in," Grysat said. "And I'll put John Doe in the Visitors Center until King calls him, right?"

Six nodded grimly as the steel elevator doors opened. He would feel a little more at ease with Kyntak in the lockup — out of the way, for the moment.

"Good-bye, Six!" Kyntak called as Six walked towards the elevator. Six glared back at him, but didn't say anything. He stepped into the elevator, and the doors closed behind him.

He was alone this time. No irritating chatter, probably because it was noon and no one else was arriving. His vertical journey was a lonely one. There was nothing to distract him from his thoughts, but at this point he might have welcomed an interruption. He glared at his reflection in the stainless steel doors.

No one else really knew what had made Six the way he was. Most people, of course, didn't know that he was a Code-breaking genetic experiment, but even King couldn't pinpoint the cause of his contempt for the human race. Six himself wasn't sure, either — he had never really thought about it in great detail; he just lived his life in what seemed to be the easiest way. He had no friends or family, apart from King. He spoke when he had to, and trusted no one. He disliked sports except for fitness purposes. He had little use for money other than to sustain his existence for another day. Everyone else did things to be happy, but Six did things for no reason at all. He kept himself alive because it was better than the alternative. The only emotion he had ever really felt was fear, and even that didn't come very often.

Perhaps a man who doesn't believe he is human will never do the things that humans do. Six had known since he first awoke that he wasn't a part of society, because right from the start, he had been alone with others looking in at him. He was in his glass enclosure and everyone else was a part of the real world. He was an experiment of humankind, not a part of it.

The elevator doors slid open for him. Six stepped out into the corridor and turned, his slightly damp shoes squeaking on the linoleum.

This was why Kyntak seemed so alien to him. Kyntak smiled and joked and talked like humans, even though he was no more human than Six. If God had intended us to be humans, Six thought, then he would have given us parents.

He smiled wryly at that. He wasn't religious, of course. Only humans were religious. But somehow the idea of God having any say in his life seemed amusing. God created humans, and humans created Six. No matter how far above the rest of the world Six believed he was, humans had created him — they were his gods.

Imagine trying to get through the gates of heaven, Six thought, *when you're not God's creation. But hell requires a soul, so I'm not headed there, either.*

I'd be headed for limbo, he thought.

He touched the handle on King's door and waited for the buzzer.

"So who is he?" King asked. "And why do I have to meet him?"

"The name he gave me is Kyntak," Six said. "He's obnoxious, loud, stupid, and seemingly suicidal. He was one of the guards at the Lab, but he helped me escape, and he says he has the evidence and information we need about Code-breaking activity in the Lab. But with all these things aside —"

"Excuse me!" King interrupted. "You were captured? And then you needed help escaping? *You?*"

"They were shooting on sight," Six said bluntly. "No 'who's there?' no 'freeze,' no 'put your hands on your head.' I'm lucky to be alive. I might have been able to get out on my own. It doesn't matter whether I needed help or not; he gave it anyway."

"I thought that having any company at all was a liability in your view," King said.

"In many ways, he was a liability. But physically, he could do everything I could do, and more."

King leaned forward. "What?"

"He claims to be from the same experiment as me. Apparently I wasn't the only creation of the Lab — Kyntak says his DNA is identical to mine. I think he's telling the truth; there's no way a normal human being could've done the things we did this morning."

King looked stunned. Then he put his face in his hands. "Another Six hanging around the Deck," he groaned. "That's all we need."

"No!" Six said, tensing up. He had half lifted his body out of the chair, every muscle taut. He saw King staring at him and tried to relax.

"Kyntak is nothing like me," Six said coldly, his composure regained. "He is unprofessional, uncontrolled, unpredictable, and possibly very dangerous. I do not trust him, and I advise you not to trust him, either. His motives are extremely questionable. Even if he's not a ChaoSonic spy, he sure needs to grow up."

King sighed. "Six, maybe it's you who needs to grow up."

Six's eyes narrowed. His hands clenched. But he said nothing.

"I blame myself for the way you've become," said King. "You believe that you're better than everyone else, and that's understandable given that, in many ways, you are."

You're right I am, Six thought.

"But unfortunately," King continued, "you seem to believe that no one besides you has any value at all, and that's not as easy to forgive. Physical and mental superiority does not give you the right to show contempt for those you feel are inferior to you. A lot of people in this City can't run as fast as you can — and if you hate them all, you'll never be happy."

Six was silent.

"I know you understand what I'm saying, Six. As a consequence of your persistent efforts to avoid the rest of humanity, you have no purpose in life — and I think it's time for you to decide whether or not that's a worthwhile sacrifice. We are brought into life upon this earth, then we exist for a comparatively short period of time, then we die. In the meantime, many of us enjoy ourselves. And if you don't like it, well," — he shrugged — "tough. You're stuck with us, so you might as well try to grin and bear it. And as for Kyntak, I know what qualifies as 'unprofessional, uncontrolled, and unpredictable' for you — it's the same as your description of everyone you've ever met. The reason you're so upset now is not because Kyntak is psychologically abnormal. It's because, physically, you think you may have met your match."

"You can't trust him!" Six said loudly. "The Lab is up to something big, something worth killing for — and he is working for them!"

"I have no intention of trusting him — until I meet him. But given, as you say, the Lab is up to something big . . ." King clasped his hands together and put them on the desk. "I think we have more important things to worry about than your personal dislike. Don't you?"

Six glared at him across the table.

"In fact, here's some food for thought," King continued. "If Kyntak has the same 'perfect' DNA as you, but he's 'obnoxious, loud, stupid, and seemingly suicidal,' on what grounds have you declared your own superiority?"

"My actions speak for themselves," Six protested.

"Indeed," King said evenly. "Now sit down. Your next

mission is lined up. We need to find out where the Project Falcon lab is."

Six sat.

"Good. So let's look at Kyntak's disk." King put the disk into his computer.

Six gasped as images appeared on-screen.

"What the hell is going on here?" he breathed.

MISSION FOUR

LONG LIFE

"I've been all over the City, Six," King said, "and I've seen a lot of things, but I'm at a loss to explain this."

The pictures were all of faces. But, Six thought, such *strange* faces.

They were creased, crinkled — like the wrinkles of old people, but much deeper and more widespread. Their skin sagged, their hair was thin, and their flesh was loose and pockmarked.

The faces were like clay, covered in water and melted slightly before going into the kiln and erupting in tiny cracks.

"Who are they? What happened to these people?" Six asked.

"These are old people," King said.

Ridiculous, Six thought. *No one lives to be* that *old.*

"Average life spans have been dropping sharply since Takeover, Six," King said. "But people used to be able to live to eighty or even ninety years old, before the fog came down on us. You've probably never seen anyone older than sixty, but I remember people approaching their eighth decade." He tapped the screen. "They used to look like this."

"This bad?" Six asked.

"Well, never this bad," King said. "These people would have to be . . . at least a hundred or a hundred and ten years old, but it's hard to tell without a comparison — I've never seen pictures of anyone over about ninety-five. One way or the other," King continued, "I'm very curious to find out what this is all about."

"Could the photos have been taken before Takeover?" Six suggested.

"No, the pictures were taken with a ChaoSonic camera."

Maybe so, Six thought, *but I don't trust Kyntak as far as I can throw him.*

"Could these be photos of rich recluses?" Six frowned. "People live longer if they've got expensive air-purifiers in their homes, particularly if they never go outside."

"It's certainly possible," King said. "But if the Lab has been kidnapping ancient millionaires, why? And why haven't we heard something about it? A dozen rich people vanishing, particularly ones who've been around for a long time, doesn't happen without somebody noticing."

"Perhaps it's . . ." Six paused, thinking. "Perhaps it's not a matter of kidnapping. Perhaps the Lab is approaching these people for funding. They make pharmaceuticals, right?"

"Ah, I see," King said. "You think that maybe the Lab has developed some kind of life-span extending therapy, and is selling it to these people in order to fund Project Falcon?"

"It's possible," Six said.

"It certainly is. Have you ever heard of Chelsea Tridya?"

"No."

"She was a Gear research scientist. For the past few years she has been working on exactly the kind of therapy you've mentioned. She was interested in the science of life and aging. She claimed she'd made a breakthrough quite recently, wherein she'd been able to control the rate of cell division and replication in mice, effectively slowing down their rate of aging."

"You think she could be helping the Lab?" Six asked, not quite convinced. In his experience, different branches of ChaoSonic were too greedy to cooperate.

"If so, I doubt she's doing it willingly. She vanished, along with all her data and equipment, about six months ago."

"That sounds more like Crexe's style," Six said.

"It all seems to fit," King said, "except for one thing." He frowned. "If the Lab has had her data for months, that's certainly long enough to perfect the technique. But look at these photographs!" He tapped the screen.

Six looked down at the saggy, wrinkled faces. *They all look miserable,* he thought. *Desperate.*

"These people haven't had their natural lives extended for six months — they're much further gone than that. No matter how rich, no one lives beyond seventy these days, and these people are well past a hundred. So the treatment has to have been going on for at least thirty or forty *years.*" He sighed. "And if the Lab has had this treatment technique for that long . . ."

". . . why steal it from Tridya," Six finished. "I see."

There was a long silence.

"Perhaps they just wanted the exclusive," Six suggested. "A therapy that makes people live longer is worth a fortune, and they abducted or killed Tridya so they could keep the edge."

"Possibly," King responded. "But if they'd had the treatment for thirty years, why haven't they released it before now?"

"Maybe there's a limited supply," Six said. "Highest bidders only."

King raised an eyebrow. "Maybe so," he said. "But they don't look like satisfied customers to me."

Six looked back at the screen. The desperate, lonely eyes of twelve men and women stared back at him.

"Perhaps it's nothing," King said. "Or perhaps it's everything. Either way, bear it in mind when you're on your next mission. You remember the pictures I showed you last time?"

Six nodded.

"In that case, I only need to show you this one."

King slid a photograph across the desk. It showed a short, plump man in his forties, with thin black hair and large grey eyes.

"This is Ungrelor Ludden. He's in charge of providing weapons and allotting pay to the soldiers in ChaoSonic security. He's our ticket to catching the Lab. He's arranged to meet Methryn Crexe at sunset tomorrow."

"What interest does a security official have with this project?" asked Six. "If Ludden wanted someone killed, why couldn't he just hire someone, or use one of his own strike teams? Why take an interest in the assassin project?"

"I don't know what Ludden wants with Crexe," King said. "But he's connected somehow. We need to find out how. I want you to be at that meeting, using a digi-mike to tape the conversation. If we can't find out from the conversation where the Project Falcon laboratory is located, then we'll just have to arrest him."

"How did we find out about the meeting?"

"The information came from Kyntak. He called me just before you arrived."

"I thought he was in the lockup."

"Visitors Center," King said reprovingly. "And yes, he was, but they let him out, on special orders from one of the Jokers."

191

Six's jaw dropped. "You're kidding."

"No."

"You mean he's only been in the cell for half an hour and one of the *Jokers* orders us to let him go?"

King didn't blink. "That's exactly what I mean."

Six's eyes were wide. "That has 'ChaoSonic spy' written all over it — and one of the Jokers is involved!"

"I know, Six," King hissed. "But if the Spades get wind of it, they won't just check out Kyntak and start looking for the Joker — they'll snoop around everywhere. And Kyntak will lead them straight to you."

Six's palms were sweaty. "So what do we do?"

"I keep my head down. And tomorrow, you go to that

meeting. Find out what Crexe and Ludden are up to." He leaned forward, eyes narrow. "We can't act when we don't know what's going on. It's up to you to find out."

Six nodded. "Is that everything?"

"Almost. Here are the coordinates for Crexe and Ludden's meeting. Go and see Queen. She'll brief you for this mission." King handed over a sheet of paper. "Be careful out there. I know this is hard for you."

"It's not," Six said, turning away.

"I'm serious. I don't want anything to happen to you."

Six grunted and walked towards the door. "Incidentally," he said, pausing, "Grysat's been practically insubordinate to me lately — he often seems to forget that he's just a receptionist and I'm a Heart. Is there any chance you can get one of the Jokers to talk to him, and let him know that his behavior isn't appropriate?"

"Grysat *is* one of the Jokers," King said without looking up. "He sits on reception to keep an eye on everybody — and he's not the one who bailed Kyntak out." He put his papers in a desk drawer and locked eyes with Six. "I hope you can keep a secret."

Six gulped. "Of course," he said, and left, embarrassed.

"So," Jack said, "you'll need some surveillance gadgets?"

Six nodded. Jack beamed happily at him.

"In that case," he said dramatically, "you're in luck! I've just whipped up something that I think you'll love!" He dodged Six's cold glare. "Take a look at this!"

In his hand, Six saw a small, silver mp3 player. Jack waited for a reaction, but received none, so he explained.

"This is many gizmos in one. It's a two-way radio, an audio recorder, a digi-cam, a beacon, and . . . well, an mp3 player. I know they're ancient, but some of the lower-class civilians kept them from pre-ChaoSonic times."

Six was silent. He had seen mp3 players before.

Jack was fiddling around with the buttons. "When this memory stick is inside, all of the special functions are activated. The 'radio' button is self-explanatory — it turns on the radio. Convenient, yes?" He looked up at Six.

Six didn't reply.

"Yeah, I know. 'Get on with it,' right?" Jack sighed. "Okay, Six. The play button activates the microphone, which is inside this ridge here. Push it again to turn it off. The stop button takes a picture with the digi-cam through the hidden lens here. Just point and click — there's no flash. A screen lifts up out of the lid here so you can see the picture you've taken without a computer. The fast-forward button turns on the beacon and sends a help signal to the Deck. I doubt that you'll need that. But if worst comes to worst, push the rewind button three times. That's if you think you're about to get searched — it melts all the secret gadgets inside but leaves the player itself intact. And finally, if you flick off the stereo switch, then you'll get a perfectly innocent music recording out of the disk. In mono, I'm afraid. I hope you like funk!"

Six grimaced.

"Hey, come on." Jack sounded hurt. "It'll do the job, and

it'll do it well. It's inconspicuous, efficient, safe to use, and glitch-free. I'm sorry to hear that you don't like the music, but you shouldn't need it anyway."

"No makeover this time?" asked Six.

"Well, I think you'll be fine without it. When you're out on the streets I doubt you'll need one, especially since the people you're watching will never have seen you before anyway. Most people enjoy having a makeover, and I certainly like helping them out. Why not you, Six? You're so . . . different."

"I have a job to do," Six said. "I don't like to waste time."

He snatched up the mp3 player and made to leave the room.

"I found out who Sender J. Lawson was," Jack said.

Six grimaced. He touched his dog tags reflectively and stopped moving, his hand on the door handle.

"The files say he was caught in the firing line of his own squadron," Jack said. "That's why he was never on your mission stats."

Six was silent.

"I'm sorry, Six. I didn't mean to be so tactless. Sometimes you get stuck between a rock and a hard place, and you have to do something you might not like. It happens to the best of us. Why do you wear the dog tags?"

Six turned and made eye contact with Jack. "I wear them," he said, "to remind myself that I *have* to be better than the best of you."

The door swung shut.

SENDER J. LAWSON

This had to be a joke. Or a mistake, or something. Because, *the fourteen-year-old boy thought,* I can't just die down here, they won't just let me die, and someone will be coming to rescue me.

The sound of a hundred booted feet down the stairwell towards the office was deafening to Six's ears.

"I'm sorry, Six," *the radio buzzed.* "I'm sorry."

Sorry is wrong. Sorry must be a mistake, *thought Six,* because sorry isn't the cavalry. Sorry won't stop bullets.

The only door was the one he had come in. He searched the floor. About four meters by five meters — wood paneling, over six-meter-deep concrete, no trapdoors. No good. The ceiling was steel, with no service holes, and above it there were at least twenty-five meters of limestone between him and the night outside. Limestone was a soft rock, but even if Six could get through the steel, he'd have nothing to dig with.

Six threw the bookshelf to the floor. It cracked against the panels, sending books and chunks of mahogany skittering to the corners of the room. He punched the wall where the bookshelf had stood, shattering the surface plaster, crying out when the bones in his hand fractured against the concrete.

The footsteps had stopped. Had the soldiers given up?

No. They were right outside the door.

Desperate now, he picked up a chunk of bookshelf and threw it at the light globe. The light fizzed out as glass tinkled to the floor. Darkness would at least give him some advantage when the troops stormed the room.

Six almost laughed at the thought of a hundred soldiers trying to fit into a four-by-five-meter office with a bookshelf on the floor and only one doorway. He actually did laugh, bitterly, when he heard the night-vision goggles click on outside the office door. Killing the light had been a waste of time.

He drew his Raven X59 pistol for the first time. Although it was an old model, the Deck had given it to him brand-new, and until now it had never been used. The grip felt alien.

I hope it works, he thought. I've never tested it. If it jams up, I'm dead for sure.

Six's thoughts were suddenly shattered as the door was broken down.

A PGC387 stun grenade was thrown in. Six caught it with his left hand and threw it back over the commando blocking the doorway, then shot him in the head with his right.

Instinct had made the decision for him.

The soldier slumped forward uncomplainingly as Six squeezed his eyes shut, moments before the PGC detonated.

Like black roses blown over by a gust of wind, the troops outside fell backward. The blinding shock wave rippled through them, a lethal splash of light. Many of them had very quick reflexes and turned away before the flash. Some didn't, and were nearly knocked unconscious by the shocking light, amplified by their night-vision goggles.

Six hesitated, then dropped his Raven to the floor. No more guns, *he thought numbly.* Ever. *He ripped off the dog tags from around the neck of the soldier he had killed before springing into action.*

The blinded soldiers were pushed forward in the struggle to get through the door. But when the troops who could still see arrived in the office, it was empty. Six had slipped outside among the others.

It was only a moment before a commando noticed that a man dressed like one of his colleagues was pushing in the direction opposite from the rest of them. He saw that the man wasn't wearing goggles or carrying any weapons. He opened fire with his Owl.

By the time the soldier's finger had hit the trigger, Six was no longer in front of him. Instead, four other commandos were shot in the back. One was protected by armor, and he turned around, searching for the source of the attack.

"About-face," he roared, seeing Six vanish into the crowd. He pulled the trigger and sent a hail of bullets after him. Two soldiers were hit in the legs, and they went down firing. Confusion and fear took over as those who had been blinded or disoriented by the flash started firing, too, and soon the air was shredded by the gunfire.

Six gasped as a few rounds pierced his left thigh. He thrashed his way out of the line of fire, but his movement caught the eye of a commando in front of him, who suddenly leveled his Owl. Six grabbed the man's knees and threw him to the ground as sparks flew off the body armor of soldiers above his head. By the time he had hit the floor, the soldier was already dead, shot by his comrades. Six found himself standing in front of another commando, who learned from the mistake of the previous one and scurried out of Six's way like a cockroach caught in the light as the bullets of his colleagues sliced the air around him.

By the time the other Hearts had arrived at the entrance to the underground base, there was no movement on the floor below.

Only a cold, bleak silence.

No one stopped them from breaching the outer door and no one raised the alarm when they crossed the polished threshold. Even when they were inside, the only sound was of neon bulbs humming softly and indifferently.

But before they climbed downstairs to see the aftermath, they witnessed a miracle.

When Six dragged himself out of the elevator, he had two broken knuckles, a shattered femur, five bullets in his body, and a pair of dog tags around his neck.

Six kept seeing the bullet, his bullet, disappearing into Lawson's face over and over again. His imagination worked like a slow-motion X-ray — he could see that fatal, perfect shot breaking

Lawson's nose, cracking a hole in his skull, and finally separating his spine from his brain.

Inside he was pulling that trigger repeatedly, like a psychopath, with each shot striking him like an accusation.

Murderer. Murderer. Murderer.

NO ONE MUST ESCAPE

Six's fingers played idly on the record button as he sat at the bus stop in the City Square. With each tap he gave the player, there was a resounding click from the speakers in his ears. He had deliberately adopted a slumped and relaxed pose — head back, shoulders loose, legs spread — but his eyes were keen and alert behind his dark glasses.

The Square was a relic from pre-Takeover times, a rash of red clay tiles providing temporary relief from the monotonous fields of huge grey buildings that surrounded it. Because it was right in the middle of the City, there were many people passing through it at any given time. No one stayed. Few even lingered, except for those who sat on the benches briefly, for one reason or another. But people seemed to be drawn towards the Square from all over the City, led to it by all the old roads and paths and rusted signs. The tiles were worn smooth by millions of feet. The Square was never silent — voices and footsteps always spread through it, duplicating and dividing, bouncing off walls, replicating like a disease.

Across the Square, Six saw a chicken salesman gesticulating wildly at his stock, trying to be noticed by pedestrians. Inside their tank, the boneless, legless, beakless birds splashed in the water, trying to flap with bald, floppy wings. Their gills heaved, and their empty eye sockets stared at the prospective customers.

Modern chickens were designed before Six was. The fast-food branches of ChaoSonic had saved a fortune by lacing normal chickens with altered DNA, removing all the inedible pieces and adding gills to make them more hygienic and cost-effective. There was no longer a need to scrape the meat from the bones — chicken was now just meat: muscles and organs. There was nothing inedible inside a chicken, so they were blind, deaf, dumb creatures, cloned on demand and ready to be thrown in a deep fryer.

Things haven't changed much for centuries, Six thought, looking at the struggling chickens. *Humans have been using living things as tools since the invention of the horse and cart for heavy loads, or the caged canary for testing air. They've been improving on these tools for almost as long — selective breeding for better crops, or special training to make guide dogs. The chickens are not a testament to a more exploitative human nature, but to the new and better technology to exploit nature with.*

And, of course, I'm just like the chickens, he thought. *A tool, but used as weaponry instead of food. Unlike the chickens, the humans made me stronger and better than I once was. But the purpose was the same — I was also modified to be more useful.*

Crexe and Ludden were due to arrive at any minute now.

Six had been in the area for more than half an hour, but he hadn't sat down at the bus stop until the last bus had left.

His finger twitched rhythmically against the player. Six could stay completely motionless if he had to, but that would have looked unnatural. A boy sitting motionlessly on a bench is much more suspicious than one wiggling his fingers for no apparent reason. A good agent could sit immobile for days, and Six was a very good agent. He could stay motionless for weeks if he wanted to. Boredom was for humans, he had always thought.

I wonder if Kyntak ever gets bored, he wondered suddenly. *How long has he been copying humans? Has he begun to think like one as well?*

Six shook his head. He had to stop this. The more he thought about the events of the last two days, the more he seemed to lose control of his thoughts. He had to concentrate on the mission.

Suddenly he saw what he was looking for. A man in the crowd: leather jacket, light sneakers, sunglasses, and the telltale bulge of a radio in his pocket.

They're here, Six thought. Though he displayed no outward signs of change, he now began to search the crowd with feverish intensity. So far, three guys with radios. No, four. Three of them had guns, too — he could see the shapes in their jackets. Probably from Ludden's side. Then there were two more guys, neither with guns.

Six paused. One of the new men on the scene was staring straight at him. Six slowly and casually turned his head away, but kept examining the starer from behind his sunglasses. The man was of average height, and lithe, with close-cropped dark hair, deep blue eyes, and powerful muscles hidden under his clothes. He had a long scar on his neck, evidence of a vicious gash. He was staring at Six incredulously, as though he couldn't believe what he was seeing.

What's going on? Six wondered. *Has he recognized me from yesterday? He must know me from somewhere.*

Maybe he was the one watching me in the parking lot the other day.

The scarred man moved first.

Six was on his feet instinctively, drawing a silenced gun from his belt. The man was reaching for his radio, but Six was quicker. As the man's fingers touched the switch on the radio, two bullets pierced it. The man dropped the ruined receiver to the ground and turned to run, with Six already hot on his heels.

"Six, what are you doing?" Queen crackled through Six's radio.

He ignored her, roughly pushing people out of his way as he tore after the stranger. Amazingly, he found that he wasn't gaining any ground at all on the other man. This guy was fast. He was better than fast — he was getting away!

The chicken salesman lunged forward, reaching into his tank and pulling out a Crow KOT45. Water dripped off his arm as he aimed for Six's skull and pulled the trigger. Six dived forward, ducking his head and turning his shoulder. The bullets whined over him as he rolled along the tiles and jumped back to his feet.

KOT45s fired from a closed bolt, making them impervious to wet or sandy conditions. However, this slowed the firing rate, and Six dodged the bullets without too much trouble. He barely noticed the soldier — he was still chasing the scarred man.

The other Deck agents, however, did take note of the gunfire directed at Six. So did the civilians, who panicked.

"Move in! Go!" Six's radio buzzed. *"Lock and load!"*

Their original mission now abandoned, the other Hearts agents moved into action, clambering up from manholes, leaping out of shops, and drawing pistols from their civilian outfits. The ChaoSonic agent ducked behind the steel base of his chicken tank. Pedestrians screamed and fled the scene, jamming the streets around the Square.

Six snarled and pushed through the throngs of bystanders. He could still see the scarred man sprinting away. *No one must escape,* Six thought. The tiled Square became a crimson blur beneath his feet. The people around him lost their human shapes and became flying blobs zipping past his body like comets. Still the man ahead remained out of his reach.

Soon they were each moving so fast that everything else seemed to be happening in slow motion. The people were like shop-window dummies, frozen in place as Six darted in between them.

They were out of the Square now. No more clumsy civilians to barge through, only narrow side streets and randomly parked vehicles. *This is where I'll get him,* thought Six. *I'll catch him, knock him out if need be, and take him back to the Deck.*

As he was running, he unscrewed the silencer from his Hawk and fired a shot up into the air. The explosion echoed loudly around the streets.

"Freeze!" Six yelled, but the man ahead of him had suddenly disappeared.

One moment he'd been running up ahead, and then the street was empty.

"What the . . ." Then Six saw the side street on the left. The man must have gone down there. Six slipped between the buildings and kept sprinting. But still he couldn't see his quarry. The street stretched out ahead of him for at least three hundred meters, but it was empty. It was a very narrow street, with no doors or windows in the buildings on either side. Where did the guy go?

He looked up. The scarred man was hopping quickly between the two walls, moving higher and higher out of Six's reach.

"Oh, no you don't," Six whispered. He jumped into the air, soaring between the buildings. He stretched up and grabbed the man's ankle. The scarred man cried out in surprise and lost his foothold on the wall. They both fell down towards the concrete. Six shoved his feet against one wall in midair and was propelled back towards the other, briefly slamming the other man against it. Then they landed, and Six hit the ground. He immediately scrambled to his feet but was knocked down when a lean muscular fist hit him in the face.

Immediately he sprang up again, but the other man was gone, sprinting down the street.

Who is this guy? Six wondered.

He powered along after his quarry, gaining velocity with each step, going faster and faster until it felt like nothing and no one could ever stop him. Suddenly he was out of the alley and the man was still running; he'd turned a corner and was speeding alongside the building. Six continued the chase, and realized he could now overtake the man. The blasting wind whistled past him as he put his feet on the wall and continued running, with the sky on his left and the ground on his right, and the running man in front of him still. Six ran up the wall a little farther, putting all his energy into the sprint. The speed levitated him, holding the ground at bay just out of arm's reach. Within a moment he was directly above the man, and he deftly reached down and grabbed his fluttering dark hair. The man looked up, and his jaw dropped as Six overtook him, whirled around on the wall, and flipped his feet down to the ground. Then he stopped dead, and the man cannoned into him, unable to turn around in time. Six stayed still as he took the impact, and the man fell to the ground. Six whipped out the Hawk as the man scrambled to his feet.

"No more games — you're coming with me," Six panted. He swallowed. "Understand?"

The man looked him in the eye, apparently unafraid, and nodded.

"Good. Tell me —"

There was a whirl of hair, a flash of white teeth, and suddenly the man was gone again. Six gasped. The front half of his gun had completely disappeared.

It had been *bitten off.*

Six looked up. The other man was rapidly receding into the distance. He gave chase again, discarding the useless weapon. His feet pounded the dirt into dust behind him as he saw the man dive into a ChaoSonic Chariot and start it up.

Six sighed, and jumped over the door of a nearby convertible, an old ChaoSonic Landmark. Car security systems were simpler than ever before — by skillfully jamming a clip of bullets in between the card slot and the exposed side of the cube, and using all his strength, Six was able to prize the lid off. He slid the ignition tube out swiftly, slipped his long fingers inside the hole, and connected the battery to the coil wire. The lights on the dashboard flicked on. With a little more wire crossing, the engine started, the motor roared, and suddenly he was in pursuit of the man again.

The hot-wiring had taken eighteen seconds.

The other driver was already far ahead of Six, but the Landmark was well built and powerful, and he had no difficulty closing the distance. Within moments he had slammed into fifth gear and was screaming after the smaller car.

"No one escapes Agent Six," he muttered. "Ever."

Six watched the car ahead tearing up the road and matched its every move. At a T-intersection it feinted left and turned right, but Six spun the wheel and screeched after it without losing any ground.

He saw his quarry's eyes flick to the rearview mirror.

"Yep," Six said aloud, "I'm still here."

As if in response, the Chariot swung left and screeched

into the entrance of a shopping center parking lot. Other drivers honked as they swerved aside to avoid him.

Six followed unhesitatingly — a second later his car was zooming up the ramp.

Once his Landmark was inside, it wasn't hard to find the Chariot. He just followed the noise of screeching tires and beeping horns.

The exit ramp was just ahead, so he accelerated forward to block it . . .

. . . just as he saw the Chariot drive up the *other* ramp, the one that led to the next floor.

Six revved the engine, and his Landmark shot up the ramp.

Once he was up on the next floor, he could see the Chariot in the second row, but it wasn't moving. Had it broken down? Or had he made a run for it?

There was a screaming of engines and a squealing of tires from the other side of the parking lot, and he saw a different car, a Trenlan IV race car, zoom forward.

In a storm of exploding glass, *it disappeared into the shopping center.*

The metal framework that had been holding the glass doors in place screeched as it was flattened against the ground. People screamed from inside.

The scarred man had switched cars and decided to go shopping. *But,* thought Six, *if he thinks I'm not going to follow him there, he's dead wrong.*

Six revved the Landmark, put his hand on the horn, and shot through the smashed entrance.

This wasn't about finding out where the man had recognized Six from anymore. Nor was it about making sure none of Crexe or Ludden's security crew escaped and spread the word to other Lab officials that the Deck was after them.

This was about competition. By nearly escaping Six's clutches, the scarred man had challenged Six's ability. And Six wasn't going to give up.

People in the shopping center yelped and dived aside as the two cars tore down the arcade. Signs were slammed against the floor. Papers and plastic bags swirled out of trash bins as the bins were knocked over. The litter was temporarily dragged behind the cars in the vacuum left in their wake.

The Landmark pulled alongside the Trenlan IV.

Six wrenched the wheel to the right.

The Trenlan was slammed against the shop windows on its right-hand side.

The scarred man kept his foot on the accelerator, even as his car was crushed between the Landmark and the shops. The sparkle of bursting windows along one side of the arcade looked like a comet tearing through space.

Civilians covered their heads with their arms and ran into the cover of the shops on the other side.

The scarred man slammed on the brakes.

Six suddenly lost what he had been pushing against, and the Landmark lurched violently to the right. It glanced off a shop wall, cracking one of its headlights, and the Trenlan sped by on his left.

With a crackle of splintering glass, the Trenlan was

outside again, this time in the parking lot at the other end of the mall.

"You're *not* getting away from me!" Six roared. The motor of his Landmark screamed as the big car squealed over the floor tiles.

But once he was outside again, he saw that the game was nearly up.

As he was still coming out through the doorway of the shopping center, the Trenlan was already screeching down the exit ramp. In a second it would be on the streets again — Six would never have time to drive all the way down to the opposite corner of the parking lot to reach the entrance to the ramp. The Trenlan and its driver would be well and truly gone by the time he got there.

Give up, Six, a voice inside him said. *There's no point anymore.*

Yes, there is, he answered.

You'll never catch him now, said the voice obstinately.

Yes, I will.

Six shifted into first and floored it.

The Landmark zoomed forward.

Into second. Floored it.

The Trenlan was halfway down the exit ramp.

Six was headed straight for the fifty-centimeter-high concrete barrier. The one supposed to stop cars from falling off the parking lot onto the exit ramp.

Into third. Floored it.

Into fourth.

The Trenlan was three-quarters of the way down the ramp.

Floored it.

Fifth.

The Trenlan was right underneath him.

Six spun the wheel.

The Landmark flipped sideways . . .

. . . hit the concrete . . .

and rolled over the barrier.

The Trenlan turned out onto the street. Despite the smashed-up state of the car, its driver tried to look casual and inconspicuous.

He glanced in the rearview mirror . . .

And his eyes widened as the Landmark dropped out of the sky, motor screaming, spinning like a corkscrew, slamming down onto the asphalt right-way up, immediately behind him.

Six nodded coolly to the other driver. *Yep. Still here.*

The Trenlan blasted off down the road, and a second later, Agent Six of Hearts was right behind it.

Another T-intersection was coming up — and on the other side of it, Six could see the Seawall. *I'm back at the coast,* he thought. *Have we really gone that far?*

The driver in front veered from side to side, not giving Six any hints as to whether he would go left or right.

Which way will he go this time? Six thought. *Do I just guess and take a fifty-fifty chance I'll lose him?* He edged his car over to the right-hand side of the road. If the Trenlan went left, Six would have plenty of room to turn, and if it went right he could block it, or smash into it.

The car in front went *straight ahead,* smashing through the safety barrier and vanishing into the foggy void.

Over the edge of the cliff.

Six's eyes widened.

He slammed his foot down on the accelerator. "I said *no more games*," he growled as the ground fell away beneath his wheels and he took the plunge earthward.

His back wheels hit the cliff and bounced. Immediately he saw that the cliff face wasn't vertical; it curved down at about a sixty-five-degree angle before hitting a road that ran alongside it below. Six could see the Trenlan speeding down the cliff towards that road.

After a moment of flight, the Landmark was hurtling down the face of the cliff. Dust and rocks poured into the convertible from above — Six couldn't find the button that activated the roof. He slammed his foot on the brakes and changed back down into second gear. Stalling would be a very bad move. The engine howled crazily at him as the revs went off the scale. The front wheels slammed into the cliff face, sending a spray of dust and dirt flying up across the windshield. Six fought to keep the wheel steady.

He changed the gears up and accelerated, wheels sliding over the dirt, raising a dusty cloud above him. He could see the other car far below, driving towards the road. It was nearly there, and seemed to be swinging left. *No problem*, Six thought.

I'll land on him. If that doesn't stop him, nothing will. Six twisted the wheel.

The wheels of the Landmark tore at the dust, and the car started to slide, sideways, down the cliff. "Uh-oh!" Six yelled. Bad idea, bad idea . . .

Suddenly the car was spinning out of control, and the wheels had lost their grip on the side of the cliff. Six was flipped upside down as the Landmark began to fall; he looked up and saw the ground racing towards him. Crying out, he pushed himself out of the seat and flipped in midair until he was the right way up again, still falling towards the road. The convertible was spinning and twisting above him, and the ground was flying up to meet him.

Three two one . . .

Six slammed his feet down onto the asphalt, and quickly rolled out of the way as nearly a ton of automobile crashed down beside him. It slid across the cliff face, slowly coming to a twisted stop. By the time the vehicle was finally at rest, Six had already gone — following the Trenlan on foot.

Six sprinted furiously, trying to catch up. He could run at about fifty kilometers per hour, and the Trenlan could do four times that amount but the road was narrow, windy, and rough, and the car hadn't yet begun to accelerate. Six's sneakers whipped the asphalt, his arms flew by his sides, and he was getting closer.

The driver leaned out of the car window and looked behind him. He raised his eyebrows in surprise when he saw

Six. But this was quickly replaced by a grin. He reached back into the car and then came out again holding an Eagle automatic.

Six gasped. The gun must have been in the car when the other man stole it — he certainly hadn't been carrying it when Six had been chasing him on foot.

Six leaped into the air, threw up his arms, and flipped over — grabbing a plant growing on the cliff for support. He heard bullets from the machine gun whine past as he swung off the branch, springing into the air, then digging into the cliff with his left hand. He flipped over again and thudded into the rock, face first, hugging it tightly as bullets chattered around him.

And then the car was out of sight around a corner, and Six was safe. He dropped down to the road, spitting out dirt and chiding himself.

I let him get away!

He clenched his fists angrily. He could feel his 100 percent mission success rate becoming a jarring 99.9.

"Failure," he told himself sternly, "is for humans."

But he no longer believed it quite so firmly.

AN EMPTY DECK

It was dark outside by the time Six had walked all the way back to the Deck. The freezing wind stung his skin, but it had blown some of the fog away; the moon was shining among the stars. The many cars on the road had left to make room for shadows, and the ground was being spattered with a light shower of rain.

He wondered how the mission had gone, but there was no one he could ask — it was against Deck protocol to communicate via radio over long distances as it increased the risk of the transmissions being intercepted.

His forehead creased with worry. If Crexe and Ludden had been arrested with all their plainclothes bodyguards, then there was a chance they would have told the agents all about Six and Kyntak. *As soon as I walk in the door I could be arrested by the Spades,* Six thought, *for being the product of an illegal experiment.* Or, if Crexe and Ludden hadn't been caught, and they'd rendezvoused with the scarred man, they could have worked out who Six was and sent a hit team for him by now.

Or, even if the Lab had no idea about Six, but Crexe and Ludden had gotten away, then they would still be up to whatever they were up to.

And it's all my fault, Six thought. *I chased the scarred man instead of helping the others, and I let him get away.*

Six stopped for a moment, just outside the pool of halogen light surrounding the Deck. He stared up at the stars — sparse pinpricks piercing the carbon mist.

They say that God created humans, he thought. *But humans created me. I am better than humans, therefore humans think they are better than God.*

But who has the right to make me so strong that when a suspect escapes, I am to blame? Why should I be given the power to kill Sender J. Lawson, and then hold myself responsible when I do? Why is it fair that I should be able to do everything, so everything is my fault?

Six bowed his head and cursed Methryn Crexe, fingering the tags around his neck. Crexe and the Lab, he thought, playing God and making him suffer.

With a sigh, he walked in out of the cold. Inside the Deck, lights were blazing, and the warm yellow bulbs had an aura of comfort and coziness, especially after the night outside. He couldn't see Grysat (the Joker, he reminded himself) anywhere, and was surprised at his own disappointment. Shaking his head, he buzzed himself in and headed for the elevator.

Agent Two was standing in it. "Howdy, Six!" he said.

Agent Two had only been employed by the Deck for eighteen months, but he'd already gained much respect from King and the others. He was clever, fit, and dedicated. Six had thought that Two's incessant socializing and sentimentality were inexcusably unprofessional, and so he had avoided him — except when they had been forced to communicate via radio on the Shuji mission. But tonight, Six was glad the elevator wasn't empty. He didn't want to think about the day's events.

"Hello, Two. How are you tonight?"

Two looked taken aback, but recovered quickly. *Comes with the job,* Six thought wryly.

"I've been all right, thanks," Two replied calmly. "I'm just riding the elevators up and down — I don't feel like going home yet, but everyone else has, and there's nothing else to do." He smiled. "Probably someday one of the Spades will see me doing this on the surveillance cameras, and I'll get into trouble for acting suspiciously and wasting time. But for now . . ." He pushed the button for the top floor.

"When in Rome . . ." Six murmured, and pushed the button for King's floor. Two grinned at him.

"So how are you?" Two asked. "Where have you been? I haven't seen you today."

"I was sent out to the City Square at the southside pavilion. I should have been back long before this, but I wrecked a car on the cliffs at Stratsville."

Two's eyes widened. "Really? Are you hurt?"

Six shook his head. "Just annoyed. It was a nice car, a Landmark, and it wasn't even mine. And the guy I was chasing got away."

"How'd you wreck it? Did you wrap it around the posts

on the side of the road, or did you hit the cliff on one of the bends?"

"No, no. It never touched the road — not while I was in it, anyway. I wrecked it on the cliff. I was driving down it at the time, and I rolled it."

Two eyed Six carefully, probably trying to decide if he was joking. Six looked right back at him. "What?" he asked.

Two burst into laughter. "I heard you did some crazy things, but — whoa! Are you serious?"

Six nodded blankly. Two laughed even harder.

"You drove down the side of the Stratsville cliffs? That's insane! That's even better than the stuff you did on the Shuji project the other day! I can't believe you're still alive!" He giggled. "And you're complaining about losing your car?"

"It wasn't my car," Six said. He almost smiled, but stopped himself. *This isn't normal,* he thought.

We are brought into life upon this earth, we exist for a comparatively short period of time, then we die. In the meantime, many of us enjoy ourselves.

Cheers, King, Six thought. He sighed. "I messed up the mission; the suspect was better than I was. Today hasn't been a good day."

Two stopped laughing and patted Six on the back. Six tensed slightly at the touch.

"Hey, don't worry about it," Two said. "We all make mistakes. Everyone has good days and bad days, and from the sound of it, you have more good days than most of us."

Six smiled faintly. "You have no idea."

Two laughed. "Yeah, I bet. Don't fret over one bad day. We all have 'em. It's only human."

"Yes," Six said softly. "Only human."

The elevator pinged at the top floor. The silver doors slid silently open.

"Are you going to get off here?" Six asked. "Or are you going to keep riding up and down?"

"I guess I'll get off." Two shrugged. "Where are you headed?"

"Floor Eleven," Six said, gesturing at the button he had already pressed. "I'm going to find King and talk to him about the mission." He looked outside the elevator, seeing nothing and hearing silence. "Is it usually so empty at this time of night?"

Two shrugged. "No. But it's not unheard of. It's been a bit weird for me, because I always stick around, and people say good-bye and stuff before they go. But today I got all my work done early, so I went for a walk to stretch my legs. When I got back, nearly everyone had already left."

"I see. I'm never here this late; I'm not used to it. Has King left yet?"

"Nope, don't think so. I'll stop in and see him with you, if that's okay."

"No problem."

The elevator purred as it slid downward. Six frowned. He'd never seen the Deck so silent before. It disturbed him. Normally, even alone in an elevator, his sharp and sensitive ears could pick up the hustle-bustle and chatter of people conducting business in the corridors and offices of the building. But now all he could hear was Two's breathing.

"You know," Two began, "before I started work here, I never guessed that being a secret agent would involve so much paperwork. James Bond never had to do any, I'm sure."

Six smiled as Two talked. It seemed that he was not the only one who'd seen some old movies.

The elevator pinged and the doors slid open. Two and Six stepped out, turned, and began walking towards King's office. Six paused midstep. "Do you hear something?"

"Well, I certainly do," Kyntak said, walking towards them. "For secret agents, you guys aren't very secretive."

Six turned. "Kyntak! What are you doing here?"

Kyntak grinned. "You brought me here, remember?"

"No," Six said, frowning. "I heard you got out of the Visitors Center, so why are you still hanging around?"

"You need me. But no one brought me any dinner and I was hungry, so I went for a wander. Who's your friend?"

"I'm Agent Two," Two said, with a friendly smile. "Nice to meet you."

"Likewise," Kyntak responded, shaking his hand.

"How do you know Six?" Two asked.

"I met him when he was on a mission. After he destroyed the building I worked in, I had nowhere to go. So here I am!"

"Me!" Six hissed. "I'm not the one who smashed up the building!"

Kyntak laughed. Six's eye twitched.

"We're going to see King," Two told Kyntak.

"I'll follow you." Kyntak grinned. "Which way?"

They walked down the corridor to King's room, their footsteps echoing through the silent corridors. They found King's office door unlocked, but no one was inside. The computer was still on, papers were still on the desk, and a warm cup of coffee was beside them.

"Looks like he'll be back soon," Two said. "Shall we wait here?"

"Yeah, okay," Kyntak agreed. "You don't mind that, do you, Six?"

Six shook his head. "Fine by me." He felt surprisingly comfortable enduring the company of Kyntak and Two and listening to them talk, but that was Kyntak's gift. He made people relax, made them trust him. *Observe his behavior,* Six ordered himself. *Is he a spy, or just a freak?*

Ten minutes later, Six looked at his watch. "King's still not back," he said, frowning. *It's not that far to the bathroom,* he thought.

Two blinked. "Tell you what, I'll go down to reception, use the central computer, and find out where he is. He must be in someone else's office, right?" He shrugged. "You guys stay here in case he comes back."

Two disappeared down the corridor.

"How did the mission go today?" Kyntak asked.

"Badly. I let the guy I was chasing get away."

"Why the sudden urge for charity?"

"I tried to catch him, and I failed."

Kyntak stared. "No way."

"Yep."

"That's not normal at all for you, is it? How are you coping?"

"I'm all right. Everyone makes mistakes, don't they?"

Kyntak grinned warmly. "Yep, they sure do. Nobody's perfect, after all." He paused. "You know, I'm very relieved to hear you say that."

"Why?"

"Because from the instant you woke up in that cell, you seemed so determined, so cold, so mechanical! But now, it's like you've loosened up a bit. Like you're one of us again."

"Us?"

"Human."

Six chuckled. "Humans."

Kyntak laughed. "You're not losing it, are you?"

"Losing it?"

"Yeah. It's great that you're coping, but you just laughed at something that wasn't actually funny. And laughing seems weird from you at the best of times. Has losing a bad guy sent you over the edge?"

Six laughed again. "Me, over the edge? Never! But on the other hand, today has been a very unusual day. Maybe I am. I've certainly never behaved this way before."

If anything has sent me over the edge, it's King's little speech, not losing a bad guy, he thought.

"Well." Kyntak shrugged. "Just as long as you're okay."

"Yes," Six said. "I'm fine. Better than ever." His smile faded. "Tell me about the photographs on the disk."

Kyntak shivered. "Creepy, aren't they?"

"Where'd you get them?"

"Where you found me," he said. "I came across the old people in their cells, and had no clue as to why they were there. I figured they were evidence of weird stuff going on, so the next day I smuggled in a camera and took some shots. The day after that, they left."

"What condition were they in?" Six asked.

"Physically they were completely healthy, except for being at least twice as old as anyone I'd ever seen before. But mentally . . . they were freaky."

Six frowned. "Can you be more specific?"

"They were, I dunno, senile, I guess. They looked at me but it was a really confused, empty look. Mindless. And none of them spoke English, that's for sure. They made noises all right, but it was just yelling, gibberish. It was like their brains had been melted."

Doesn't sound like a group of old millionaires, Six thought. Unless they'd been tortured.

"How were they brought in?"

Kyntak shrugged. "Actually, I have no idea how they got there. I mean, I saw soldiers drag in a few people on the day I first saw the old people. Some of them were obviously agents or vigilantes, like there was a really, really big guy who tried to escape past me, and he was agile, let me tell you. But mostly I think they were just civilians who saw too much. There was a guy who was some kind of lunatic priest; a woman who looked like an office worker; there was even a bunch of babies that they'd kidnapped for one reason or another. And that's not even beginning to tell you about the animals I saw!"

"Animals?"

"Yeah — dogs, cats, birds, even tanks of fish. I assume they wanted them for experiments of some type, the ones they weren't ready to try on humans. But anyway, no old people. Not one person over forty ever entered."

"Could they have come in the night before?" Six asked.

"I thought they might've, but I asked the night shift guy, and he said he hadn't seen anything. So there's obviously something special about them — if they were smuggled in without either of us knowing, it must've been through a hidden entrance somewhere.

"The weird thing is, they left by the main gate, dragged out by soldiers, kicking and screaming. One of them even managed to worm out of her guard's grip, but when she tried to walk, her legs couldn't support her, and she fell down. I tell you, these people were *really* old."

"Why would they cover up their arrival but not their departure?" Six asked.

"I figured that they needed them for something while they were inside," Kyntak said. "An experiment or something. Once they'd got in, it didn't matter who knew that they were there."

Six rubbed his chin. Something still didn't add up. Where had people that old been hiding?

Maybe on another continent, he thought suddenly. *Outside the City.* Perhaps people lived longer out beyond the Seawall; Kyntak said they didn't speak English.

Who could say for sure that the lethal fog had stained the entire globe? There could be holes in it, with islands in them, places where people could . . .

"Did you know that you and I were once birds?" Kyntak asked suddenly.

"Pardon?" Six said.

"Birds," Kyntak repeated. "Like, originally."

"What do you mean?"

"Well . . . how much do you know about how genetic science works?"

Six considered this. He'd read a few standard textbooks, he knew the basic history of the Human Genome Project that had paved the way for his creation, but he hadn't ever really studied it properly.

"I know a little," he said.

"Well, you know how DNA is just like a code, one that governs the growth of your body? Basically."

"Basically," Six agreed.

"So you know that we didn't always have bodies like ours? That we didn't start out as superhumans, we grew into it in our first few years as infants?"

"I had always assumed so, yes," Six said.

"Well, they didn't implant the DNA into human embryos. They used birds."

Six's eyes widened. "Bird embryos?"

"Yep. Peregrine falcons, believe it or not. In the really early stages of growth, they spliced in the human DNA, laced with a bit of cheetah muscle, bloodhound nose, shark skin, elephant brain, that sort of thing, and so from then on the birds slowly became us."

"Wow . . ." It had never occurred to Six that the embryos used may not have been human. But it made sense, of course. Human embryos wouldn't have been easy to obtain, legally or otherwise. And testing on animals would have been more easily justifiable than experimentation on humans. But still . . .

"Kind of makes you think about destiny," Kyntak said.

"What?"

"Well, every cell in your body is replaced about once every four years. So four years after the human genes were spliced in, there would have been no traces of peregrine falcon left in us, except the genes in the doctored DNA to make our bones lighter and eyesight better. But there were no beaks, no feathers, nothing like that. We've been pure human for three cycles now. Right?"

"Three point two, if you count from the beginning of gestation," Six said. "But we're not pure human being — there's the flesh of many different animals under our skins."

"True, but if a surgeon were to open one of us up and do an in-depth study . . ."

Six shivered. *Or an autopsy,* he thought.

". . . they would find an incredibly healthy but otherwise normal human body. The animal DNA has been used to modify human organs; we're not jumbled-up bits and pieces of animal, right?"

"That's correct."

"The point is, we're not birds anymore, and haven't been

for twelve years now. But look at the way we behave," Kyntak continued. "We don't have our wings anymore, but we still jump off buildings and try to fly. We've come so far from where we started, but we still act as though we have to follow the same rules. We should be acting how we are, not how we were . . ."

". . . or how we were supposed to be," Six finished. "Was that your point?"

Kyntak was silent.

"Interesting," Six murmured, his voice echoing slightly through the empty office. Kyntak smiled, apparently relieved that Six had not immediately dismissed his idea.

Six shoved his hands into his pockets and balled them into fists. His forehead creased in thought.

"Two hasn't come back," Kyntak observed, finally breaking the silence.

"Yes, you're right," Six said awkwardly. He wondered where the other agent was. "Don't worry, I'll find him. You wait here, okay?"

Kyntak nodded, and Six wandered away down the quiet corridor. "See you soon," Kyntak called out to him, his voice bouncing off the walls. Six didn't reply.

"I'm better off on my own," he murmured to himself.

The polished linoleum clicked in time to his footsteps.

Why? a voice inside him asked. *Why fight it? Why not just behave like normal people do?*

Because I'm not a normal person, he answered. *I'm not even a real human being. I never have been, and I never will be. Grief is for humans. Love is for humans. Friendship, failure, sympathy, and regret are all things that humans experience, but things that I will never suffer.*

He felt better already. He felt enriched, relieved, and clearheaded. *I am Agent Six,* he thought. *I am the finest agent the Deck has ever or will ever have. I am the cleverest, most physically powerful man in the world, and no one can stop me from doing whatever I want to do.*

He considered for a moment. Maybe he wouldn't even bother looking for Two. Leave him wandering, leave Kyntak wondering, and find King in his office in the morning. It wasn't Six's problem that King had vanished, and Two had followed . . .

Along with everyone else in the Deck.

Six's blood ran cold. King hadn't just gone to the bathroom. Two hadn't just been unable to find him. No one had gone home. Six whirled around, and saw an empty corridor.

There is no way that everyone just left work early tonight. There are no coincidences.

The Deck wouldn't have been an easy target, even for professionals. But an attack like this wasn't impossible. Much of the Deck's security depended on the secret location of its headquarters. If that were discovered and exposed, then enemy forces could take over. They could send in a dozen agents in disguise with some chloroform in their pockets, wait until people were alone, and then knock them out. It wouldn't be too hard to get everyone, even in a building this size . . . but who? Why? Who even knew they were here? And who would dare to attempt an operation that big?

Six quivered with fear. The Lab agents must have followed the surveillance team back to base, and now everyone in the Deck had been kidnapped, or worse. . . .

And the Lab security forces are inside the building.

Six wasted no more time. Within a moment he was gone, and a closet door was swinging shut.

He lay waiting in the darkness, like a coiled spring. Who knew how many of them could be out there. They could be trained killers, they could have guns. . . .

Click, click, click.

Footsteps in the corridor.

Six tensed up all the muscles in his body. His heart pounded like a drum.

Could they be with ChaoSonic security? Who had followed the surveillance team, Six wondered, Lab agents or ChaoSonic soldiers? Surely Ludden's forces would be more likely to try to take Deck agents away for questioning, not silence them one by one.

So, probably not his side, then. And if these were Lab professionals, Six thought grimly, then they would do anything to cover up what they'd done.

The footsteps came closer. *High heels,* Six thought, listening.

Could it be Queen?

But Six had never seen Queen wear high heels. He ran

through the list of other female agents in his mind. *It could be Ace,* he thought, *or Eight.*

Six put his hand on the door handle, about to warn the woman outside . . .

. . . when he froze.

There was *another* sound, more distant than the first one — the sound of padded sneakers on the floor, treading softly, stealthily. Six bit his lip.

Someone was sneaking up behind that woman.

He wanted to rescue her, but he couldn't. He didn't know who was out there. He couldn't see. He didn't know what they were armed with. He didn't know who the woman was. There were many reasons to stay where he was.

Could he just let the woman outside die, when he had the power to stop it?

Did he have the power to stop it?

These were the people he had been running from all his life. These were the only people who understood his abilities, except for himself, King, and Kyntak. These were the people who wanted to hunt him down.

And they were drawing closer all the time.

The City's big, Kyntak's voice echoed in his head. *But you can't hide from anyone forever — friend or foe.*

Six heard the chloroformed sponge cover the woman's mouth. He heard the muffled scream of horror and the brief struggle. He heard the grunt of satisfaction from the man in sneakers as the movement stopped.

And he heard, too late, the tin bucket behind him fall over as he brushed against it.

Six held his breath as the clattering ceased. Had the soldier heard it? There was silence outside the door. No one was coming towards him, but no one was walking away, either. Six searched the inside of the closet. It was very small. There was nowhere to hide if the man came to look. There were shelves stretching up to the ceiling. More buckets on the floor. A light fixture high above.

And then the first footstep fell. Very light, very careful, very slow, but Six heard it. The man was heading for the closet.

Six desperately tried to think of a way out. The light fixture. What about the light fixture? The ceiling, a very high ceiling, with a light on it. As he heard the hand close on the door handle, he tensed up his whole body, waiting. A high ceiling.

As he heard the handle turn, he jumped. His body sprang up through the blackness of the closet, his hands found the top shelf and pushed it away, his back collided with the wall above the door, he whirled around, and landed lightly on the top of the door as it started to open.

Crouching on the edge, he held on with his hands to keep his balance as the door was pushed all the way open and a gun barrel appeared below him. The man came through the doorway; he was dressed in black and wearing a ski mask. He had a Raptor GD933 in his hand.

He stepped inside and swung the door back.

Six rolled his hands into fists, one finger at a time. *When the man looks up,* he plotted, *I can drop down onto his head, feet first. When I land, I'll grab the door handle and slam it shut. If he gets in the way, I'll close the door on him once, then push him inside and shut it properly. If he's too bewildered from the kick in the face to get to the door, no problem, I'll lock him in, and make a break for it. He'll never find his way out of there, anyway. The tricky bit will be getting out of the building — the place could be crawling with armed agents, and they've already taken out the other Deck agents, so they must be competent — I'd never be able to get out the front door. My best bet is to steal one of the Twin-900 stealth choppers or jump out of a window.*

Then the man with the ski mask silently backed out of the closet, closing the door behind him. Six slipped off the top of the door as his feet touched the wall, and then he landed softly on the floor. He pressed his ear up against the door, and heard footsteps fading away into the distance. When they had gone, Six continued listening, but only silence reached his ears.

Six sat down in a daze. The agents were gone, the Deck was empty, and there was no one to help him. There was no place to hide from the Lab now.

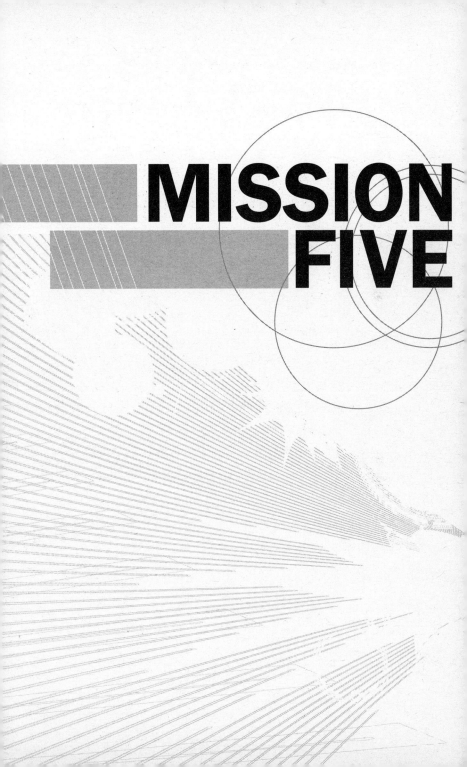

MISSION FIVE

TO BOLDLY GO

Earle Shuji looked up, surprised, as Agent Six entered the cell.

She raised an eyebrow. "Who are you?"

"My name is Agent Six of Hearts," Six said. "Also known as Scott Macintyre." It wouldn't do her any harm to know what he was capable of, he thought.

Shuji blinked. "Well," she said, "you looked older then."

"Our makeup artist is very good," Six said. "I'm actually only sixteen."

"You still look older than that," Shuji said, frowning.

"I was a product of the superhuman assassin project that the Lab started twenty years ago," Six confessed. *There, I said it,* he thought. "I matured physically pretty quickly."

Shuji's eyes widened. Then her expression changed. She was now looking at him as an object, a tool, rather than as a person. This was how Six had always known people would treat him if his secret was ever found out.

Six held her gaze and she grimaced. "That explains a lot," she said finally.

Six nodded grimly. "If it makes you feel any better, your bot was the toughest opponent I'd had in years." He sat down opposite her. "But I didn't come in here for idle chitchat. I came to make a deal."

King's words floated through his head again. *They'll be dealing with some very rich, and therefore very dangerous people.*

"What deal?" Shuji asked suspiciously.

"If you know where the Project Falcon lab is," Six said, "I'll let you go free."

"You won't let me go free," Shuji said. "I've killed too many people for that."

"I don't believe in justice," Six said. "Justice is a widely accepted construct of humanity's desire for revenge. I believe that punishment has two practical uses. One, as a preventative measure. If a man is imprisoned for engaging in immoral activities that inflict suffering on others, he will usually be unable to continue these activities while he is imprisoned. Two, as a deterrent. People try not to participate in activities that will draw the attention of the Deck for fear of the penalties if they are caught. Fewer crimes are committed if more Code-breakers are punished — and penalties deter repeat offenders as well.

"If 'justice' were done upon you, Dr. Shuji," he continued, "you would be tortured, starved, beaten, imprisoned, and forced into a fight to the death with an invincible machine. This would be repeated around a hundred times."

Shuji said nothing.

"But," Six continued, "that would not bring your victims back from the dead. That would not do anyone any good, in fact, except for bloodthirsty 'justice' addicts, who are only slightly higher on the moral spectrum than you."

"What's your point?" Shuji asked coldly.

"My point is that the Deck has decided to put you in this reasonably comfortable cell, with plenty of food, water, and safety. You are imprisoned so you cannot repeat your immoral actions, and your money has been taken so that we can save more lives in the City. Beyond that, we are not interested in you." He leaned forward. "This is not justice, this is reason.

"If I were to release you into the City, with enough money to set you up until you can find employment, then that would not do anyone any harm. Your victims cannot die again. And I know you will not break the Code anymore, because that would draw our attention, and while today you have something that I want, next time you might not be so lucky. Am I making myself clear?"

Shuji nodded.

"So, is it worth one criminal going free if lives could be saved because of it? I have decided yes — but the deal is not negotiable. You of all people should know that there are other ways of getting information from someone . . ." He paused, trying to read her expression. ". . . and that I will do things much worse than freeing a murderer in the interest of the greater good."

Shuji gave him the coordinates without any further hesitation. Six got up to leave, but paused in the doorway.

"The bots you designed — were they programmed with the ability to fly a helicopter?"

Six slipped on his weapon belt and began loading up. He stuffed his backpack full of ammunition, including spark bullets — rounds that would explode brightly on impact. These were perfect for stunning enemies, or distracting them.

Six also slid a few sleeping-gas canisters into the bag, as well as a water bottle, a blowpipe with tranquilizer darts, and a Soni-Cell laptop computer. He had loaded his two silver pistols with 12-millimeter bullets, and clipped them to his sides. He had attached a holster to his lower back, and slid an Eagle automatic rifle into it. And finally, he had strapped magnetic clasps to his right calf and used them to hold a twenty-seven-centimeter combat blade, ready to be drawn at short notice.

You never know, he reflected.

As well as photographs, Kyntak had provided diagrams of the interior of Project Falcon's lab, and Six studied them now. *Clever,* he thought, tracing the lines with his finger. Hidden, yet unsuspicious if found. And the shape . . .

The building was three floors high, but only the top one was above ground. There was another similar one below that, labeled as the basement. But below that, there was a secret floor — one that officially did not exist.

The whole building was like a maze, full of loops, one-way doors, dead ends, and corridors that led into one another in circles. There were three elevators in the building. Two only went to the top and middle floors, and they were easy to find, at the northeast and southwest corners of the building. The third only went to the middle and bottom floors, and it was tucked away in an obscure corner of the maze. The maze only covered the top two floors — the bottom floor was straightforward and functional. It also contained the doorway to a tunnel that led to a nearby tower, which Six was certain belonged to the Lab as well. The bottom floor and the tower, Six guessed, were where the testing and experimentation were done. That way, only employees with good knowledge of the building could get to the secret areas. They would have to find one of the top two elevators and take it to the middle floor, then find their way through the maze to the third elevator, where, presumably, there would be some sort of security.

So, how was Six supposed to get in?

Easily. This was not the first time he'd done something like this. Six rolled up the blueprint, having committed it to memory. He put the roll in his backpack. The tougher question was, how was he supposed to find the other Deck personnel?

Slightly less simple, but still straightforward. Follow the soldiers. Wherever there were armed guards, there was bound to be something worth hiding.

They'd be in a room that was large enough to hold them all, but with only one exit, so they could be guarded easily. It would almost certainly be on the middle floor, too. If they were in the bottom level, there would be a risk of them seeing too much, or doing something dangerous near the equipment. And if they were on the top floor, they could theoretically escape or be found more easily.

All this was assuming they were still alive, Six reminded himself. But if the Lab was planning to kill them, why the soldiers and chloroform? Why not just blow up the Deck?

Six paused as he climbed into the helicopter. He could run, if he wanted. No one knew where he was. He could leave now and get as far away from the Lab's reach as possible.

Six had faced a lot of tough life-or-death decisions in his life. In some cases, he'd felt he'd made the wrong one. But this was the easiest choice he'd ever had to make.

No, he decided. *I'm going into the lion's den. I'm going to find the other agents.* He stepped into the chopper.

The Twin-900 silently ascended towards the sky, vanishing into the night. The Deck was completely empty.

SHADOW MAN

The guard rubbed his goggles, trying to erase the fog. His vision cleared for a moment; he looked around and saw nothing suspicious — just concrete pillars, an inky black sky, and the parking lot below. The rooftop was completely still. He sighed, tapping his loaded Eagle idly with one finger.

As far as he could tell, no one had ever tried to break in. He was always on his toes, but there didn't seem to be any point . . . nobody ever saw anything suspicious.

He wobbled slightly as a gust of wind hit him. Regaining his balance, he straightened up and glanced around. *Crazy weather around here,* he thought.

A tiny scuffling noise.

The guard whirled around, leveling his rifle in the same motion. His body became perfectly still, except for his eyes darting around behind the goggles. *Something or nothing?* he wondered. He held still, waiting.

Another noise. Tiny, almost inaudible, but the guard

heard it. He grinned wryly. *Now here's the fun part of my job. Rat hunting.*

Was an unauthorized rat trying to sneak onto the company's premises? If so, he would terminate it with extreme prejudice.

He stepped forward silently. The padded soles of his boots gripped the concrete. He eased around the corner of a cement slab, searching. *Where'd the critter go?* he wondered.

He looked around him and saw only more concrete slabs, a few skylights, and the low wall that surrounded the roof.

A thud from his left.

He spun around to face it. That sounded bigger than a rat. But there was still nothing in sight. He walked forward, and glanced down at the thick steel trapdoor below his feet.

Could it be . . . no. No way.

He turned around and walked back to his post. It took three men to open that huge trapdoor. No one could possibly have opened it by themselves.

He almost laughed out loud. *I need more sleep,* he thought. *What exactly am I worried about?* Unless some unbelievably strong, super-fast intruder dropped out of the sky, landed safely with no more than a scuffle, then sneaked silently into the building through a hole no one could open on his own, his job was still secure.

The guard grinned to himself, relaxing gradually. *It's been a long night,* he thought.

But then he glimpsed something on the ground in the concrete parking lot. Walking to the low parapet, he squinted into the darkness, peering over the side.

Was that helicopter there before?

Six lowered his ear from the cold underside of the steel trapdoor, satisfied. He seemed to have remained undetected — for the moment. But as always, a moment had been all he needed.

He crept swiftly down the ladder and landed on the polished tiles. He was on the top floor, ready for the maze.

I'm inside, he thought. *I'm inside the Lab. And I've got no way out.* He shivered slightly as he scanned his surroundings for danger.

The lighting was good — fluorescent tubes glowed on the ceiling, reflecting off the floor. This was bad for Six. He could see in the dark while others were blind. In this cold neon, he would be visible and therefore vulnerable.

When subtlety is no longer an issue, he thought, *perhaps I can short out the power somehow.*

The ceiling and walls were made of thin softwood paneling, held in place by a metal grid. Six presumed that the walls were hollow, and that there'd be a shallow gap between the floors.

According to the blueprints, he knew he should take the next three lefts.

Six was suspicious of the blueprints. Kyntak had supplied them, after all. But so far they had been accurate, and he had no choice but to trust them.

He walked down the corridor to its end, turned left, and was faced with another identical corridor. So far, so good. He continued walking, seeing his next left turnoff up ahead. Fluorescent tubes buzzed above his head. He rounded the next corridor, then jumped back immediately and flattened his back against the wall. Surveillance digi-cam. Tuning his ears slightly, he could hear it humming — he had been careless and had missed the sound as he'd approached. He cursed inwardly. He doubted that anyone had seen him — he had only been in the camera's line of sight for a moment before he'd spotted it and turned back. But still, he had been clumsy.

It was weird that this was the first camera he'd come across. It wasn't like the Lab (or any part of ChaoSonic, for that matter) to be under-cautious.

Something isn't right here, he thought, *but I have no choice except to go on. So how do I get around the camera? There's no other way, no separate corridors that lead to where I want to go. The camera is at the other end of the corridor, so it covers the whole length; I can't just duck past it.*

Six crouched down to the floor, still thinking. It probably filmed at about twelve frames per second. Could he run down the whole corridor in less than one-twelfth of a second? He calculated quickly. Possibly, but he'd have to get a run-up of at least fifty meters. That was impossible — he had to get around the corner, so he couldn't have any run-up at all.

If he tried to round a ninety-degree corner at that speed, he'd end up on the ceiling. . . .

Six glanced up, and his eyes widened. The ceiling! Of course! He took another swift glance at the camera around the corner. It was angled downward, so it covered the whole floor of the corridor and most of the walls, but it couldn't see upward! He smiled slightly.

He put his hands on the wall and lifted himself up, using the metal grid for handholds. It seemed to be able to support his weight. Delicately he climbed up to the ceiling.

The metal was soft and began to bend towards him, but each beam could hold him for about a second. He dropped to the floor. He could climb it, but he'd have to be quick so it wouldn't collapse.

Scrambling back up, Six started to crawl across the ceiling. His arms and legs moved simultaneously, constantly finding new handholds and footholds. The metal grid sagged under his weight, but held. Every hand or foot movement took him a bit closer to the end of the corridor.

He crawled upside down like a spider, hanging on to the metal with strong hands and soft shoes. He could see the camera humming away, but it remained oblivious to his presence. He clambered forward eagerly, gripping the grid and pressing his body to the ceiling.

Then he froze. Footsteps.

He could feel the metal in his hands twisting, buckling under his weight.

The ceiling moaned. The camera hummed. Six sweated.

He couldn't tell from the sound how far away the guard was. He could be two corridors away, leaving Six safe to round the corner without being seen. Or the guard could be in the next corridor, getting closer and closer to where Six hid.

Every second I wait makes him nearer, Six realized. *It's much too late to turn back.*

Suddenly, the ceiling framework collapsed. The metal snapped, and his hands slipped off. He started to fall. He reached out and grabbed the support struts for the video camera, and swung backward on them, rounding the corner and thumping into the wall. He dropped to the floor and scrambled to his feet immediately.

He could still hear the footsteps, but no one was in sight. Brushing himself down, he started walking down yet another identical corridor. Within a second, the guard had rounded the corner in front of him, holding an Eagle.

Six's heart raced. The soldier looked up and saw him.

Take it easy, Six cautioned himself. *Just bluff it out.*

Six kept walking. Out of the corner of his eye, he watched the guard come closer. Then, when they were about to pass, he looked up and nodded to the guard, who nodded back and passed in silence.

How good is the security in this place? he wondered. *What systems will they use to check who's authorized to enter? Keycard passes, finger ID, retina scans, what? Obviously not simple facial recognition, or the guard would have stopped me by now. And, more important, what weapons will they have? I know that the last few guards I've seen have been armed with . . .*

A gun butt hit him in the back.

He sprawled across the linoleum, but as soon as his hands touched the ground, he pushed up desperately and flipped himself backward onto the guard.

Taken by surprise as Six's boots hit him in the chest, the guard staggered back but did not fall. He swung his Eagle to point at Six, and reached for the trigger. Before he could pull, Six grabbed the gun barrel and twisted it away from him. Then he yanked it. The guard held on determinedly, apparently sensing that his weapon was his only useful defense against Six. Six pulled harder, but the guard was dragged along with the gun, refusing to let go.

"Okay," Six said matter-of-factly, and he swung the gun to his right, whipping the guard off his feet and sending him flying into the wall. The wooden paneling shattered and the guard plunged through, splintering the metal framework with his velocity. He hit the wall on the other side of the hole and clung on with one hand, the other still gripping his Eagle.

They had opened up a whole new fighting arena — the dark hollow between the walls of the maze.

Six dived in as the guard aimed his Eagle. The gun sliced past Six's chest as he, too, hit the wall on the other side. He looked down and saw nothing but blackness.

According to the blueprints, the walls were about eighty-five centimeters thick. In reality, they seemed to be hollow. If the gaps stretched down right through all three floors, Six thought, then there was probably about an eleven-meter drop below him.

His thoughts were again interrupted by the guard, who had gallantly taken a swing at Six's hand where it gripped the framework. Six dodged, then smoothly slid out of the ring of light from the hole in the wall, into the darkness behind him.

He dangled there in the blackness, watching the solider look around blindly. He focused his eyes on the spot where Six had vanished, and lashed out into the shadows with his foot.

Six grabbed the soldier's leg and wrapped his arm around it. The guard cried out in surprise as he suddenly found himself dangling from his left leg. Then he yelped as Six swung him up and threw him into the wall again. The guard crashed through it and slid along the floor of a new corridor, leaving a hole for Six to slip through. Six landed safely on the tiles, squinting against the neon glare of the new location. As the guard reached for his gun, Six kicked it out of his hands.

Click.

Six sprang up and clung to the ceiling.

He had heard the sound of a safety catch being switched off behind him.

He scrambled forward across the ceiling as the corridor was suddenly filled with the sound of a rapidly chattering assault rifle. A hailstorm of bullets filled the air.

Standard issue for these guards is an Eagle automatic, he thought immediately, *which has eighty rounds.*

As Six's train of thought sped up, time seemed to slow down and he could count each shot of the machine-gun fire as it left the gun.

When the soldier readjusted his aim, Six heard the first shot hit the panels behind him.

Six swung to his left and collided with the wall.

Forty shots fired, he thought.

He rebounded off the wall, hit the ground, and slid across the floor to the other side of the corridor. Fifty. He heard scraping sounds as shots tore across the floor underneath him. From behind him there was a sickening thud; a bullet had hit the first guard, who was still lying on the ground.

Sixty shots now, Six thought. *He's three-quarters of the way through his ammo.* Six scrambled up the wall on the other side of the corridor as the panels under his feet were torn to shreds by bullets. *Seventy . . .*

He jumped off the wall and bounced along the floor as bullets whirred through the corridor around him. Then he landed directly in front of the gun barrel just as it clicked empty.

Eighty, he thought.

The guard had only a moment to look astonished before Six knocked him unconscious with a flying fist. Holding open the stunned guard's eyelids, Six took a quick look at the rolled-back eyes. He'd be out for at least an hour and a half. More time than Six needed.

Six returned to the other guard. He was lying on the ground, moaning and writhing, with blood pouring out of his leg. Six knelt over him and examined the wound. He tore the guard's sleeve into strips and knotted them together, wrapping them tightly around the injury. The blood flow stopped quickly.

"You'll be fine," Six assured him, and touched his neck lightly. The guard lapsed into deep sleep.

Agent Six pondered his position as he stripped the uniform from the other soldier, including a ChaoSonic buzz-belt that would tell him when the guards were put on alert. This little detour had positioned him in a place he had never intended to go — this corridor was of no use to him. He could always, of course, clamber back through the two holes he had made and resume his journey. He would then be no worse off, but for a few minutes lost.

On the other hand, he thought, this could be turned to his advantage. It'd be good to avoid the other guards. Six leaned into the hole in the wall and looked down. Below this, the second floor; below that, the laboratory. He didn't need to go through the top floor of the maze at all.

Six slipped down into the darkness.

On the way down, he examined his location. If he remembered correctly, the blueprints of the building placed him just a few turns away from his best guess at where the Deck agents were being held. So if he dropped down five meters . . .

He did the math. Five meters free fall, less than a second.

Six let go and plummeted through the darkness.

So if I stop about now, he thought as he grabbed the grid in front of him and broke through the wall into the light, *I should be on the second floor.*

He glanced around. The corridor looked the same as

the ones on the top floor, but he knew he was in the right place.

He broke into a jog. The blueprints said that his first guess for the cell was just a few corridors away. His shoes padded silently across the floor. A maze was actually a pretty good security system in itself, he thought. It was unsuspicious, it was reasonably cheap compared to many alternatives, and it was reliable.

He jumped back from the corner he had just been turning. There were still a few soldiers to get around. He hoped they hadn't seen him.

These two guards looked bored out of their minds. Neither of them seemed to be very alert. They glanced around, but with curiosity rather than real intent.

What was that sound? Six listened carefully.

He paled. It was not a sound he was intimately familiar with, but he could now tell what it was.

It was the sound of people screaming.

Six began to run. *I have to hurry,* he thought. *My friends are being tortured.*

But at least they were still alive. If the Lab staff was torturing them, then they had something that the officials wanted. He still had time to save them.

He pulled the blowpipe swiftly out of his thin backpack, loaded it with a tranquilizer dart, and blew.

Even as the guard was slumping to the floor, Six was reloading the tube. The other guard looked at his fallen comrade in alarm, then reached for his weapon.

Too late. He fell to his knees and collapsed facedown. Six ran forward silently and stepped over the two sleeping soldiers. He opened the door they had been guarding and braced himself for the worst.

But what lay behind the door was not what he had been expecting. He looked in horror.

THE CHILD WITHIN

The old people.

The twelve old people from the photographs were in prison cells. Their clothes were stained and their skin was warped. They screamed and screamed and screamed. Six smelled before he saw that there were no toilets in any of these cells. The concrete floors and the prison outfits were stained with muck.

The old people were dragging themselves on their cracked, skeletal hands, moving in pointless circles around their barred prisons. Some of them had managed to get onto their hands and knees, but that was it. It was as if their legs weren't working. Their wrinkled, saggy skin was filthy with grime from the cell floors, and their faces were stained with the smeary congealed remains of food.

The man nearest Six grabbed the prison bars.

"*Nyaaaagarameee!*" he screamed hoarsely.

Six stepped back, and moved along the cells. What were they doing here? What use could the Lab possibly have for a bunch of old people? And what had the Lab done to them to drive them out of their minds like this?

Soon he came to an old woman who was not screaming. She looked up at him curiously.

He crouched down beside the bars.

"What's happened to you?" he asked her.

She laughed, a gurgling, hiccup-like giggle.

And then something clicked in Six's mind.

Have you ever heard of Chelsea Tridya?

She was interested in the science of life and aging. She claimed she'd made a breakthrough quite recently, wherein she'd been able to control the rate of cell division and replication in mice, effectively slowing down their rate of aging.

She vanished, along with all her data and equipment, about six months ago.

They don't look like satisfied customers to me.

All the clues he'd collected snapped together suddenly, in a new and alarming way — like a picture that makes no sense until it is turned upside down.

Physically they were completely healthy, except for being at least twice as old as anyone I'd ever seen before. But mentally . . . they were freaky.

None of them spoke English. They made noises, but it was just yelling, gibberish. It was like their brains had been melted.

There was even a bunch of babies that they'd kidnapped. They left by the main gate, kicking and screaming. One of them even managed to worm out of her guard's grip, but when she tried to walk, her legs couldn't support her, and she fell down.

Six's brain started to compute at top speed.

Chelsea Tridya.

Control the rate of cell division and replication.

Data and equipment stolen.

Babies dragged into the Lab.

Old people dragged out.

Six's skin erupted in goose bumps. The old woman kept laughing — a giggly, gurgling laugh.

And just as Six realized that he was looking into the wrinkly, sagging face of a child, a woman's voice spoke behind him.

"It wasn't supposed to be like this," she said.

Chelsea Tridya was a very small woman, an impression accentuated by her stooping posture and the tiny, youthful hands clutching the bars of her cage. Six thought she was about thirty-five. Her face seemed too large for her head, or what could be seen of it from behind thick strands of dirty, blond hair. Her large, sorrowful eyes stared up at Six.

"I wanted to help people," she said, as if pleading for forgiveness. "Not to hurt them. Not to kill them."

"What are they being used for?" Six asked, gesturing at the ancient children in their cages.

"Nothing, now," Tridya said. "Just subjects in a successful test. I assume the Lab will kill them once they work out a way to profit from their deaths. I will suffer the same fate."

Her voice had no bitterness or fear. She spoke with resignation, staring all the time at Six. He assumed that all hope had been burned out of her in the six months she had been missing.

"What do they plan to do with your aging therapy, now that they have it?"

She lowered her head finally. "You *know* what they're going to do. I can hear it in your voice."

Six's chest tightened. "Make an army?"

"Yes. An army of genetically engineered supersoldiers." She looked at Six again, with neither judgment nor emotion. "Clones of you."

Six said nothing.

"That *is* who you are, isn't it?" She wasn't asking. "You're one of the Project Falcon kids."

"Why?" Six said. "What's the army for? Who is left to fight?"

But there was no time for her to reply. The door swung open, and Kligos Stadil stepped into the cellblock.

Stadil glared suspiciously along the cells. He was sure he had seen a flicker of movement as he entered. Someone was in here.

Almost certainly the agent, he thought. He hefted his weapon: a heavy Owl 5525 sidearm, fully loaded with 9-millimeter rounds. Time to put a stop to this game.

But before he moved in any farther, he wanted to know where the agent was. He had seen the footage and the data of this creature, and the thing was *fast.*

Stadil hated this prison block. These aged children were ugly, stinking, and downright unnerving, particularly when they were screaming — he could hardly hear himself think. Right now they were just grumbling and shuffling, which could work to his advantage. The agent wouldn't hear him coming.

He had nearly reached the last cell. With the smooth manner of a professional killer, he eased himself into stillness, coiling his muscles, preparing to make a low dive around the corner.

He put both hands on his gun.

He jumped and flew into the open.

The cell came into view.

Empty!

Midair, Stadil's eyes widened in dismay. *There was the old, dribbling prisoner, but where was the agent?*

Six landed on Stadil's wrist with one foot, and pressed the other firmly against Stadil's throat. Stadil cried out and the Owl fell from his hands.

Six had been on the ceiling, following Stadil the whole time. That was the trouble with professionals, he thought. They were predictable to others of the same profession — unless you happened to be the best.

Six lifted Stadil up, held his arms still with his own hands, and forced his knee onto Stadil's thighs so neither of his legs could move.

Letting go of one of Stadil's arms, Six picked up the Owl and held it against Stadil's temple. Stadil stopped struggling immediately.

"This," Six said, picking up and unrolling the blue prints, "is a map of this floor. I want to know where the Deck agents are being held. As you are head of security, please do not waste my time by pleading ignorance."

Stadil raised an eyebrow coolly. This wasn't the first time someone had held a gun to his head.

"I have visited several of these rooms, and established that my colleagues are not in them," Six said. "If you point to a room I have visited before, I will kill you. If you refuse to tell me, I will kill you. If you take too long, I will know you are plotting against my interests, and I will kill you. If you cooperate, you will be left here. Alive." His gaze hardened. "If my proposal takes much consideration, then I have clearly underestimated your intellect."

Stadil pointed out a room on the map wordlessly. Six was right — there was nothing else he could do.

Six pulled the earpiece from Stadil's ear and quickly bent the bars of the cell. Then he shoved Stadil through the bars, and bent them back to parallel immediately. He turned to Chelsea's cage, leaving Stadil trapped in the cell.

Stadil sat down on the bed as Six and Chelsea left the cell-block. His cellmate grinned mindlessly at him and laughed a stupid, gurgling laugh.

ALL HEART

"So when the Lab stole your research on cell division rate control," Six said as they ran, "they used it not to slow down aging, but to speed it up."

"That's right," Chelsea confirmed. "Methryn Crexe is making an army for Ungrelor Ludden. In the past, the assassin project would have only been useful to create lone killers — it was never cost-effective to have enough equipment or resources to create many infants at once. And because each one would've needed a gestation period of nine months before it was able to leave the tube, it would take many, many years to have even a small strike team of clones."

"But with growth acceleration," Six said, "so powerful that a group of toddlers could be kidnapped and be physically aged to more than a hundred years old days later, Crexe could create an army in only months. Right?"

"Less," she said grimly. "Weeks. They would need to be trained, of course — but I bet Ludden could take care of that."

"Who's he attacking? Who's threatened ChaoSonic?"

"This is just a suspicion," Chelsea panted, "but I think there are continents free of ChaoSonic, outside the Seawall."

Six gasped. It made sense! In fact, perhaps the Seawall itself was built not to stop people leaving, but to stop others getting in. Now Ludden was going to eliminate the threat once and for all.

Maybe the other continents weren't even attacking.

Perhaps they are trying to rescue us.

Right now, though, all this was just speculation. There was something more pertinent bothering Six.

"Stadil had a radio earpiece on him," he said. "Why didn't he call the rest of Lab security for help?"

"I don't know. Perhaps his radio wasn't working, or maybe . . ." Chelsea hesitated. "Maybe Stadil coming alone was part of some greater plan. You noticed the strange architecture — the thin walls and the lack of cameras?"

"Yes," Six said.

"There's something else going on here, something neither of us understands yet."

This is what frightened Six most — the thought that he was participating in some kind of intricately choreographed plot, the aim of which was invisible to him.

He took Chelsea's arm. They'd arrived.

Six took a quick glance around the corner to confirm what he'd expected — yes, the place was being guarded.

To get to the cell, they had to go through an anteroom first — this was the room at the end of the next corridor. The door appeared to be locked, and next to the door was a large window. Behind the glass he could see several guards wandering around the anteroom. There was a crimson alarm button on the wall inside.

If they raise that alarm, Six thought, quivering, *we're as good as dead. Hundreds of soldiers will come running, they'll take Chelsea back to her cell, and I'll be locked up, injected, examined, and pinned like a butterfly in a display case before the night is out. No one will ever know what became of me. And the others from the Deck — they'll never see daylight again.*

Six gritted his teeth. *If I fail at this point . . .*

He looked at the window again. It had a slightly dull sheen to it; Six could tell it was a pane of bulletproof glass. The door was heavy steel — he wouldn't be able to break it down before someone saw him and raised the alarm.

There was a grate in the ceiling above the door — an entrance to the ventilation shafts. If he could get into the shafts, he knew he could climb into the anteroom. But how could he get into the shafts without the soldiers inside seeing him and getting to the alarm?

Six took the spark bullets from his bag.

There was nothing better to exploit in the human mind, he contemplated, than panic.

"Who is *that*?"

Through the glass, the guards could see a figure advancing. Before they'd had time to realize that he was not one of their colleagues, the figure broke into a run towards the glass and leveled his rifle.

"Duck!" one of the guards shouted, and dived for cover as a hail of fire swept up the corridor towards the glass. As the bullets hit it, they disintegrated into showers of sparks and filled the room with harsh, glaring light. The soldier scrunched up his eyes against the brightness, cowering on the floor. Then it was over, and no evidence remained except for the ringing in his ears. The glass was intact. The door was still closed.

But the corridor was empty.

"Did you see that?" one of the others slurred.

"I sure did!" the soldier said, still seeing stars. "Raise the alarm."

One of the others tried to stand, but slipped over backward, landing on his behind.

Another guard staggered towards the red button.

He reached out a hand to press it . . . just as something dropped out of the ceiling and landed between him and the button.

The something grinned.

Then it shoved him back, a shove that sent him flying into the wall. He slid down it, dazed and groggy.

Agent Six nodded politely to the other two guards. "Pardon me," he said.

The still half-blinded guards moved to draw their weapons, but as they did, Six deftly produced a grey canister from his pocket. He picked up the air vent cover from below his feet and cracked the canister against it. He tossed the canister to one of the guards. The guard caught it bewilderedly as it started to spray forth thick blue gas. The other tried to aim his weapon at Six, but he was already groggy from the gas.

As their eyes began to close, Six crossed the room, and opened the door to let Chelsea in. They swept through into the holding room without looking back.

Six closed the door behind them.

He turned.

And he saw the faces of those he'd come to find. All the Hearts were there, plus Grysat. They all looked up as Six came in, and stared at him.

"Umm," he said, "I'm here to rescue you."

"What happened to the guards?" King asked.

Six jerked his thumb back towards the door. "Asleep at their post."

King walked up to Six and grinned, placing a hand on Six's shoulder.

"What took you so long?" he asked.

ON THE RUN

"You were taking a big risk, you know, coming in here without a professional makeup artist disguising you first," Jack chided.

"I figured that no one would mind just this once," Six said.

"I'd fix you up now, but I don't have the kit with me," Jack apologized. "I have my pocket brush, but . . ."

". . . but that wouldn't be enough on its own, I understand." Six laughed. "Thanks for the offer, just the same."

Jack put his hairbrush back in his pocket.

Six looked around again. "Was Kyntak brought in with you guys?" he asked.

"Not with us." King shook his head. "I don't know if he was even captured."

Six frowned. He still didn't trust Kyntak. Was he a double agent, spying on the Deck for ChaoSonic? But if that was the case, why had he given King an accurate map of the building? Without it Six would never have found the others.

These questions can be answered later, Six thought. Right now, these people were depending on him.

"Okay," he said. "You need to hold your breath when we go through the next room. I gassed it on the way in."

Everyone in the room nodded, inhaled, and closed their mouths as Six opened the door.

"Incredible," King said, as they ran down the corridor. He and Six were in front, with Ace of Hearts watching the rear and all the other agents in between. "They're speeding up growth rather than slowing down aging. I never thought of that."

"We have to stop them," Six said. "If they build an army of soldiers —"

"Clones of you," King interjected.

"Then the other continents won't have a chance," Six continued. "They'll be massacred. Who knows how many assassins Ludden has contracted Crexe to grow from the genome."

"We can launch a full-scale attack on the Lab when we get back to the Deck," King said. "Once we get there we can collect equipment and formulate a strategy. We'll call in the most senior Clubs, the ones who've done the most training —"

"Where's the other Joker?" Six interrupted. "Grysat's here — why didn't the Lab kidnap the other guy?"

"They don't know who he is, probably," Grysat said from behind them. "Makes sense — I don't."

He ran up alongside Six.

"You don't know who he is?" Six asked incredulously.

"Nope. He makes donations to our cause, provides key intelligence for every mission, and sends information to me via private encrypted satellite — but I've never actually met him. He's always avoided all of my questions about who he is or where he gets his information about the inner workings of ChaoSonic. And you don't bite the hand that feeds you."

"How'd he tell you to release Kyntak from the Visitors Center two days ago?" Six asked, remembering.

"That was the most direct contact I've ever had with him. He phoned my terminal at the front desk and ordered me to release the prisoner who'd just come in. He wouldn't say why, and he wouldn't say how he knew Kyntak was in there, when he'd only been taken in a few minutes previously. He whispered the message, so all I could tell about him from his voice was that he was male."

Six had assumed this meant that Kyntak and the Joker were both involved with ChaoSonic. But Kyntak's information had been genuine, so what was the Joker's real agenda? How did he know they had detained Kyntak, and why did he set him free?

"So chances are," Six said, "that the Joker knows we're missing, and he's working on another mission plan as we speak."

"With any luck," Grysat panted, "yes."

Six kept outwardly alert, but inside he relaxed a little. Things were looking up — and help was on the way.

Six had suggested that instead of finding their way through the maze until they got to the elevator (which would probably have at least one camera in it), it would be quicker and safer to remove some of the panels on the ceiling and climb up to the next floor. The others had all agreed, so Six had jumped into the air and knocked out some panels. He had then jumped again, punched a hole in the linoleum of the floor above, and prized it open far enough for a person to climb through.

He raised his head through the hole. No cameras, he thought, and no guards. Too easy. He dropped back down to the floor.

"All clear?" Two asked.

"Don't move, don't talk," Six said sharply. He had heard footsteps.

"What —"

"*Shhh,*" King hissed, staring at Six.

The footsteps were distinct now, and getting louder.

Six made his decision. "We bluff it," he said, and began herding his colleagues down the corridor towards the corner where the footsteps were coming from. "Try to look apprehensive," he said to them.

"We *are* apprehensive," Jack said. But he turned his eyes to the floor. Two stared at his hands. King hung his head, while Queen sniffled convincingly.

They marched down the corridor, a somber crowd of

defeated prisoners, with Six walking confidently behind them. He kept the guard's gun trained on their backs, and prodded King every now and then to complete the effect.

The owner of the footsteps appeared from around the corner. It was another guard, tall and wide. He held his gun loosely in one hand, and clicked his fingers with the other in time with his footsteps.

Six looked up and acknowledged the guard's presence with a nod of his head. He walked faster and overtook his prisoners, then turned to face them. He waved his gun at them menacingly, and they all moved to one side of the corridor to let the guard pass. Six turned back to the approaching man and nodded again, hoping that the guard would just see Six's stolen uniform and not look too hard at his face.

The guard nodded back, and walked casually past them. Still keeping up the pretense, Six rounded the prisoners up again. He walked around to the back of the group, and began marching impassively forward, jabbing his gun at them to get them moving. They stopped as soon as they got around the corner, and listened as the guard's footsteps faded into the distance.

Six breathed a sigh of relief.

They walked back down the corridor towards the hole Six had made in the ceiling. "Okay, you all know the drill now," King said. "We see another guard, we do the same thing — bluff our way through." He looked at Six. "You'll warn us, right?"

Six didn't have time to answer. Everyone froze as they heard the sudden scuffle and the yell.

All the air was snatched from Six's lungs as something thudded into him, hard. His feet left the ground and suddenly the world was upside down — and there was a guard in it, who was somehow the right way up.

Six spun around in midair like a falling cat, and snatched at the rapidly approaching floor with both his hands. Pushing against it with his palms, he twisted his torso, propelled his left knee towards the ground, and landed. His right foot was immediately down, ready to throw his body forward at his opponent.

He suddenly realized what had happened. The guard had fallen through the hole in the ceiling, and had landed on top of him.

Six wasted no time — he lunged forward. The guard had been scrambling to his feet, but when he saw Six coming he dropped suddenly to the floor. Six flew over him, surprised at the soldier's reflexes.

He was even more impressed when the guard threw a fist at his solar plexus as he drifted over.

For someone stupid enough to fall through a hole in the floor in front of him, Six thought, this guy sure was quick on the draw.

Six caught the punching hand and clenched it tightly, then rolled across the linoleum. As his back hit the floor, his momentum lifted the guard up by his arm. Six's heels landed, and he found himself staring up at the ceiling as the guard sailed over him, arm first. Six tugged at the arm again. The guard jerked in midair and slammed into the ground, back first. He wheezed.

Giving him no time to recover, Six rapped on his neck with his knuckles, knocking him out.

Six stood up. He glanced around at his slack-jawed companions. *Well*, he thought, *my secret is out. They've seen too much.*

King was grinning. "It's been a long time since I saw you do that, Six."

Six nodded. "There's been a lot of call for it lately." He turned to face the others. "We need to move quickly. That's seven incapacitated bodies lying around now, so it can't be too long before they realize something's amiss."

King nodded in agreement. "Let's go."

A LONG WAY DOWN

The guard on the rooftop sighed. Still half an hour to go. *I could really use some coffee,* he thought, yawning.

His ChaoSonic buzz-belt zapped him. He jumped.

There was an orange light flashing on the buckle.

No, it couldn't be. . . .

The guard raised his rifle, double-checking it. Ammo in, safety off, sights straight, laser on. He was ready.

An actual alert, he thought. Maybe it was a drill . . . but they never had drills. On the other hand, they never had alerts, either.

Then he saw them, climbing down the fire escape — twelve, no, thirteen of them.

They moved stealthily and silently. The guard slipped into a crouch and aimed his rifle.

The time had come, it seemed, for him to finally earn his keep.

Another electric hum from his buzz-belt. He glanced

down, and the light was no longer flashing. It simply stayed illuminated.

The guard blinked unbelievingly. An illuminated light meant that all the security measures had been implemented — every soldier called in, all the land mines around the gates armed, and all staff and personnel, excluding the hundreds of troops, moved to bomb shelters under the second floor.

The guard shivered apprehensively and gripped his gun. They had talked about it, of course. They had talked about it and trained for it each and every day, but it had never been done before.

The intruders had reached the bottom of the ladder — they were now on the ground in the parking lot. The guard could see the other soldiers in the area and on the roofs. At least a hundred rifles were leveled at the escapees. The guard held his aim — he didn't know yet whether they were the source of the alert. Even if they were, the soldiers would probably be asked to take them alive, and they would be tranquilized for transport.

He gazed through the scope of his gun to get a closer look. The one in the lead was a wiry, dark-haired boy in Lab security fatigues, moving quickly and quietly across the dusty concrete. The guard squinted — the kid looked familiar. Could he have seen him before? Yes, just a couple of hours earlier, before the start of his shift, he'd seen him enter the facility through the front door; only he thought the boy had bleached-blond hair.

The boy looked back, staring straight at the guard's scope.

The guard frowned. *No way, it's too dark,* he said to himself. *The boy couldn't possibly see me at this range.*

The boy swiftly dropped into a crouch and drew a pistol. He took aim at the guard, who gasped and ducked below the cover of the parapet.

There was no noise from below. The guard swore and peered back over the parapet. At first he couldn't see the escapees at all. Then he caught a glimpse of them running on the other side of the parking lot.

The kid had only aimed at him to get him to take cover.

The guard glared down at the boy, who was moving at an incredible speed across the terrain. He aimed his gun again, but the order to fire still hadn't arrived. And they were moving fast, with urgency. He wouldn't have an easy shot.

Still, they were unlikely to escape. Even if the instructions came too late, and they managed to avoid being shot, stunned, or captured, the land mines stationed around the perimeter would finish them off.

But they seemed to think there was hope. Led by the dark-haired boy, they were sprinting across the dirty concrete towards . . . the helicopter!

The guard rested his gun on the parapet and tightened his grip, squinting down at the targets. He was prepared to shoot the moment the order to do so came through. A helicopter wouldn't trigger the land mines, so if it got away, the only option would be to give chase in some kind of air vehicle. That'd be expensive and conspicuous, so the company wouldn't want this helicopter to leave.

And maybe I'm the man to handle it, he thought.

The guard watched as the intruders piled into the Twin-900 and its blades began to spin. The boy had let everyone else get on first, while he stayed low, taking scope of the surroundings carefully. He appeared to have spotted the stations of each and every soldier on duty. He must have been wearing some kind of night-vision lenses, the guard presumed, because a naked human eye surely couldn't see the other soldiers. He marveled at this kid's confidence, standing outside the helicopter in plain view with a hundred rifles trained on him and not even looking nervous. How did he know they wouldn't just shoot him where he stood?

Then the guard saw the boy was wearing a guard-issue ChaoSonic buzz-belt.

He knows our orders are not to shoot, the guard thought. *That cocky little —*

Then his buzz-belt crackled. A voice hissed, *"Open fire! Repeat, open fire! Shoot to kill!"*

The guard jammed his finger to the trigger. The gun shuddered and sent forty lead cones into the dirt. But the boy was gone, and all the others were in the helicopter.

The soldier re-aimed his sights. But before he could fire —

Splatsplatsplatsplatsplatsplat! He fell over, partly from the impact, and partly from the shock, as six shots smacked into his chest armor.

He took cover behind the parapet and examined his armor. What the . . .

His chest was splattered with slippery, translucent goo.

"Where are those shots coming from?" his radio hissed. *"Is that a* robot?"

Six was sprinting, already halfway to the gate, with small explosions of dust marking his steps along the way. He was nearly at the gate when a stray bullet hit the ground on the other side and activated one of the land mines.

The blast smashed the gate down to the ground. The concrete underfoot splintered. Six felt the impact vibrate through his legs first, and he halted as the wave of energy shoved against his forehead. Then the real force of the blast hit, and his whole body was thrown backward into the superheated air.

No sooner had he hit the dirt than he was up again. He began sprinting away from the gate, towards the parked cars. He hoped that the soldiers couldn't see him through the dust, although he could still see them — blurry grey smudges against the pitch-black sky. *A car,* he thought. *I need a car!*

"Harry," he yelled, tapping his earpiece, "keep up the firing until everyone is clear, or you run out of paintballs. Whichever comes first."

"Yes, Agent Six of Hearts," came the reply.

"And go for their eyes," Six said, running towards a high-powered armored jeep. "Get some paint on the lenses of their night-vision goggles. Six out."

He dived forward and hung in midair for a moment, shots streaking through the air around him.

Then he slid over the hood of a jeep, pulled open the

driver's door, and landed in the cab. Six ducked behind the thick metal door as the gunfire slammed into it, hoping the windows were bulletproof. He jammed the buckle of his buzz-belt into the key slot and ripped it out of the cube, then pushed the plug wires aside, grabbed the coil wire, and jammed it into the battery. The lights on the dash clicked on. Holding the kill switch up with one hand, he used the other to cross the smaller wire with the battery cable.

The motor roared.

Under thirteen seconds, Six thought. *My best time ever.*

He slipped the buzz-belt back on and then slammed his foot down on the accelerator.

The dust had almost cleared, and Six could see the helicopter, which had already taken off. It had been knocked back by the blast from the land mine, but no apparent structural damage had been done. It had just crossed over the fence and was slowly gaining speed.

The soldiers resumed their shooting. Lead pinged off the steel casing of the jeep, but none penetrated. This was what the jeep had been designed to do.

The others are going to be all right, thought Six. *Now how do I get out of here?*

Six's eyes widened as he heard the hiss of a Drifter missile.

Looking up, he saw the massive rocket float over his head, powering its way towards the Twin. Though heavy and bulky, the missile moved forward inexorably, leaving a trail of steam and exhaust behind it. This, Six knew, was why it was known as the Drifter.

Six's backpack was still on his shoulders. Within a moment he had reached over his shoulder and brought out the two silver pistols. He pressed down on the accelerator, straightened the steering wheel, and then took his hands off it, concentrating on his aim.

Drifters had heavy armored hulls, so they could not be shredded by super machine-gun fire — this was the main defense of most aircraft against missile attack. But the armor came at the cost of a good navigation system. If a Drifter was bumped off course, it stayed off course until something touched its exhaust emission valve or its warhead.

Six fired with the left gun first, and a bullet sparked off the side of the missile. The Drifter veered very slightly to the right. But not enough to save the chopper, Six thought, as the jeep roared along beneath him.

He fired twice more.

The missile gently pitched farther away from the helicopter. It overtook it with half a meter's clearance, and plunged into the black night. Six took aim at where the steam trail had vanished, and fired another shot.

The bullet went straight into the exhaust valve, and the missile detonated.

Boom.

Six shielded his eyes with his arm as the blackness of the night was impaled by a ferocious rippling firestorm. He was pressed down into his seat by the blazing wall of energy that bore down on him from above. The jeep's motor whined as it struggled to keep moving against the pressure. The helicopter lurched to one side before righting itself a few seconds later. Six's ears were assaulted by the shrieking sound of burning fuel and of the exploding nitroglycerin twisting the tungsten hull of the missile.

The blast had burned up most of the air within a radius of fifteen meters, and Six was nearly sucked out the window as the wind rushed to fill the resulting vacuum. All the dust was drawn into a huge airborne ball.

Then it was suddenly over. The missile was gone, the dust ball had disintegrated, and the helicopter was still in the air.

Twin-900s are built tough, Six thought. But now he was left to face the immediate problem of trying to steer the jeep across the cement that had been splintered by the earlier explosion of the land mine.

It is, Six thought, *a difficult situation to be in.* Land mines no doubt ringed the entire perimeter, or there would have been no point in placing the one the bullets had set off. Only one mine had exploded, so the others were still there, hidden and presumably armed.

The only safe way out of the Lab's clutches was the route that had already been cleared. Which, unfortunately, Six thought, was a smoking chasm in the concrete.

Six floored the accelerator. The wheels spun faster and faster as dozens of bullets thudded into the jeep's sides. *Maybe I can jump the gap,* he thought.

The engine howled. The wheels slid. Six's knuckles were white on the steering wheel.

Then, as he heard the hiss of a second Drifter blasting overhead towards the Twin, he knew what he had to do.

Agent Six wrenched the wheel to the left and jammed his foot on the accelerator. The jeep swerved violently away from the chasm, heading in the direction of the helicopter.

The wheels spun across innocent, safe-looking concrete. Six took his hands off the wheel and reloaded the silver pistols. He braked, sending the car into a spin, then braced himself by pressing one foot against the passenger seat and one against the door as the tires touched the land mine.

The concrete below him hiccuped.

Blam! The explosion of the land mine hurled the armored jeep up into Six. It hit him feet first, and like a rocket taking off, the ground burst into flames and the jeep shot into the sky. It was like being inside a elevator traveling up at hundreds of kilometers an hour. The jeep's metal floor bent and twisted underneath him, warping with the force of the explosion, and suddenly he was below it, surrounded by dust and chunks of concrete.

And a very long way above the ground.

Six twisted the already loose and rattling roof, and ripped it free of the chassis, suddenly making the jeep a convertible. The roof spun out into the void. He clambered towards the backseat as the car spun heavenward through the air.

It flew higher, and higher, and higher.

When he looked up, he saw the dust cloud he had arisen

from. As the car flipped forward, he was looking at the sky. Then as the wreck of shredded steel whirled to one side, he found himself looking at the helicopter, which was moving slowly away.

The wind howled in his ears as the ground below disappeared. The wind blasted his hair back flat against his head, and he squinted against it. He leveled his silver pistols, waiting for the right moment as the jeep spun up through the night.

Then, as he saw the massive Drifter missile looming in front of him, he fired three times.

The first shot pinged off the underbelly of the Drifter. The nose cone rose a few degrees towards Six.

The second whizzed across the side of the missile, redirecting it away from the helicopter in a shower of sparks. The jeep was slowing down in the air — Six could feel in his stomach that it was reaching the upper limit of its trajectory. The missile roared slowly towards him. *There isn't much time,* he thought.

The third shot made a last-second adjustment to the course of the Drifter; nose slightly down, and left.

The jeep stopped, hanging in the air for a precious second, almost two hundred fifty meters above the surface of the earth.

Six dropped his pistols and launched himself into the void, jumping as far as he could towards the helicopter . . . as the Drifter collided with the jeep.

BOOM!

Six was surrounded by a storm of blazing chemicals and burning air.

The helicopter vanished.

The sky vanished.

Six couldn't see. He couldn't breathe. His skin and flesh were cooking on his bones.

And then the true blast reached him — and his body was smashed out farther into the air.

Six felt his chest being crushed like a tin can, every bone in his body being broken or pulled from its socket. The heat squeezed his flesh against his skeleton. He held his eyes shut for fear that the force or the heat might blind him. Behind his closed lids he was still dazzled by the blazing light.

It was like being in heaven. Everything was so bright that all Six could see was pure, clean white. And the noise was so loud that he could hear nothing. Silence. The explosion had deafened him, maybe even torn off his ears.

And still the firestorm blazed around him, inside him, through him, all over his body. He curled himself into a ball, using his disintegrating arms to draw up his legs, trying to protect his internal organs.

Six gritted his teeth as he felt flames lick across his back. His clothes were no protection at all against this much heat. The buckle of his buzz-belt and the blade of the combat knife attached to his shin were burning hot. His wristwatch melted — liquid plastic seared his arm. Six realized he couldn't feel his fingers anymore, and hoped they were still there.

He reached out with both hands, but they gripped only empty air. Scalding, empty air.

As some of the smoke cleared, Six forced his burning eyes open against the heat, and saw the helicopter above him.

He had jumped as far as he could, but had missed the helicopter.

Agent Six's luck had finally run out.

He knew he had begun to fall, he could feel it in his guts, though the familiar sensations were overpowered by the agony of his burning flesh. But which way was he falling—which way was down? He didn't know.

He was going to die.

"Nooooooo!" He expended what breath he had left by howling against the fiery wind. He flailed his arms and twisted and turned in the searing air, screaming silently.

Superheated carbon dioxide roasted his lungs as he tried to breathe, and he choked. His tongue dried and cracked in the heat, and he shut his mouth, but his lips still burned.

His head ached with the force of the thoughts racing through it. Still a hundred ninety meters above surface, he thought furiously, falling speed of twenty-seven meters per second, accelerating by nine meters every second. He'd be at sixty-three meters per second when he hit bottom. He could flatten his body, create as much surface area as he could to slow him down . . . if a moment before impact he pulled up his legs and put his arms forward, it would break his bones but he might survive . . . he had to somehow get his head up, he must be falling headfirst right now, and if he landed like this, he'd be killed instantly.

But he realized there was nothing he could do. A fall that far onto concrete would kill anything, no matter how strong. If a creature could live — it could die.

This time there would be no miracle. He was headed for solid concrete. He had no padding, nothing to cushion the blow. No dangling chains to grab hold of. No crane to ride. No parachute to open. No falling car or jeep to hold beneath him. His hands gripped the burning, empty air. He had nothing.

His mind turned briefly to his old fantasy, riding a speedboat out into the open ocean, looking for new lands to conquer. His burned and torn lips twisted into a smile as he pictured it.

He bowed his head in acceptance. His time had come.

I hope the others made it out okay, he prayed.

283

CRASH LANDING

The guard watched, dumbfounded, as the falling kid slammed into the ground like a rag doll. His left arm flopped sickeningly, no longer completely attached to the shoulder.

The guard peered through his rifle scope as the bot bent over the body. *No hope,* he thought. He didn't see —

Movement?

The boy was moving. Definitely.

It looked like an after-death spasm. The boy's body twitched momentarily. Then there was nothing.

The bot touched him, apparently scanning for a pulse.

The guard held his breath.

Could this mysterious boy have survived the whole ordeal?

Even as the Lab ambulance screeched towards the scene, the bot was standing up. It jumped, and then disappeared into the darkness, leaving the dead boy sprawled uncomplainingly on the concrete, like a child in a soft bed who hadn't slept for days.

THE PERFECT SOLDIER

I think, therefore I am.

Descartes. He meant that he could be deceived about the nature or existence of anything around him, but he could have complete faith in his own existence, because in order to be deceived about anything, he must first exist.

I can think, too. I am thinking. I think, therefore I am. I am thinking. Therefore I am alive.

Agent Six opened his eyes.

He ached and stung in every joint, every limb, every muscle — and he felt as weak as a newborn kitten. There was ringing in his ears and throbbing in his head. But he was thinking. He was breathing.

He was alive.

He checked to see he had feeling everywhere. He blinked his eyes. He wrinkled his nose. He pursed his lips and moved his jaw and wiggled his ears. So far, so good.

He tested his mind for brain damage. *My name is Agent*

Six of Hearts, I have no family, I live east of the Square: 87 multiplied by 379 is 32,973.

Six gently moved his shoulders and flexed his forearms. He curled his fingers and bent his wrists. Slowly he worked through every muscle until he reached his toes. Excellent. All his limbs were still attached, and his spine was in one piece, at least. All his joints were very stiff and sore, but apart from that, he seemed to be in good shape.

His eyes narrowed. Unsettlingly good shape, he thought, as he remembered the fall from the sky. What was going on here?

Six sat up. Blue walls. Glass ceiling. White tiled floor. He was in a cell similar to the one in which he had met Kyntak. But this time, the door was locked. He was wearing a white T-shirt and grey cotton track pants. He had no weapons anymore. They had all either been stripped from him or he'd lost them in the fall. He checked his calf. Even his combat knife was gone. Only the magnetic binders he'd used to sheath it were still there.

That was a bad fall, he thought. *I should be dead.*

He glanced around. There was a digi-cam in the room, a directional microphone, and a guard, who was pointing a Hawk at Six's head.

The guard nodded to Six. "You're awake," he observed.

"I'm as surprised as you," Six said, stretching his neck by tilting his head from side to side. He was sure that he was fine, but it would perhaps work to his advantage to appear incapacitated.

Then he recognized the guard. Muscular but small, dark hair and eyes, and a scar on his neck. Six tensed up his muscles, preparing to fight.

"Don't bother," the guard said. "I am aware that you recognize me. You held your ground impressively through that chase, although you lost out in the end. But please, Agent Six, relax. You have passed your final test."

Test? thought Six.

"I know how well armed you are even in the absence of weapons," the scarred man continued. "However, I want you to hear what I have to say. If there's fighting to be done, believe me, you will neither start nor finish it."

Six raised an eyebrow.

"In other words, my brother," the man continued, "you are out of your depth. Attempt to fight me and you will never leave this building." He shrugged. "But, as I'm certain you are aware, if I planned to kill you, you would be dead by now. I have a proposition for you."

He put the Hawk on the floor and kicked it under his chair.

"I'm listening," Six said.

"You have been invited into the employ of the Lab. Should you choose to accept employment, you will receive very handsome sums of money in return for your services to us, which will come in two separate categories."

Six screwed his eyes shut. *No way.* "Guinea pig, and . . . ?"

"A crude analogy, and far from accurate. You would indeed be studied and rated for the benefit of the company, as an employee, as a creation, and, of course, as a threat. Hence the gun." He smiled icily. "No offense, I hope."

"None taken." *They want me to work for them,* Six thought. Things were starting to make sense.

"The second part of the package is much like your previous job — espionage, undercover work for us. You would be assigned to duties of protection for the company. Much like the common Lab soldiers, but with more emphasis on the, er . . . *offensive* side of things. The best form of defense is attack, after all."

"Explain some of these duties," Six said.

"That's why I'm here. As you no doubt have guessed, I am the offspring of the same experiment as you — Project Falcon. As such, I am useful to the company, and my usefulness is well rewarded —"

"Why don't you look like me?" Six asked.

"Plastic surgery." The man's expression was unreadable. "Just a precaution. Some examples of the jobs I do are . . ." He paused, as though pondering. ". . . protecting Methryn Crexe. I am present at all of his prescheduled events. I have also often been assigned to liberate research from competing companies, although they are becoming few and far between. Sometimes a scientist stumbles across an idea that can be remembered without computers, and I am asked to eliminate them inconspicuously." He grinned wolfishly. "I'm told that your organization doesn't do that sort of thing, so I'm sure you will be pleasantly surprised at how well it pays."

Six said nothing.

"I also have similar tasks regarding people who discover the nature of the company or its experiments. They can be bribed or eliminated at my discretion. I find that both together is the most effective method — the money is easy to reclaim."

So, thought Six, *I'm being offered money to kill people for the Lab.* He doubted that refusal would be met graciously.

"Now I'd like you to meet Mr. Crexe, so he can explain how valuable you will be to his organization." The man held Six's stare. "I can guarantee that you'll never regret the decision to stay. I didn't. The work is good, and the money is better. I look forward to having you on our side."

The man began to walk towards the door. He gestured at the security camera, and the door swung open.

"What's your name?" Six asked.

The man raised an eyebrow. "Why do you ask?"

"You outran me. I like to know the name of someone who has beaten me."

"Neither of us has names. You know that perfectly well. But when we are on duty, you may call me Sevadonn. That's my employee code name, and it's the only identification I've ever had. Life is simpler this way, don't you agree?"

The man stepped through the door. Six got to his feet and followed.

He found himself in a very familiar place. Everything was a clean, crisp white. He was surrounded by monitors, bright lights, staff in white coats, and glass windows with slow, careful activity going on behind them. Six couldn't tell what was happening in those sealed glass chambers, but he knew it was some type of experimentation, probably dangerous. Certainly immoral.

Looking up, Six saw that the ceiling was made of glass, and that the next floor was visible. He could see that the floor above also had a glass ceiling, and he could vaguely make out moving shapes above it. He wondered how far underground they were, and how many floors had only glass separating them.

Wait, he thought, *of course. I'm in the tower attached to the Project Falcon lab.*

This sterilized laboratory reminded him of his birthplace. Well, not exactly "birth." It was thanks to places and people like these that he had never technically been born. Six knew that this couldn't be the same laboratory he had been spawned in, because that lab had been ransacked and torched. But the resemblance was uncanny — this lab must have been modeled on the last one.

"Agent Six!" Methryn Crexe grinned from across the room, as he strode in the door. "Finally we meet in person!"

Six sized him up. Methryn Crexe was shorter and wider than Six, although not overweight. He had a thin, dark mustache and neatly trimmed hair. He wore a symmetrically creased black business suit, with the bulge of a handgun in the right breast pocket. His eyes were dark and sparkling.

Crexe stepped confidently towards Six. "At last!" he said. He extended his hand, and Six shook it.

"It's a pleasure," Six said. Like most humans, Crexe blinked once every nine seconds. Each time Crexe's eyes closed, Six scanned the room for threats. There were three armed guards on the floor above — he could see them through the glass, and he had no doubt they were watching him. There was one in the laboratory. He presumed there would be three guards behind the entrance to the room (a steel door), as was the standard practice. One to look one way, one to look the other, and a third to spring into action should one of the others become incapacitated. Six also took into account the gun in Crexe's suit.

"I take it Sevadonn has already voiced our offer?" Crexe said.

"He has," Six answered. "There are a few questions I'd like to ask you."

"Please, be my guest." Crexe flashed a chillingly perfect smile.

"First and foremost, how am I still alive?"

"Ah!" Crexe laughed. "Yes, your stunt in the parking lot. That was most impressive, by the way. You passed the final test with flying colors." He chuckled. "No pun intended, of course. But in answer to your question, most of you died. You are not who you were two days ago. As soon as we recovered your body, we put it on ice so your brain didn't disintegrate. Then we grew a clone of you."

Six's eyes widened.

"We replaced most of your organs with new ones from the clone, including your lungs, your heart, your kidneys, both your ears, your left arm, and most of your skin. We did some reconstruction on your other broken limbs, then we started your new heart and thawed your brain. After that we injected you with growth hormones, and then took a large sample of your blood.

"Your new organs were accepted by your body, so the growth hormones forced your system to burn up the food we were drip-feeding you, and to create more blood. Once the pressure was back up, we returned the blood sample to your body, a bit at a time. The pressure was well above normal, but not dangerously so, and it gave you a sudden burst of energy. Your body started the healing process around all the reconstruction we'd done, and we gave you a few shots of adrenaline and our aging drug to speed up the process. The entire process took less than twenty-four hours, and you've been sleeping undisturbed for another fourteen. Of course, a proper human being would have been killed instantly, well beyond resuscitation — even with an identical copy to use for transplanting. But let's not dwell on that."

It made sense, Six thought. The repairs they had done were dangerously experimental, but possible in theory. He was still alive and not crippled or brain-damaged, so it must have worked. Six shivered. This was the closest he'd ever come to death.

"You did a good job," he told Crexe, flexing his biceps and shoulders. He stretched each leg a few times, then bent over into a hamstring stretch. On the way back up, he subtly unclipped the magnetic binders from his leg and closed his hand around them. He put his hands behind his back.

"So *why* am I still alive? Surely you didn't perform all that expensive surgery simply to have one more soldier in your crew."

Crexe laughed. "Of course not! It certainly was expensive, not worth the life of one employee. In fact, you just cost us more than the average Lab trooper earns in a lifetime. But you're going to earn us far more than that.

"You see, Agent Six, you are going to be of immense value to our project. From the original Project Falcon, you are one of three offspring. There's yourself, Sevadonn here, and the creature known as Kyntak. You all have identical DNA, and you had identical gestation periods in identical synthetic environments. Until the gestation laboratory was destroyed, you three were carbon copies of the same perfect being."

"Nobody's perfect," Six said automatically.

"Ah, and modest, too. But though it's taken more than twenty years of hard work, we've finally managed to reach our goal. Unfortunately, Kyntak is worthless. He's unpredictable, emotional, and dangerous, and therefore he's of no use to anyone. We plan to have him terminated as soon as we can. Sevadonn here is suitably clever, resourceful, and unsympathetic, but, unfortunately, he has the will to lead inside him. He is devious and ambitious, therefore useless for a soldier, despite being a truly excellent agent for us."

Sevadonn's face remained expressionless.

"But you!" Crexe continued. "You are exactly what the project was supposed to achieve. You value logic and reason instead of sentimentality and morals. You are prodigiously intelligent, and well trained for any challenge you may face. But you are neither greedy nor ambitious. You follow orders without question, and even when they ask the impossible of you, you somehow succeed. You are the perfect soldier. You are everything we hoped for, and more.

"As you may know, personality can't be programmed into genes. A personality is something that a creature earns through its experiences, through its triumphs and losses, through its mistakes and successes. And you have the perfect personality, in genes and in mind."

"You want my life story," Six realized. "You want me to tell you everything that has happened to me, and everything I believe, so you can duplicate it with . . . with the next batch."

Methryn Crexe's sinister grin blazed. "Exactly! The genome of the new model is very different from the one we used for you — new and improved, you might say — but we still want it to have your personality."

Something else clicked in Six's mind.

"The fire sixteen years ago wasn't an accident, was it?" he said. "You arranged it yourself, to send me, Kyntak, and Sevadonn our separate ways."

"Right again," Crexe said. "That was your first test — can he make it out of a burning building, having never walked before?" He smiled. "As with all your tests so far, you scored a hundred percent."

All my tests? Six thought. That feeling of being watched —
it was starting to make chilling sense.

"Kligos Stadil said you wouldn't make it," Crexe said. "He
said I was pushing you too far when I sent all those men after
you in the Lab headquarters. He said that no one could escape
his prized security there. And he wasn't expecting you to survive that car chase with Sevadonn, that's for sure.

"But now who's laughing? He's still in the cell you put
him in, and you survived a free fall!" Crexe chuckled
delightedly.

"You arranged all this," Six realized. "No one was ever trying to kill me at all. You were just testing my abilities!"

"No, we *were* trying to kill you," Crexe admitted. "At
least, the orders we gave to the troops were to kill you. We
only gave you favors from time to time — letting you and
Kyntak escape, for example, and not sounding the alarm
today until after you'd found the other Deck agents, even
though we already knew you were here. It was a win-win situation. If you died somehow, the greatest threat to our
operation was eliminated. If you survived, we had created the
perfect soldier."

"That's why the facility was so badly made," Six said.
"With thin walls, cheap metal framework, few digi-cams . . ."

"Yes, the digi-cams were just for show," Crexe said. "We
made the walls thin so that we could watch your movements
with an infrared thermal camera and a noise detection unit
from outside — the digi-cams were just there so we could see
how you would avoid them."

"I admire your commitment to the customer," Six said. "Clearly you are keen to provide Ungrelor Ludden with very high-quality products."

Crexe coughed. "Actually, Ludden's dead. Lerke tried to make a private deal with him behind my back. Lerke wanted to sell a sample of your DNA to him before he got the soldiers. This would have been proof of quality, but the money went straight into Lerke's pocket, and we couldn't allow that. Unfortunately, Ludden had already examined the cells, so Sevadonn had to terminate him. I know where Lerke is hiding, so I'll send Sevadonn after him soon. But you know as well as I do that in ChaoSonic, there is always someone waiting in the wings, ready to take over."

Six kept his face expressionless as he nodded. His knuckles whitened around the magnets.

"So Ludden's death doesn't mean that the assault on the other continents has been called off?" he asked.

Crexe raised an eyebrow. "I'm sorry?"

"Will you still grow the army of supersoldiers, and send them to attack the other continents beyond the Seawall?"

Crexe laughed. "Oh, I see. Yes, that's an easy mistake to make." He put a hand on Six's shoulder. Six tensed, trying not to recoil from his touch.

"Six," Methryn Crexe said, "there *are* no other continents. There is nothing beyond the Seawall."

Six gasped. "What?"

"The City is the only continent left in the world. When the fog descended, it changed the climate and melted the ice, so the whole world became flooded — except for the City, because we put up the Seawall. The City is only about seven and a half million square kilometers in area, but it supports more than nine billion people, and that's the population of the whole world. All the continents from pre-Takeover times are now completely underwater, except for this one."

"Then why trick people?" Six demanded. "Why the captive market? Why did you shoot down the planes that tried to leave? Why didn't ChaoSonic tell the public there was nowhere else to go?"

Crexe sighed. "If we'd left the ocean open to the public, and people kept trying to leave, then sooner or later they would've realized that there was nothing out there. Once it became accepted that there was nowhere else to go, the public would want to fix things up here. They'd want to overthrow ChaoSonic, break free — and no one wanted that.

"Even if they didn't try to bring down ChaoSonic, they might actually manage to fix things up in the City. And people buy fewer things when they're happy.

"So, it's easier this way — everyone believes that there's something better out beyond the wall, and no one protests. A few people try to escape, but no one ever succeeds. A whole world of empty ocean is the perfect security system."

"Then why build the army?" Six asked. "Who is left to attack?"

Crexe grinned. "You know who. The only threat left to ChaoSonic."

"The vigilantes," Six said. "The Deck."

"Bingo," Crexe said. "Once they're gone, the company can do whatever it wants — and an army of cloned super-human assassins is definitely the best way to do it. In just one night, very soon, hundreds of supersoldiers will storm the headquarters of each and every vigilante group in the City, and kill everyone on sight. Then ChaoSonic will have *ultimate* control." He paused. "But not the Deck. Not this way."

Six raised an eyebrow. "Why not?" he asked.

"They already know too much," Crexe said. "Your first assignment will be to terminate all of the Hearts and Diamonds, and both the Jokers, to prevent them from revealing information about us. Sevadonn can assist you with that."

Sevadonn nodded solemnly.

"Actually," Crexe went on, "I'm mystified as to why you didn't do that when you found them here. The whole point of kidnapping them was so you would come to terminate them in case they spilled any of your secrets to the torturers. A rescue mission, though impressive, was not what I was expecting. Why not kill them?"

"I was keeping my options open," Six said. "Without them alive, I'd have to rely on your generosity for employment, which I couldn't guarantee. Provided they escaped, I would still have income, and be able to join your side at a later date if the option so arose."

Crexe nodded. "I see. No matter, I trust you can dispose of the problem. You will still be paid handsomely, despite your partial responsibility for the difficulty." He grinned. "I can hardly blame you — you did what I would have done under the circumstances."

Six shivered involuntarily. Sevadonn was watching him suspiciously.

Crexe clapped his hands together. "Well, I'd love to show you around — I'm very proud of everything I've achieved — but your first assignment is rather urgent. The Deck agents have been back at their headquarters for nearly forty-eight hours now, and they're bringing in reinforcements from the other suits for an assault on this facility. We don't want a full-scale battle on our hands, Six. Even though we'll win, my forces may still sustain casualties, and afterward the survivors could scatter in any direction, and it would take months to find and terminate them all. So, are you ready to go?"

"No," Six replied.

"No?" Methryn Crexe appeared puzzled. "Why not?"

"Grateful though I am for your offer, and for saving my life, I'm refusing the job," Six said.

Crexe's jaw dropped. "What?"

"I can't endanger the men and women who work at the Deck. I am obliged to protect them." He paused. "They are my friends," he said finally.

Crexe's eyes narrowed. "Then you're not the perfect weapon we hoped for."

Six laughed. "No, that's right. I'm better." And with that, he flicked the magnets backward out of his hands — and they stuck to the computer console behind him.

No one ever expects the magnet, Six thought.

The machinery squealed like wounded cats as the circuitry corrupted itself and erupted in flames. The staff in white coats immediately ran to the computer, shouting hysterically.

Crexe drew his Raptor, but Agent Six had vanished.

A guard was firing at the space Six had occupied moments before, and there was a splash of blood from a scientist who was standing nearby. The machinery in the enclosed areas exploded, shattering the glass. The scientist yelped as he fell to the floor, and the others all ducked. Crexe waved his pistol wildly around through the smoke, searching for Six.

"Behind you," Six shouted.

Crexe whirled around, but saw nothing. Then his pistol was snatched out of his hand. Instinctively he ducked, but as he covered his head he felt a foot press down on his back, and a gun barrel touch the back of his skull.

"What's the quickest way out of here?" Six demanded.

"You can die first!" Crexe screamed.

Six was about to insist when he detected movement to the right. He jumped into a backward flip as a black shape flitted past beneath him. *Sevadonn,* he thought, just as a boot thudded into his chest. Six heard the crunch of ribs as he was tossed back across the room, bashing into the tiles. He gasped for air, but found none as a fist hit him in the stomach, and another in the collarbone.

Six couldn't even see the attacker. Sevadonn was moving too fast to hit, and Six had dropped the gun. He couldn't see that, either. He was helpless before his assailant, blind and injured — and still weak from the surgery that they had performed on him.

He feigned choking on the smoke. Another fist lashed out, at his head this time, and he caught it. There was not the usual cry of surprise from his opponent — but, Six thought, Sevadonn was hardly his usual opponent.

Six twisted the arm as it tried to pull back. He thought he heard a bone snap, but the roaring of the flames and the wail of the alarms made it hard to tell. He immediately pressed his feet against the wall and dived forward, letting go of the arm as he did so.

He had expected Sevadonn to roll with the impact, but instead he reached up and wrapped his forearm around Six's neck. He squeezed, and Six fell to the floor, unable to breathe.

"Nice working with you," Sevadonn spat as he choked the life out of Six.

Six pushed his legs off the floor and somersaulted, catapulting the soles of his shoes towards Sevadonn's face. Sevadonn dodged nimbly, but had to let go of Six's neck to do it. The moment he fell to the floor, Six grabbed Sevadonn's calves and held them together with his arms. Sevadonn lost his balance and slipped down headfirst through the air. Immediately Six was falling towards the back of Sevadonn's head, boots first, but Sevadonn rolled to one side and Six landed nimbly on the tiles.

The smoke made Six's eyes water. The acrid stench of boiling chemicals filled his nostrils and the constant blaring of the alarms squeezed his eardrums. He lifted his feet off the ground to avoid a sweeping trip-kick from Sevadonn. He dived in the direction he had seen the kick come from, and landed hands first on the tiles. Sevadonn was no longer there.

Six immediately rolled to one side and sprang to his feet. He still couldn't see Sevadonn, so he ducked. His instincts proved correct: A vicious forearm cleaved the air where his head had been a second before.

Six bowed his head, crouched, and jumped back towards Sevadonn, aiming to knock him over with all of his weight. But he was stopped very suddenly. His spine bent backward over Sevadonn's knee, and he cried out. Then he was kicked forward onto the tiles.

I'm not going to win this fight, Six realized, as he lay on the floor. *He's fitter, stronger, and cleverer than I am. He'll kill me if I stand my ground.* Six looked up from the tiles to see Sevadonn looming over him.

Six sprang to his feet and tried to run towards the elevator. But no sooner was he off the ground than he felt two strong hands grabbing him, one on the back of his shirt and one on his neck. He was lifted bodily into the air and hurled forward. He could see nothing but a smoky haze as he flew head over heels.

Thud. His side hit the inner wall of the elevator, and he cried out in agony as he slid to the floor.

But he had made it to the elevator. Seizing his chance, he planted his foot on the button panel. The doors began to close.

Sevadonn burst headlong through the smoky fog and flew through the door. It slid shut behind his heels. Six rolled out of the way as Sevadonn's weight shook the floor.

The elevator began to hum gently upward.

Sevadonn tried to pick himself off the floor of the elevator, but Six was on him in a flash. He punched, kicked, elbowed, head-butted, and kneed Sevadonn in the ribs. The other man yelled in surprise and moved his arm down to protect his side. This was what Six had expected, and so he drove his fist into the side of Sevadonn's head.

Sevadonn was thrown over by the force of the impact, but the blow had missed his temple and he wasn't badly hurt. He roared and jumped back towards Six, chopping at Six's neck with his forearms and lashing out at Six's belly with his boots.

Six felt the blows bruise his muscles and break his bones. He gritted his teeth and tried to block the assault, but each rapid strike was just too fast. He was driven into the floor by a steady thumping on his torso. He was utterly at Sevadonn's mercy.

"Help me," he whispered to no one. He needed a miracle.

The elevator door pinged as it slid open.

Six struck out with both legs, slamming them into Sevadonn's chest. Sevadonn was thrown backward out of the elevator, and slid across the glass floor outside. Six pounced on him, Sevadonn punched Six, and they continued to brawl across the floor.

Six saw that he was now on the fourth level. He could see three layers of glass between him and the laboratory far below. The glass was cold to the touch.

Sevadonn swung his elbow into Six's ribs, and Six was thrown sideways. He bounced across the floor, gasping with pain as his broken bones collided with the glass. Out of the corner of his eye he saw Sevadonn leap towards him like a pouncing cat. He tried to roll out of the way, but he was too slow. Sevadonn's knee drove down into Six's back, pinning him to the floor.

Life is so cruel, Six thought bitterly. Snatched from a grisly death by a miracle, only to be beaten to death immediately upon awakening. He would have sighed, but just then Sevadonn's forearm snaked around his neck, cutting off his air supply. He choked and gasped, limbs flailing and whirling, slowly becoming weaker and weaker.

Then he saw something down below. From the ground floor, where he had begun the fight, Methryn Crexe was looking up at him. Six thought he could make out a smile on the man's face. And a gun in his hand, aimed upward.

Six let his limbs slowly go limp. Holding his breath, he feigned a last desperate shudder to dislodge his captor. Sevadonn didn't budge, of course, and Six collapsed facedown on the glass floor.

He watched.

He waited.

And when Crexe sent the bullet up through the first glass barrier, Six flipped back against Sevadonn's weight. He tossed the man off his shoulders as though shedding a coat, and dived to one side as the bullet spat up through the floor where he had been lying.

Sevadonn let out a shocked yelp. Mid-leap, Six turned his head and saw the blood spill from Sevadonn's leg where the bullet had hit.

Cracks spread across the glass floor like lightning, spiraling out from the bullet hole like a frosted spiderweb. Six tumbled to the ground, raising his arms to cover his head.

He thumped on the glass with his tiny fists.

Six's elbows shattered the glass. He and Sevadonn both plummeted earthward. Laboratory windows flashed by, like a train in the night. "I'm going to die," he whispered.

Kicked it with his stubby feet.

Six thudded into the next floor, smashing right through it. The air around him filled with tiny flecks of crystal. Barely slowing down, he dropped like a stone. "No! I have to fight it!" he rasped.

He beat on the glass with his palms, harder and faster.

The glass below swept up to greet him. He curled into a ball and rolled to one side, aiming to hit it feetfirst. He plunged through it like a cannonball, spraying the air with shimmering fragments. "I'm going to make it," he growled. "I'm going to make it."

Then Six slammed down onto the tiles. His feet touched first, and his knees buckled. His legs were too far to one side and they slipped out from under him. He cried out as he felt his spine crunch underneath his weight. The back of his skull bounced against the floor, and suddenly there was a pounding noise in his brain.

"No miracle this time, Six? You can jump off dams, you can dive off buildings, you can leap off cranes, drive down cliffs, ride flying jeeps into missiles, but a four-story drop onto some broken glass finishes you off?"

Six tried to focus. There was a dark shape looming over him, pointing at him with a long dark finger. He blinked a few times, and saw it was a gun.

"I'm glad I didn't hire you," Crexe continued. "Your rebellious spirit is bad enough, but it seems that you're weak physically as well. Maybe, up until now, you've just been lucky."

Six heard a gurgling sound to his right. Blinking blood out of his eyes, he rolled his head over to look, and saw Sevadonn. Sevadonn's legs were both broken, and one of his arms was mangled. He was dragging himself towards Six with his good arm, staring at him through filmy crimson eyes.

Crexe fired twice, and Sevadonn stopped moving. "Sorry, but you were always dispensable, and I've wasted quite enough money for one day."

Six tried to throw himself at Crexe, but could barely even raise himself off the floor. He couldn't feel his legs, his ribs ached, and the pounding in his head seemed to be blinding him. A syrupy metallic stench filled his nostrils, mingling with the smoke.

"Pathetic," Crexe said. "I had hopes for you — but now you're nothing but a hindrance. A genetic experiment gone wrong, lying helpless in a puddle of its own fluids." He sighed. "Such a terrible waste. You were, as you've probably guessed, somewhat expensive."

Six tried to speak, but choked. He spat out a tooth.

"Why didn't you join me, Six?" Crexe said. "You had nothing to lose, and everything to gain. It would have been a beneficial situation for both of us. You owed nobody anything. Why should you have qualms about such easy work? You're not even human. You don't have to be moral."

"More human than you," Six rasped.

Crexe laughed. "Indeed. You think you are, at any rate. You even seem to be under the impression that you have a soul." Crexe leaned forward, looming over Six. "I was *there*. I watched Lerke design you, and I oversaw your growth from day one. If there was any humanity, any spirit incubating in that tube, I would have known about it and I would have flushed it out. You are artificial. You are a parody of a human being."

Six winced as Crexe aimed the pistol at his chest. His finger tightened on the trigger.

"A soul is like a personality," Six whispered hoarsely. "It's something that a creature earns through its experiences. You aren't born with it; it is life's gradual gift to you. I think, therefore I am."

He closed his eyes.

I did it, he thought.

I know who I am. At last.

As Methryn Crexe aimed the gun at Six's head, his eyes suddenly rolled into the back of his head. Crexe slumped backward and Kyntak lowered him to the ground.

THE NEXT GENERATION

"How do you do it, Six?" Kyntak laughed.

He wrapped one arm around Six's back and helped him to his feet. Six tried to support his own weight, but his legs buckled underneath him.

"Whoa," Kyntak said, catching Six neatly. "Relax, buddy. It'd be a shame for you to fight off all those psychopaths and then bleed to death. Let me get you out of here."

"How'd you find me?" Six asked.

"I found the Lab's central computer system, and used it to track you. You don't need to be afraid of them anymore."

Kyntak was blurry. Six closed his eyes. "I owe you one."

"Nah, don't mention it. You'd have done the same for me. And anyway, I got to knock my boss unconscious!"

"You were a double agent?"

"I told you that right from the beginning! I was working for the Lab so I could spy on them, getting information about the inner workings of ChaoSonic."

Six smiled. "I knew we couldn't trust you."

"By the way, I was really touched by what you said over there. I never knew you had a spiritual side."

Six coughed. "Neither did I."

"You and I are very different people, Six, but our genes are the same. We may not have been born the same as most people, but if it's the outside world that gives us souls, then we're just as human as everyone else."

Six smiled. "Maybe we're not so different after all."

"Maybe not." Kyntak chuckled.

"Did you hear what Crexe said?" Six rasped. "About the Seawall?"

"No," Kyntak said, "but I can guess what it was. I learned the same thing from the mainframe. There are still nine billion people to save, though."

They were almost at the door when Six choked. His eyes widened.

"Are you all right?" Kyntak asked, alarmed.

"Look!" Six whispered.

The smoke parted to reveal a shining pillar of glass. It was perfectly round and smooth, like a giant flashlight balanced on the flat end. Inside, a small bundle of flesh slowly drifted up and down in water. As they got closer, Six could make out tiny arms and legs, little hands and feet, and the smooth dome of the head.

"They made another one," Kyntak breathed.

Six remembered Crexe talking about "the next batch." He had wanted Six to tell the story of his upbringing, so that the next experimental soldier might have the same capacity to follow orders, fight blindly, and cheat death so effortlessly. But Six had never imagined that they would be growing the first infant already.

Probably a test subject, Six thought. *Start with one, test it, then build the army.*

"If anyone finds this — if they realize what this is . . ." Kyntak stammered.

"I know," Six said. He thought of all the things that had happened to him since he was in this state. Escaping from the fire, finding King. Working at the Deck, meeting his friends. Finding Kyntak, learning about life. Always learning.

"Please," Six said. "Take me closer."

Kyntak silently helped him forward.

With his last ounce of strength, Six drove his fist through the glass. It shattered, and he staggered back.

The water drained out of the pillar, and the baby coughed, blinking its big eyes and flexing its tiny limbs. It moved to its hands and knees and stared up at Six.

"Take it with us," Six whispered.

"Shh. Sleep." Kyntak picked up the infant and held it to his chest, then slung Agent Six of Hearts over his shoulder. He carried them both out of the door in silence.

"Kyntak," Six whispered.

"That's my name. Yes?"

"Are you the other Joker?"

Kyntak smiled, but didn't answer.

EPILOGUE

The man watched through ChaoSonic night-vision binoculars as the boy with the bleached-blond hair placed the other gently inside the car. Then he placed a small bundle on the sleeping boy's lap. The baby looked up at him curiously with her large dark eyes.

The watcher smiled. Excellent. The children of Project Falcon were as predictable as ever.

The boy started up the car and pulled out onto the road.

The watcher pulled his beanie tighter over his bald head and stared at the car as it disappeared into the City's haze of neon lights.

"There'll be no mistakes next time," Retuni Lerke whispered into the darkness. "You're my baby girl, and you belong with me. One day, you're going to be a great soldier."

He vanished into the night.